KAREL SCHOEMAN

THIS LIFE

Translated from the Afrikaans by Else Silke

archipelago books

Archipelago Books
232 3rd Street #A111
Brooklyn, NY 11215
www.archipelagobooks.org

Library of Congress Cataloging-in-Publication Data
Schoeman, Karel, author.
[Hierdie lewe. English. 2015]
This life / Karel Shoeman ; translated from the Afrikaans by Else Silke.
pages cm
English, translated from Afrikaans.
Summary: "THIS LIFE considers both the past and future of the Afrikaner people
through four generations of one South African [family]. Told from the perspective
of one woman in her final days, it is a lyrical account of a 200 year old culture and history
that has been irrevocably lost." – Publisher's note.
"First published in English in 2005 by Human & Rousseau,
an imprint of NB Publishers, Cape Town South Africa."
ISBN 978-0-914671-15-2 – ISBN 978-0-914671-16-9
1. Afrikaners – Fiction. 2. Rural families – South Africa – Northern Cape –
Fiction. 3. Family farms – South Africa – Northern Cape – Fiction. 4. Northern Cape
(South Africa) – Fiction. I. Silke, Elsa, translator. II. Title.
PT6592.29.C5H5413 2015
839.3635–dc23   2014035212

Archipelago gratefully acknowledges the generous support from
Lannan Foundation, the National Endowment for the Arts and the
New York State Council on the Arts, a state agency.

PRINTED IN THE UNITED STATES OF AMERICA

THIS LIFE

THE NIGHT-LIGHT FLICKERS and goes out; I lie awake in the dark, listening to the regular breathing of the girl asleep on the cot at the foot of my bed. It does not matter, nothing matters now, for to wait is all that remains, and light or darkness no longer matters. I know this room where I slept as a child, this old house on the ridge with Maans's new house some distance below, the kraals, the dams, and the low hills of the flat, faded land. I do not even have to close my eyes: wide-eyed in the dark I see the house where I was born, the farm where I grew up and, if I were to get up, I would still be able to find my way blindly over the dung floor of the bedroom and Stienie's new wooden floor in the voorhuis. I would feel my way to the bolt on the front door, without hesitation I would pull open the heavy old door, careful not to let the hinges creak, and step out into the yard. There is no moon, but I do not need moonlight to recognise the farm of my youth or to find the footpath. I feel no pain as I step barefoot over the stones, past the outbuildings and the kraal, and over the ridge to the graveyard, to stand there, my hand resting on the stacked stones of the wall. And then? What then? I am no longer certain what I have come to look for here. The silver glow of the night becomes shrouded, the greyish landscape grows dim before my eyes, and I no longer know where I am.

But no. No.

Where am I? I lie trapped in the dark, listening to someone breathing near me in the dark. Is it Dulsie who has stayed to sleep on the skin-rug in front of my bed, watching over me on my sickbed; is it Sofie who has fallen asleep, waiting for the knock on the shutter? But no, I am no longer a child and Dulsie is long dead and Sofie too; it is Annie's daughter who is watching over me here and who has fallen asleep because she is young and tired out from the day's work, and because a dying old woman in a bed means nothing to her – why should she feel anything for me, who is no relation of hers, and why should she be grateful for Maans's generosity? She is asleep and it does not matter, for what more can I possibly need now and what cause would I have to call her? Annie's daughter – her name I cannot remember, but that is no longer important either.

It is my own room, now I know it again, the room where I slept as a child: there is the door to the voorhuis and there the small window with its inner shutter, set deep in the wall, with its view over the yard and the shed and the outbuildings. Why can I not see it? Through the chink between shutter and sash the moon would shine into the room to show where the window was, through the small chink the narrow beam of moonlight would fall into the room to flash in the mirror. If I wait I shall see once more that dark square outlined by the moonlight, the shutter opening soundlessly and the moonlight spilling over the floor, and my brother Pieter outside, placing his hands on the window-sill and hoisting himself up to land inside.

But no, no more; no, I remember now, and in the darkness certainty comes to my bewildered thoughts and memories. In later years the windows were fitted with glass panes: how would Pieter hoist himself through the window if he should come now? And the shed and the outside room where he used to sleep fell into ruins, so that Maans had them demolished and Pieter himself is dead and rests under the chiselled stone I ordered from Oom Appie and paid for myself.

There is no reason to get up now, even if I could still move; there is nothing more I could do and no one I could search for, for over the years everyone has gone, one after the other. Where are you in this vast darkness, and can you hear me? Speak to me if you are near, here where I lie alone in the night, unable to sleep, trapped with my bewildered thoughts and memories at the end of my life; speak to me, you who know more than I do, and explain to me what I cannot understand. But there is nothing, no voice in the dark or even the swish of a dress, black in the depth of the shadows: I am alone here where I lie, speechless and paralysed, with the thoughts I am power-less to control and the memories I can no longer evade, the relentless knowledge I would rather avoid.

I remember too much, for during my entire life I had too much occasion to look and listen, to see and hear, and to remember. I sat with them and helped pour the coffee, handed round the plates, took away the tray; I heard them talk, about the marriages and the deaths, the consistorial meetings and the auction sales, the shiny black horse-drawn cart and the white marble stone, everything they considered important, and now that they are dead, I still remember it all. I sat with them and heard the silences between the words, the hesitation before the answer, the scarcely perceptible evasion; I saw the look in the eyes or the quick movement of the hands that the others missed because their minds were on more important affairs, and I still remember it. I did not gather this information intentionally, nor did I ask to retain it, but here at the end of my life, reflecting on all this accumulated wis-dom, I suddenly realise that it is not meaningless, like the incidental swelling of the soil that indicates the hidden paths where the mole has tunnelled. All that is left is this knowledge; all that remains to me of this life is this collected wisdom.

How far should I go back? As far as I can remember, to the day we took out the honey, Jakob and Pieter and Gert, and they carried me back on their shoulders because I was so young that I was tired out and could not walk home, that long trek home with the young men laughing and jesting about the accomplishments of the day, with the harsh, faded landscape aglow for a moment in the light of the setting sun and the dams glittering in the distance? Or further still, to a time that has come to seem just as real to me through anecdotes and tales and inference, to the ramshackle cart and the small herd of scabby sheep, to the pleated caps and the embroidered apron and the bright red and blue of the bowls displayed in the wall-cupboard? I do not know: I am tired and I want to rest but sleep will not come, and there is no sign that this night will end; only the thoughts and memories remain, and avoiding them is no longer possible.

The darkness before my eyes, the helpless body, and this banked mass of memories through which I have to feel my way blindly. Words and images of more than seventy years, fragments of conversation, an incidental remark from servants gossiping in the kitchen, a few words spoken by a herdsman in the veld, anecdotes and tales, verses, rhymes, and the psalms sung around the table in the voorhuis of an evening, or later in the little village church, flashes I no longer know where to place, the house and yard in the moonlight, the moonlight glittering in the mirror and the distant glitter as the water in the dams catches the daylight, the spekbos clear-white on the ridges in springtime, the luminous silver of the renosterbos in the diffused sunlight of the late afternoon, and the dead lamb, its eyes pecked out by crows, the reebok slung sideways across the saddle, dried blood around its jaws; the quill pen, the pocket knife, the candlestick on the bedside table; the coolness of the pane against my fingers and the coolness of the stone, the hard, straight edge of the splashboard under my hand as I stand beside the Cape cart. This is what I have left, and all that remains for me, awake here in the dark, is to sift through it, alone, with no hand to guide me along, no whispering voice in my ear. I was a quiet, timid child, whose presence went unnoticed by all, an inquisitive child with alert, attentive eyes, who observed and remembered, and my memory and mind are no less clear now, even though they are the only faculties I have retained. To sift through and arrange the bits and pebbles and chips, the patches and threads and ribbons and notes, and finally to piece together from these the story in which I have figured over all these years, silent and vigilant in the corner or at the edge of the company, and perhaps also to understand, and even to forgive, to have all the unspoken anxieties, reproaches and sorrows eliminated, the last scores settled. To remember.

I must get up and journey back into the past, through the dark, alone across the years. I must move through the darkness of the sleeping house, soundlessly so no one will hear me, and pull open the front door; I must cross the threshhold and venture outside.

The moon has not yet risen, but in the faded, diffused glow of the stars I can recognise the world of my youth, the wide landscape of my life, the bleak, faded land of shrub and stone, the harsh land of frost, snow and drought. Bitter land where I was born, meagre shaly soil where they will dig my grave inside the stone walls of the graveyard. I should like to move out through the sleeping house once more, to take leave of my life; I should like to go out one last time and behold the land, in sunlight and starlight, and follow the narrow path to the graveyard beyond the ridge, my hand groping among the stacked stones of the encircling wall. Never again. Only in my memories, sleepless in the dark, shall I still tread the old paths; only in my thoughts shall I still move soundlessly through the familiar darkness of the house, back across all the years.

Get up and go, get up and walk through that darkness; pull open the door and leave the sleeping house, cross the threshhold to the yard where the land stretches out in starlight. Again and again I follow that familiar path, unnoticed in the dark, again and again I waver at that door, waver on the threshhold, only then reaching for the bolt and pulling open the door, only then venturing out into the night.

Meagre land, bitter land, beloved land. How did I come to spend my entire life here yet never really notice you, or notice you so rarely, even then sparing you barely a glance, that even now I remain unfulfilled, always yearning to see you again? Meagre land, sparse land, harsh land of shrub and stone, dry springs and fountains of brackish water; our fountains were the only ones never to run dry and our dams the only ones to glitter in the light. Land without mercy where the wild cat savages the sheep and the eagle swoops down on the lamb, where the herdsman is found dead in his shelter, covered with the fine, sifting snow, and the hunter loses his footing on the rock; unforgiving land, where brother is set against brother and servant against master, where the trespass remains unforgiven and the written word perpetuates the lie, the chiselled inscription is rendered untrue.

I must carry on, barefoot in the half-light of the night, step by step, on the trail of every memory; every remembered word I must examine, and every half-forgotten one attempt to recall; along the rocky ridges, in the dry crevices and hollows of this arid land, borne from one disclosure to the next. I must search for the rare fountain, the dripping of water and the moisture of soil that may have retained a footprint.

Bright land, gleaming silver-grey land drifting away from me in the night, where I marvel at the way every branch of the harpuisbos sparkles as its dense, whorled leaves reflect the glimmer of the light, and every rock glows dimly on the ridges. The porcupine disappears into the shadows between the shrubs, the yellow cobra slithers past my feet, and jackal trot along the rocky ridges, paying no heed to the grazing sheep. I have nothing more to fear, walking barefoot and alone through the veld and over the stones in my flapping nightgown until I reach the edge of the escarpment where the vertical rockface falls away, the sheer drop invisible in the depth of the shadows as if it were not there, barefoot on the rocky ledge at the edge of the world, the rock cold under my feet and the piercing wind blowing straight at me, yet I do not freeze or falter. Beneath me lie the mountain ranges, cliffs, chasms and plains of the Karoo, one mountain range after another ranked to the horizon; beneath me lie the warm lowlands filled with the herbal scent of shrubs, and one last time I survey it all; but then I turn back to the low inclines of the plateau where the wind blows so piercingly, back to the land where I was born, the bitter land, the beloved land, and slowly in the starlight, over shrubs and coarse clumps of grass, past the ridges where the jackal hides, through the dry streams with their stony beds and fissures where water has not flowed for many years, I walk back. At last I see in the distance once again the glitter of the dams and the dark shape of the house with its high thatched roof set against the ridge, the kraal and the shed and the outbuildings in the background, the radiant pear trees covered with blossoms in spring; and past the orchard the footpath leading to the graveyard with its few stone mounds and headstones in the shelter of the encircling wall of stacked stones.

1

....

The farm was granted to Father's grandfather when the first white people toiled up the passes of the Roggeveld Mountains to find grazing for their sheep flocks here along the edge of the escarpment. It must have been he or his son who had built the old stone house with its walls of stacked flat stones and its big hearth that still formed part of the outbuildings during my childhood; the thatched roof had already begun to collapse over the rafters when I got to know it, and later Maans had it demolished when the outbuildings were resited. It was not a very big farm, but it was favourably situated here on the edge of the escarpment and it was one of the best sheep farms in the district, with good grazing and dams fed by springs that ran dry only during the harshest droughts.

Of my great-grandfather and his wife I know nothing more, and not much more about my grandparents either, because they all died before I was born, and Father was a rather reserved man who was never very keen to speak of the past. Mother never spoke of the past, nor did she, even in passing, refer to anything that had happened earlier. I only know that as children we sometimes picked up arrowheads in the veld and I recall Father mentioning how, when he was a boy, they had to flee to the Karoo because they were attacked by Bushmen; men making a furrow or digging in a field would come upon beads of polished ostrich eggshells or a bracelet, and sometimes upon a grave with skulls and bones. Once Father also told of the butchers' men that were sent from the Cape in earlier days to buy sheep, and that is probably how Oupa made his money, for apparently he was a wealthy man for these parts at the time of his death. He had married a woman from the Bokkeveld, and it was he who had built the large homestead; but no, I remember Father telling us that she herself had overseen the builders while they were working, for Oupa was probably a gentle and meek man, much like Father, and so she had taken the lead. The old people moved across to the new homestead, and when Father and Mother were married, they lived in the old house – both Jakob and Pieter were born there. Only after Oupa's death did Father and Mother come to live in the new house, and that is where I was born then, in the house where I shall also die. Father added two more rooms, and after that no further changes were made to the house.

It was not a particularly large house, neither could it be called grand – Stienie always found it dark, poky and old-fashioned, and she did not rest until she had built her own home – but it was situated in a poor and remote region where most farmers had to move about constantly to find water and grazing, across the Riet River to the Nuweveld or down to the Karoo in winter, and among the simpler makeshift homes of the Roggeveld it appeared solid and impressive, and even grand through my childish eyes. Thick walls, almost two feet wide, a *brand-solder* resting on beams, under a high, thatched roof, small windows with wooden shutters on the inside, and clay floors – I was a young girl when it was decided to fit glass panes; no, it was just before Maans married Stienie, and I was a grown woman by then. Nevertheless, the house was never good enough for Stienie, though she kept her complaints to herself while Mother was still alive, and I suppose it must have been cold and dark and inconvenient, but we lived like that all the years without knowing any better, Father who died there, and Mother, we children who grew up there, Sofie during her brief stay with us and Maans who was born there – yes, and Stienie too for all those years until Maans had the new stone house built for her on the plain towards the road. After that they did not make much effort to keep up the old homestead, because only Pieter lived there, and during these past years Annie and her daughter, and what did they actually mean to Maans that he should put himself out for them? The house began to fall into disrepair, but essentially it is still as I knew it in my childhood, sixty and seventy years ago, with the long, dark voorhuis where you enter, and two small rooms on either side: Father and Mother slept in the front room on the right, the one on the left later became Jakob and Sofie's room, and behind Father and Mother's room was mine, with the window overlooking the yard and the outbuildings, until the shutters were closed and latched against the moonlight. It is to this room that they carried me, this room to which I was carried back, to lie awake in the dark, awaiting my death.

Against the furthest wall of the voorhuis as you enter, you would probably expect a hearth in this cold region, but our fire was made in the kitchen, and when a visitor once remarked on it, Father shrugged and answered, "No, but that is the way my late mother had wanted it," as if that explained everything. Did Ouma want to keep the cooking and the servants out of her voorhuis, and was it her way of establishing her own way of life in the house that had been built under her own eyes and hands? In the furthest wall, where you would expect the hearth, two small wall-cupboards with glazed doors had been built in, the only glass panes to be found in the Roggeveld in my childhood years, and in those cupboards Ouma's china was kept, cups and saucers and bowls patterned in red and white and blue with a touch of gold here and there in between. Mother never used them or even took them out of the cupboards, and as a child I sometimes stood there on a Sunday afternoon, gazing for hours through the glass panes at the red and blue and gold of the patterns on the china, the only brightness in our sombre home or in the faded, flat region where I grew up. Now Stienie probably has it all, though I cannot remember ever having seen it; once people from the Boland, who were interested in such things, called on us in our town house, and Stienie mentioned a bit disdainfully that she still had some of Great-ouma's old china, but where she kept it I do not know and she never used it, because they were old-fashioned pieces and not to her taste at all. That is all I know of Ouma, the fact that she came from the Bokkeveld and had a house built with recessed wall-cupboards to display her china. Oupa lies buried here in the graveyard behind the ridge, with a stone on which someone chiselled his name and dates carefully, for he died first and she saw to it that a headstone was made for him, but when she herself died, no one took the trouble, so she rests anonymously under one of the overgrown stone mounds beside him. Father had probably still known which grave was hers, but today no one would be able to point it out.

The brightly-coloured china in the wall-cupboards drew my attention as a child, but, even so, there was more that Oupa and Ouma had left us. When I was a child we seldom left the farm except when we moved down to the Karoo in winter, but as I grew older and we rode over to neighbouring farms more often for weddings and funerals, I came to appreciate better the modest and unobtrusive wealth that we had inherited from them: not merely the brightly-coloured china that had drawn the attention of a child, but the solid homestead with its strong walls and the few heavy, plain pieces of furniture that had not been made locally but had been brought over the mountain passes of the Boland by wagon: Father and Mother's four-poster bed, the cots, the large table in the voorhuis with its riempie chairs arranged along the walls, and the kists in which our clothes and linen were stored.

This house and this furniture which we had inherited from my grandparents seemed to set us apart from our neighbours in the Roggeveld, and as I came to realise that fact, I experienced – yes, I too – something of the pride and deadly vanity that pervaded our family, intensified and reinforced from generation to generation. The ambition I was spared, however, for it was not my task to strive and to strain ahead desperately, but to see, to hear and to remember, as I understand at last, here at the end of my life.

When you approach the farm, whether from the Karoo by way of the old road over Vloksberg Pass or from the village, the new house is the first thing you see, its shiny roof reflecting the light from a distance long before you arrive, and I am the only one who, almost instinctively, still leans forward in the cart every time we return, to look at the old house with its outbuildings against the ridge, waiting to welcome me. When I picture the arrival on the farm here before me in the dark, it appears to me as it was during all those years before the new house was built, for no matter which road you chose, from the direction of Groenfontein or Oorlogskloof – the village did not exist in those days – following the ruts of the wheels across the low hills and rocky ledges, or along the pass up the mountainside past Klipfontein, when you reached that wide, open, rolling land of the escarpment, you saw from a great distance, across the waving shrubs and grass and the glitter of the dams, the house with its high, thatched roof against the ridge, the house with the shed and stables and other out-buildings some distance behind, the orchard with its windswept pear trees, and the graveyard with its irregular wall of stacked stones. It was the world of my youth, and the surrounding farms formed its borders, except when we moved down to the Karoo in winter.

"Not that he started out with much," I heard Oom Herklaas Vlok remark after Father's funeral, "only the two farms and a handful of sheep", but by the time he died the land and the flocks of sheep had increased, and there was a measure of disapproval in Oom Herklaas's voice. Though envy may have existed in the district, I do not believe there was ever malice, not to mention enmity, for Father was never one to make enemies, a placid, silent man who stroked his beard and thought long before he voiced an opinion or answered a question, and whose words people were prepared to heed. So thorough could his deliberation be and so slow was he to decide one way or another, that it was often Mother who made the decisions, and sometimes, impetuous as she was, she became so impatient with his indecisiveness that she took the lead herself while he was still considering his course of action. She thrashed the boys with the horsewhip or sjambok even when they were all but grown-up, and sometimes it was also she who gave the herdsmen a thrashing, because Father seldom and reluctantly raised his hand against anyone. Most probably it was also she who had encouraged him over the years of their marriage to purchase those sheep flocks and that land.

As the only daughter I grew up in the house with Mother and she died before my eyes, for almost fifty years she and I lived close together, day in, day out, here on the farm or in the town house where she died, but what can I say about her now, when I must review my memories and try to explain, to understand? A slender, dark, quick woman with a fierce temper and a sharp tongue – though this much all the servants and the neighbours also knew, and all the people of my generation still remember her so today and tell stories of her explosive temper and her stubborn pride when they do not know that I am close enough to hear; and I, her own daughter, after being with her for nearly fifty years, cannot really find anything to add to that, for more than that she did not reveal even to me. But how could such a thing be possible? Something there must be among all the incidental words and gestures, shards and tiny splinters, that one can scrape together and arrange, to be able to understand and explain, to try and understand, to try and forgive.

From my childhood days I remember only what other people remember as well, though I may have had more occasion to observe it all: the diligence, the drive and the passion, the persistence that could so easily become stubbornness, the sudden attacks of blind and uncontrollable fury that scared us anew every time with their violence; drive and passion, yes, and I would almost say obsession, as if she were being swept towards some distant and scarcely perceptible goal by powers invisible to everyone but her, and unfathomable even to her. Does it sound strange when I try to explain it like this? Perhaps I exaggerate now, but I am only trying to find words to describe something of that indomitable woman in whose shadow I grew up and at whose bedside I kept vigil during her long, painful, wordless death. That is all I can still do, try, for no one has remained who can do more than that.

Passion and obsession – these probably remain the best words. And later, so many years later, when she was old and dying? In her old age the strain or tension remained, for over the years it had become part of her and it was too late for her to change, even if she had deemed it necessary, but then, right at the end of her life, that obsessiveness disappeared, as if that distant goal had been attained and all that she had striven for had been fulfilled. Was that then what she had desired all those years, without ever knowing it clearly herself: the money and the farms and the town house, Maans's education and his stylish young wife, her own status in the small community as Father's widow, the seat in the front row at church, the cape embroidered with glittering jet? Had it all been for that then, the unyielding ambition over the years, and the pride to the bitter, silent end?

Does this say something more about Mother?

There are two more things I know of her, two things from the time before I knew her myself, from a past about which she herself never mentioned a word. After her funeral, when the mourners came to our town house for coffee, I heard one of the young men in conversation with Oom Koos van Wyk ask whether she had also been from these parts. "No," Oom Koos replied, "her people trekked around in the Karoo." He said it in passing, like something of no importance or interest to anyone, unaware that I was listening, and he added nothing further to the remark, unaware that I was waiting, transfixed, to hear more, and now he is long dead, he and all his contemporaries who might have had similar information; and so it is all I have left, that single sentence and the almost contemptuous manner in which it was uttered; that, and a fragment from my own childhood memories, an image which has survived in spite of my being unable to place it in context, so that it must remain standing, uncertain and unclear as I remember it.

It was one winter when we were down in the Karoo, and I was quite young, though I am unable to say how old I was; I do not even remember whether Maans had been born yet and whether Jakob and Pieter were still with us. Only this solitary image has remained: how a trekboer company arrived at our winter quarters one day with a rickety cart, a few thin dogs and a flock of scabby sheep, and we were told it was Oom Ruben, Mother's brother. Where he and his family had come from, where they were going, how they had found us and what the reason was for their visit, of that I know nothing, and all I have retained is the image of the forlorn little group of trekkers in the sunshine of the winter's day, the woman gazing out from under the tented hood as if she were not expecting any welcome, the shy, neglected children, and the man with the wild, black beard and Mother's dark, flashing eyes, deep in their sockets like hers; but, above all, it is Mother herself

I recall, how she and this strange man greeted each other without any display of affection or even recognition, as if these were strangers who had arrived here at our stand, and how they surveyed each other warily and suspiciously from a distance, as if they knew and understood each other too well to put any trust in the other. I do not think it was a long visit or that there was much conversation: the visitor got whatever it was he had come for – money, I suppose – and then the whole strange, bedraggled company turned around and disappeared among the geelbos and thorn trees as they had come, and never was there a single mention of them or their visit, nor did I ever hear of them again.

Is this, therefore, the world Mother came from? I wonder now, looking back and remembering: the daughter of a family who moved with their stock from fountain to fountain and from farm to farm in search of a temporary stand, tolerated by the white people, despised by the coloured people, a half-wild group of drifters and hunters as still existed in the interior in those days, trekking around in the Karoo, as Oom Koos had said where he sat having coffee in our town house after her funeral. Oom Ruben and Oupa Adam – yes, where do those memories spring from all of a sudden, like echoes from the bottom of a well, things I did not even know I remembered any more? Father laboriously entering Maans's date of birth in our family Bible with the scratchy, messy quill pen, and Sofie standing behind his chair, watching, and asking whether Pieter had also received his grandfather's name. "No," Father replied, "his grandfather's name was Adam, but we did not feel it was a proper name for a child." He was referring to Mother's father, the grandfather after whom Pieter, as the second son, should have been named. Adam and Ruben – Biblical names – who was it that had decided against it? Perhaps Mother herself, who had preferred to forget the names and the world from which they came, or perhaps Ouma, who had still been alive then, Ouma from the

Bokkeveld with her wall-cupboards and her china? But if this were all so, how did it happen then that Father married Mother and brought her here, and how did they live here together all those years, with Father and Mother in the first house and Oupa and Ouma in the new homestead? Dulsie would have known, but she is dead too, and the little information she had ever disclosed had been so sketchy and confused that I would not have been able to compose any answer from what I remembered of it. Now I would never know; never would I be able to come closer to the truth than with that single memory of Oom Ruben and his shy, withdrawn family with their wary eyes who had slunk out of our lives like scraggy wolves to some distant and unknown destination; Oupa Adam and Oom Ruben with their rickety wagons and their old rifles, silent men with deepset black eyes.

At the time my earliest memories of Mother begin, she must have been around forty: her date of birth can be seen in the family Bible in Maans's house and on the big white stone in the village graveyard that had been erected for her by Maans, and for now one would still be able to look it up if it were important. I do not remember these things any more. At the time, she had already been married for more than twenty years and whatever objections or misgivings there might once have existed concerning her marriage had been removed by the deaths of Oupa and Ouma; she and Father had moved across to the new house with its wall-cupboards and its four-poster bed and had had it extended for their family, and there was no one to contest or threaten her possession of it.

Though Father may not have inherited much, as Oom Herklaas maintained, it must have been sufficient, and with time his wealth had increased; though he was not a rich man, we might have been described as well-off. We never knew any real hardship, not even in times of drought or in years when the migrant herds of antelope, the locusts or the frost caused severe damage: there was always enough food – mutton or venison, with samp or rice, fruit, fresh or dried, if the frost had not ruined the blossoms, milk and butter in summer, and sometimes even bread, for we had a field where Father could sow some wheat. There were enough clothes, enough candles; there were skin-blankets and down quilts against the cold, and firewood that had been brought from the Karoo by wagon; the solid house with its thatched roof and its shutters provided shelter. Even so, though there may always have been enough, in those years there was hardly ever much more than barely enough: with unwearied attention Mother kept the keys and locked and unlocked, measured and weighed the supplies, and patched, altered and remade our clothes; no candle was ever lit unnecessarily or allowed to burn too long and not an extra log or branch was put on the fire.

We children accepted it like that, for we were not used to anything else, and where we lived in such isolation in a bare and harsh world, it was necessary to be cautious but, looking back now, I have to wonder whether her reaction had not been extreme, driven by that familiar stubbornness. Why else do I remember so few visitors from my childhood and did I get the feeling later that people from the district avoided our house; why did they have to be lured with such difficulty to attend the dance when Jakob was married and again, years later, the dance when Maans came of age? The Roggeveld was sparsely populated and the roads were bad, so that not many people paid social visits, but travellers between the Karoo and the Roggeveld, the Karoo and the Hantam, over Vloksberg, passed quite close to us; why did so few of them stop there in those years unless they were forced to come and fill their water barrels? Did they notice that the hospitality shown them was duty-bound and guarded, and that every morsel they ate and every stub of candle that had to be lit for them were noted and every barrel of water was conceded with ill-concealed reluctance? – by Mother, I have to add, not by Father; never by Father. When neighbours rode over for advice or help, they were likewise not encouraged to stay, and I cannot remember the wives often accompanying their husbands to call on Mother: they, too, would soon have discovered that their arrival was greeted without warmth and that no effort was made to delay their departure; they, too, would have felt the reserve and lack of cordiality with which Mother usually received outsiders, and in the increasingly uncomfortable silence around the big table in the voorhuis they would have realised that every spoonful of tea was being measured out unwillingly and every lump of sugar they used was resented. For as much as the people of our district called on each other, we had no part in their social interaction, and the gatherings on neighbouring farms were seldom attended by us. Only later did things start to change, when Maans came of age and got married, when the town house was built, and when Mother took her seat among the wives of the elders in the front row at church, to hold it until her death. All that, though, was much later.

It was because of Mother, always Mother, never Father. He was not a greedy or close-fisted person, but always willing to help. He liked company, even though he never said much himself, and over a glass of brandy he could even become jovial in his unassuming way; but his path was mapped out for him like everybody else's, and usually he followed it resignedly. Only once or twice did I see him turn pale with suppressed anger and Mother yield to him without his having to raise his voice or even say much. She was the one who struggled to make ends meet and who saved so doggedly – do I exaggerate when I say anxiously, as if she were trying desperately to protect us from some danger only she was aware of, and no effort were too great to ward off the lurking danger? Perhaps this is an exaggeration, but not entirely. Perhaps it was the memory of a bitter and hungry youth that drove her to try and establish for herself safety and security, and fear was indeed interwoven with that memory. I do not know, I can only try, and cannot even say whether my efforts make sense – Oom Koos's incidental remark after her funeral and Oom Ruben's unexpected visit and that anxious scrimping and saving, these are the only means at my disposal. As a child on the farm I often played on my own near the old graveyard beyond the ridge where the old people had thrown out everything they had no further need of and among the stones I gathered shards of pottery and china or bits of blue or purplish glass. Sometimes, however, there were larger pieces among the fragments, just large enough to be able to make out something of the form or pattern of the original cup or bowl from the round shape or the ornamentation; and just so I have only the fragments of my memories from which I now have to try and recover the form and pattern of the past.

It was a lonely youth, though I was never aware of it myself, and furthermore I was the youngest child and only daughter. Between Jakob and Pieter, and again between Pieter and myself, there had been other children who had died, and only the inscriptions in the family Bible and the nameless stone mounds in the graveyard bore testimony to them, and only the three of us had survived. Jakob was the eldest son who always had to take responsibility and he was favoured slightly by Mother, as far as she ever showed any sign of favour or affection, so that there was a distance between him and me, regardless of that caused by the age difference and, besides, Jakob was a reserved and uncommunicative person. I was only a child when he died, and thus he remains scarcely more than a dark, silent figure on the fringe of my childhood world. "Blink Jakob" they called him, I remember now, and long after his death people who had known him sometimes still spoke of "Blink Jakob". Contemptuously or admiringly, or perhaps both? I cannot say, neither do I know the origin of the nickname, but later they referred to him as a handsome man, and in her old age, on several occasions when Mother spoke of him to strangers, she also mentioned with a certain smugness that he had been a handsome man. Do I remember more, or is it only the memory of the nickname that conjures up further images: can I really remember something about a sleek horse, a gleaming black stallion I had feared as a child? That could have been the horse on which he used to ride through the kloof in the evenings, to Oom Wessel's farm in the Karoo; or perhaps it is only my imagination. I was no more than a child when he died, ten or twelve years old.

Oh yes, and that he had inherited Mother's impetuous nature and her fierce temper, that I still remember. Could that be why people smiled to themselves at the thought of "Blink Jakob"? He would lose his temper in a flash and was a hard master to the farm-hands, so that he was not well-loved by any of them. Perhaps he took after Mother's people, and that might have been why she was sometimes partial to him and understood him best.

And Pieter – yes, Pieter was a different kind of person. Actually I never got to know Pieter much better than Jakob, for I lost both my brothers at an early age, when I was still a child, but between Pieter and me there was not such an age difference, and he had more time for his little sister than could be expected of an older brother. Sometimes he would make me little toys and even play with me when he was not being put to work on the farm. Pieter was more like Father's people, smaller and slimmer than Jakob, with fair hair and blue eyes, and he was also more cheerful, had a quicker tongue and a livelier imagination, and was inclined to joke and tease: Pieter singing to himself while he worked, Pieter playing an old violin, or laughing on the dance floor in a haze of candlelight and fine, powdery dust. Why do I remember this now after all the years, why does that image present itself so unexpectedly? "Oh, but he could dance well!" Hesther Vlok, by then a middle-aged woman, once sighed, and it must have been her own memories that caused her to smile like that, for she was older than me and she might have been one of his dance partners. Pieter nimble and lean on the dance floor – it must have been at New Year, the dance I remember, when Sofie came to us as a bride and there was dancing. Pieter with his slim white body gripping the sheaves on the wagon, Pieter's face at the window in the moonlight, Pieter's face by the flickering light of a candle, Pieter running through the veld, laughing, running through fields of flowers in spring, stopping, his hair blowing in the wind. Later he never laughed or even smiled any more, irrevocably withdrawn in his silence, so that no one could still say what he was thinking or remembering.

Jakob and Pieter and I, but what can I say about myself? When I was a child we had no mirror, and so I never knew what I looked like: a thin, shy, silent child I must have been, just as later I became a thin, shy, silent girl. We had all inherited Mother's passionate nature and her temper, but while the boys never learned to control their tempers or hide their feelings, I was taught at an early age to keep quiet, to obey and to accept, and the feelings I was never allowed to express must have been buried inside and continued to simmer deep under the surface. A thin, shy child on a seat in the corner, hemming a cloth or knitting a stocking, that no one took any notice of and whose presence was soon forgotten, so that they said things in front of me that otherwise would probably have remained secret, or showed feelings they would probably have tried to conceal if they had realised I was there to observe them. Mother's face, suddenly pale, Father's trembling hands, the hatred flaming from Sofie's eyes for a moment – all this I saw and more, more than they could ever guess, and I stowed much of it away, to rummage among accumulated splinters and fragments now, at the end of my life, trying to understand the meaning of it all. I bent my head over my work, however, and tried not to make any sound or movement to draw attention to my presence; I learned, one might say, to pretend and dissemble where I remained seated in the corner all the years of my life, the unnoticed girl, the unmarried daughter, the spinster aunt, always somewhere in a corner of someone else's home or at the fringe of the company where she did not belong, at the fringe of other people's lives in which she played no part, busy watching and listening, busy observing, busy remembering.

So that was our family; but then there was also old Dulsie, whom I almost forgot, as one is inclined to forget about the servants, though she was with us for as long as I can remember. She came with Ouma from the Bokkeveld as a slave when Ouma got married, for her parents had given her the child as a wedding present, and years later when the slaves were freed, she stayed with us and helped to raise me. Dulsie always looked down on our other workers because she was the Ounooi's own slave, as she said herself, and she slept in the house, in front of Ouma's bed and later in front of the hearth in the kitchen, while they, the knegte and herdsmen, Hottentots and Basters, had to find a sleeping place in the outbuildings at night, or build shelters in the veld. She must have been quite old already when I got to know her; no, she must certainly have been old, because she had also helped raise Father, but, together with Mother, she still did most of the housework. Father always treated her with a certain respect, probably for Ouma's sake; but Mother knew no respect, and when Father was not there Dulsie bore the brunt of her rage as much as anyone else.

Ouma with the gilded china teacups and bowls, Ouma who had brought along her own slave from the Bokkeveld – the only other thing

I can remember is that Dulsie often spoke to me about the Ounooi, and that there was a plaintive note in her voice when she mentioned the old days. Why had I never listened to what she told me? She described how she had to iron the pleats in the Ounooi's caps with a goffering-iron and how fastidious the Ounooi always used to be about her caps. And one evening when we were sitting together at the hearth in the kitchen, she took from some hiding-place where she kept her possessions a small bundle and unfolded it for me by the glow of the fire, a worn silk apron, embroidered with flowers, that the Ounooi used to wear for smart occasions and had later given to her when she could no longer use it. Why did I wait until now to reflect on these things; why did I never ask Dulsie about Ouma? She would have been able to remember Father and Mother's wedding and where Mother had come from, she would have overheard what Oupa and Ouma had discussed in private without noticing the presence of the slave girl, and she would have known about the tension that existed between Mother and Ouma without their realising she was aware of it; like the silent child in the corner she would have had the opportunity to observe, and she had no special loyalty to Mother to prevent her from talking. So much of what I want to know to help me understand I would have been able to find out from the servants. But now it is too late, for Dulsie is dead and lies under one of those unmarked stone mounds beyond the encircling wall of the graveyard, and Gert and Jacomyn also left and are probably long dead like her, far beyond my reach, with all the knowledge they possessed. All I can do, is try and remember their voices and listen across the years to what they can still tell me where they talk among themselves, by the kraal wall, in the yard or in front of the hearth in the kitchen, without taking notice of the white child who is listening. I forgot about them; I forgot about their knowledge.

So the servants were also there, in and around the house and in the yard, that constant presence to which I can hardly attach names or faces any more, only an occasional voice, or a few words from a half-forgotten conversation, a gibe or a curse, a song or a rhyme. Gert's name and face I can still remember, of course, for, like Dulsie, he was always there: he was a Baster, or so he always called himself, and he came to us when he was a young child, so young that in later years he no longer even knew where he had come from or who his parents had been. They just found him, Father once remarked smilingly, and so he grew up around the house and on the outskirts of our family, slept somewhere in the outbuildings, received food to eat from our table and was clothed in Father and the boys' castoffs. He was the boys' playmate, for they were more or less the same age, but between Jakob and him there was always a barely concealed animosity. "Jakob has still not forgiven Gert for the thrashing he got that day at the fountain," Pieter said one day when he was taunting Jakob, that I can remember; and how, another time, Gert grew pale and rigid with anger, a knife in his hand – "Just lay a hand on me, white man, then you know what will happen to you." Was it the same occasion, and who was he talking to? To Jakob, my memory tells me, but I do not know where that certainty comes from, only that I was a frightened onlooker in the corner of the kraal – the smell of the kraal dung I can remember, and the rough stones against my back, and my fear.

Dulsie in the house and Gert somewhere in the yard with the boys, working or fooling around, or playing – that is how I remember my childhood years. Jacomyn came only later, with Sofie, and then they left together and everything changed; but that was later. Of the herdsmen, however, I remember nothing. The men were in the veld with the sheep and built themselves shelters there, the women came to do our washing and smear our floors, and sometimes I played with the children, so that they stand out best in my memory though I cannot remember any one individual; barefoot children with ulcerous legs, in a skimpy dress or short trousers made of dressed skins or an old kaross. Later Mother did not want them near the house any longer, but later I myself had no further need of their company, later, when everything had changed; I only know that they were always around somewhere, behind the pear orchard or beyond the kraal wall, so that one accepted their constant presence without taking any further notice of them. The men were sometimes thrashed for being drunk or losing sheep, they were given notice or came to say they wanted to leave, and sometimes they simply disappeared during the night with their bundles, and only the black mark of their fireplace still showed where their shelters had stood.

In my childhood years we possessed only two farms, the one in the Roggeveld and our winter quarters in the Karoo, but an effort was already under way to extend our boundaries, and I know there was constant conflict with neighbours about disputed land ownership or beacons that had reputedly been moved, and one of my earliest memories is how Jan Baster was chased from his dwelling-place near the boundary of our land. I never learned the details of this either, but I can remember an elderly coloured man at our door, hat in hand, trembling and stammering with dismay at the injustice he had come to complain to Father about; I must have been young still, for I know I had become upset too without realising why. Father stood on the threshhold, silently, with Mother close behind him, and I remember her giving him a little nudge in the back; "Tell the Hotnot to go away!" she hissed. How well I remember it, Mother's black dress and her words and that small, impatient gesture with which she urged him on. At some time or other it was discovered or decided that the land on which Jan Baster lived was part of our farm and he was told to leave, while, from his point of view, he maintained the land had belonged to him and his people for many years and his father had lived there at the fountain before him; and then Jakob and Gert rode over one evening, or they were sent, and they burned down the few small buildings at the fountain. Jakob and Gert were enemies, but in the isolation that was our shared lifestyle, none of us could afford to surrender to our feelings of animosity or affection: Jakob and Gert struggling together to bring the ox under the yoke or to pry the rock loose with the crowbar where they were stacking the kraal wall, their heads close together; Jakob and Gert riding over to Bastersfontein together to set fire to the dry thatch of the hartbeeshuisies.

How did I know this? It was probably mentioned at the dinner-table or it was eagerly discussed in the kitchen. Yes, and one evening, much later, old Dulsie snarled at Gert: "Jan Baster's curse on you, both you and Jakob!" and Gert's face clouded with anger in the dim firelight. "Old woman, just say another word . . ." His voice trails off in my ears, his face vanishes in the wavering shadow of the firelight, and I do not remember any more. But Jan Baster left, for what resistance could he offer after all, and where could he turn for help? And he and his family crossed the Groot River to Griqualand, I later heard the servants tell. Can I really remember it, that small procession with the rickety cart struggling down the road in the distance, drifting and bobbing over the waving shrubs of the veld with us watching them from the farm, and a voice telling me, "There go Jan Baster and his people"? After that our flocks were often sent to graze at Bastersfontein and our herdsmen erected their own dwellings there, and no one gave Jan Baster another thought, trembling with outrage before our door in his shabby suit of dressed skins. Who still knows today how the fountain got its name except me, lying awake here and suddenly remembering him? I never had an opinion or passed judgement, neither did the word injustice ever occur to me. There was just an old man in a suit made of skins, and a fountain where our flocks were sent to graze all the ensuing years.

This must have been the way our land ownership expanded initially and our claim to it was secured, by disputes with the neighbours and threats or acts of violence against those who were weaker than us. Bastersfontein was the first acquisition I can remember and, after that, Kliprug; later there were the purchases and later still, when Maans was a young man, the inheritances, but it started off modestly, yet persistently, and when I reflect on it now, I realise that my early childhood was actually filled with the ongoing blurred arguments about the boundary fences and beacons of Kliprug, where Oom Barend Swanepoel's herdsmen were reputedly trespassing on our land and had to be driven off forcefully by Jakob and Gert. And once more there is such a sudden, unpleasant recollection of violence, old Oom Swanepoel with his reddish beard, slamming down his fist on the big table in the voorhuis, Mother in her black dress, leaning across the table towards him, both hands resting on the tabletop, shouting at him shrilly, the way she shouted at the farm-hands in the kitchen, and Father sitting between them, helpless or powerless, not trying to intervene in their heated argument while Mother drove the old man from the house with her words as if she were wielding a sjambok. "I won't be driven away from here like Jan Baster!" the old man shouted over his shoulder in parting, neither could they do it, for he was a white man and they could not simply burn down his house and evict his family, yet in the end he was forced to leave, how, I do not know. "Your grandfather drove to Worcester to get that piece of land," old Oom Kasper Vlok told Maans at the wedding at Gunsfontein years later, "and I don't suppose you're sorry today, are you?" They were discussing Maans's sheep that were grazing on the land that had been part of Kliprug in the old days, though nobody remembers the name today, and how good the grazing was there; I sat across the table from them and heard the old man's words, and then I remembered the name Kliprug and suddenly old Oom Swanepoel appeared before me again. I know they conferred by candlelight, Father, Mother and Jakob, and that there were documents on the table that Meester had to come and read to them, so it must have been before Jakob's wedding, when Meester was still with us. Perhaps they consulted an attorney or the magistrate, or Father might even have had his horse saddled and ridden all the way to Worcester as Oom Kasper had said, for the Vloks lived just beyond Kliprug in those days and he would probably have known. But however it may have been, the Swanepoels likewise disappeared, soundlessly and without repercussion they disappeared, and Kliprug was added to our land as if the disputed boundary fence had never existed.

Mother in her black dress – at the time I did not think about what I had seen or heard, but as I watched her become prouder and more headstrong over the years, I realised how important land and property were to her, and what a high price she was prepared to pay for what she desired, acre by acre, morgen by morgen, and farm by farm. What fired this acquisitiveness that was daunted by nothing and no one, and saw all methods as legitimate? Perhaps that old insecurity and poverty, the bitter youth, the shabby wagon, the worn skin-blankets, the small handful of tin knives and spoons? Could it be that land meant more to her than merely a specific ridge or piece of shrubland or so many fountains, and grazing for so many sheep, and did she see it as a means to everything that had once seemed unattainably distant to her, the power and the status which she finally did achieve, the town house where she hosted visiting ministers, and the seat in the front row at church? I can only try to determine and recognise the pattern; with no hope of understanding it any more.

Thus, since the beginning there must have been a goal, no matter how vague it may have been at first, and a plan, though initially it was carried out rather blindly. At the time I am actually talking about – my childhood years, when I began to take notice of what was happening around me and could remember – it gradually began to take shape, however, around Jakob as the eldest son at first, and later around Maans, his heir; but a goal there had always been, and we children were employed to help achieve it too.

Father could sign his name and read to us from the Bible painstakingly but not much more than that; at the time I can remember, it was mostly Meester who read to us from a Dutch book of sermons on Sundays, and later the task fell to one of the boys, for Meester said the letters hurt his eyes. I never saw Mother with a pen in her hand, neither do I recall her signature anywhere, nor that I ever saw her read, or write even a note. In those years and in those parts there were no schools, and there were few educated people among us; Father and Mother's contemporaries probably achieved little more than they, and the same went for their children. We had to be educated, however, and when Jakob and Pieter were still young, every effort was made to find schoolmasters for them. Where did Father find these people and how did he retain their services? There was a succession of these tutors, none of whom remained long, and in fits and starts the boys received some kind of education over the years, so that both of them could read and write and do arithmetic; Jakob did not like studying, but Pieter actually had a few old books in which I sometimes saw him read. As I remember, it was always Jakob who was summoned to consult with Father and Mother, yet when a letter had to be written, it was Pieter who had to come, while they sat watching him, dictating what they wanted him to write.

I cannot remember any of these tutors, only the last one that I still knew as Meester. By then Jakob had been confirmed and had stopped taking lessons, but Meester still taught Pieter, and, as he had ample time and no other way of passing it, he taught me a few things here and there in between, though it was not considered one of his duties. I doubt whether Mother really liked it much, but in the end I would have had to get a little education somehow in order to be confirmed, and I cannot remember her ever expressing outright disapproval.

Meester was a Dutchman, and I think that was all we ever found out about him. Dulsie once told us that Father had found him in the Karoo, barefoot in the road with his tin trunk on his shoulder, and had given him a ride out of sympathy and had brought him home to teach the boys, but Dulsie did not think much of Meester and this was not necessarily true, though he did indeed possess a tin trunk. He took his meals with us and before supper in the evenings his feet were washed with ours; yes, and as I have said, on Sundays he read the sermon to us, and I remember how I admired the enthusiasm he brought to the task, even though I did not understand the words in High Dutch. That, however, was as far as he was accepted by the family, for he lived in one of the outside rooms and Dulsie and Gert looked down on him as if they felt he should not be regarded as one of the white people.

The past is another country: where is the road leading there? You can but follow the track blindly where it stretches before your feet, unable to choose the direction in which you want to go. Why am I reminded now of the outside room with its meagre furniture where Meester stayed, and how as a little girl I would sometimes visit him there, and how formally he would welcome me then, as if it were a grown-up who had come to pay him a visit? Of course it was only a game, but to me it meant a lot, and for all I know to him too, for he must have been lonely on that isolated farm among strangers, far from his own country. What we spoke about I no longer remember, though I believe it was probably mostly he who did the talking while I sat listening, wonder-struck and uncomprehending, the way I listened to the sermons he read aloud on Sundays. Sometimes he showed me his books, and I remember some of them had pictures that I found pretty, for in our home there were few books, and pictures were unfamiliar to me. And once he unlocked his tin trunk and brought out a silk handkerchief and showed me what was wrapped inside, and it was something I had never seen before, a black and silver cross so tiny it could fit into the palm of my hand. It is the cross our Lord hung on, Meester told me, and then he wrapped it up again quickly and told me not to mention to Father or Mother that he had showed it to me. What it meant, I did not understand, as little as I understood the secrecy, but the shared confidence was like a bond between us and afterwards, when I visited him in his room, I sometimes asked to see the little cross once more and to hold it in my hand. In our home there were no pictures and no ornaments, and all I had in my youth was Ouma's brightly-coloured china in the wall-cupboards, the pictures in Meester's old books, and that tiny cross that I dared not mention, that I could not understand and about which I dared not ask questions. It must have been something Meester had brought with him from abroad that had value or significance to him in his loneliness with us on the farm.

Meester stayed with us long enough to teach me to read and write, that I know for sure, for I remember how, later, we had written each other notes that we hid in a hollow between two stones in the wall encircling the graveyard; Meester tore blank pages out of his books and tore these into narrow strips which we then rolled, and on the back of each other's notes or between the lines we wrote our replies. It was a game, nothing more, a token of affection or trust, and what we wrote to each other was unimportant. How few were the people who ever showed even just a liking for me, not to mention love; as few as

I ever loved myself. Father, Meester, Pieter, Sofie and later Maans – were these all? Yes, there was no one else and, except for Maans, they are all long dead.

Meester left us when Pieter was confirmed: he went down to Worcester with us for Nagmaal, as usual, and then he was suddenly gone. He had probably been dismissed, or possibly he realised his services would no longer be required, and to the others his disappearance was so unremarkable that they found it unnecessary to give me an explanation or even to mention it; but I had expected from him at least a word of farewell, and for days I searched for him among the Nagmaal-goers in the village and among the assembled faces in the streets and in church, but in vain. So, when we returned home I went straight to the graveyard to search for a message from him in the hollow between the stones and, groping into the narrow opening among the stones, my fingers found something, a piece of paper torn from a book, wrapped around the little cross he had left for me as a parting gift because he had known he would not be returning to the farm. I put it back between the stones, for I realised it was a secret nobody else should know about, and later I found a remnant of cloth somewhere to fold around it and a piece of sheepskin to wrap it up more securely, and so I treasured it for years without understanding the nature of the gift I had received.

2

....

That was when Jakob got married and Sofie came to us. Meester had left, and Pieter had been confirmed and had to pull his weight on the farm, so that he no longer had as much time for me; by then I was older and had more and more responsibilities around the house, where I spent most of my time with the two women, Mother and Dulsie. And then Sofie came; and I still remember how she stepped into our silent circle as we stood outside the house to welcome her and how, suddenly, she knelt down before me to hug me, and exclaimed, "Now you're my little sister!" She could not have been very much older than me, despite being a married woman: her date of birth is inscribed in the Bible along with the date of her death, and one might look it up, but if the one were a lie, the other might just as well be false, so it makes no sense to take the trouble. Seventeen or eighteen I would guess now, or perhaps even younger, for girls married young in those days, and how glad she must have been to discover in that small, secluded world and in that silent circle a child in whose company she could still be a child herself.

How can I say what Sofie was like in those years; how can I even say how she appeared to me or how beautiful she was to my childish eyes, how do I know where to begin? Sofie's face in the glow of the candlelight, yes, indeed, let me start there, for when I mention her name or think of her, that is the image rising relentlessly before my eyes in the dark, Sofie bending over the candle, her long, dark hair like a veil across her face, like a shade before the light, and then the darkness blotting out all as if it had never existed. No, not that, not that, that was not what I had wanted to remember, it was something else. Sofie with the candle in her hand, Sofie raising the candlestick slightly above her head, floating through the dark, Sofie as I saw her for the very first time; let me start there.

Every winter we, like everyone from the Roggeveld, moved down to our outspan in the Karoo with the sheep and all our household effects. Usually early winter had already set in here on the escarpment, and sometimes the first sparse snowflakes were already whirling over the ridges as we toiled down Vloksberg Pass with the loaded wagon, driving the sheep ahead of us, and from the faded grey world of renosterbos and harpuisbos, slowly we toiled down the steep slopes of the mountainside, bouncing and jolting over the rocky ledges, to the mild air and herbaceous scents of the Karoo, to the veld where the geelbos glowed in the sun and thorn tree and karee provided shade against the heat of the day. On that particular day I am thinking of, it happened once again, as often did, that something broke along the way and had to be fixed, and so we reached the far end of the kloof with the sun already setting, still a long way from our destination; yet, with that peculiar stubbornness that sometimes took hold of Father, he decided that we should push on, even if it meant we would arrive only at midnight, and, as usual when that happened, Mother did not protest. Thus we were still on the road at dusk, and so I climbed into the wagon and, leaning against Dulsie, fell asleep, only vaguely conscious of the jolting motion of the wagon over the uneven ground and the scent of crushed vegetation under the wheels. I woke up to the sound of dogs barking, and Father shouting at the oxen to halt, and, still half asleep, I knelt and looked back from under the tented hood, vaguely aware of people and voices and the trampling of horses in the dark; and somewhere I saw a light, a flickering light bobbing through the dark, and a woman's face appeared for a moment in the distance beyond the darkness as she raised the candle in her hand, before vanishing once more in the dark among the bewildering noise of voices and horses' hoofs, while I remained kneeling there, dazed and awestruck, and in the end I probably fell asleep again. The oval of her face and the symmetry of her eyebrows and her dark eyes, visible for just a moment; but stamped into my memory forever.

We had got lost in the dark and arrived on the farm where Sofie's people were camping that winter, on the near side of the kloof from our own outspan, and we must have spent the night there and taken the long way around the mountain to our own land the next morning, that was all that had happened. But that way, as I had seen her there with the candle in her hand, Jakob must also have seen her that evening, and Pieter must have seen her in the darkness for the first time, for the two of them had been on horseback, driving the sheep, and it must have been they who had been circling the wagon, invisible in the dark. Thus they, too, had seen her face as I had: did they also remember it till the end like me, did Jakob see it before him when he slipped and fell, his face against the rock; did Pieter carry it with him through the silence?

That is all I remember of that winter that distinguished it from other Karoo winters of my youth. As far as I know, we had never met Sofie's people before, for her father was a wealthy man who owned several farms in the Karoo and the Bokkeveld, and it was the first time they had camped there for the winter, but they were practically our next-door neighbours, just around the mountain from us. Could it be that Jakob had ridden over to the neighbours? I suppose so, for it was only an hour on horseback by way of the shortcut through the kloof, and in winter people used to call on each other and entertain all the time: why would he not have called on her? Oom Wessel might have been a respected man, but likewise we were well-to-do people in the Roggeveld, and Jakob was the eldest son and heir and an attractive young man to boot, handsome with his dark eyes, despite being a bit surly and temperamental. On his gleaming black horse through the kloof in the moonlight to call on Sofie, the mild air sweet with the scent of shrubs – is this something I am imagining now, or could it be a distant recollection somewhere from the depths of my memory? It must also have been that very winter that he decided to marry her, or perhaps it was decided for him that this rich man's daughter would be a suitable bride, for, as with everything that happened in our home, that, too, would have been considered and discussed, albeit not openly, and Jakob would not have acted without Mother's approval, that much I do know. Was that how it happened? I am merely guessing now; more than half of what I know is speculation and assumption, and from stepping stone to stepping stone I traverse the past, uncertain of every footstep. Much different, however, it could not have been. "You're the one who wanted it like that," Father said to Mother without raising his eyes, and his voice was flat, but his hands were trembling as he picked up the Bible, and that was the only time I ever heard him reproach her and she grew suddenly pale and turned aside and made no reply. So, it must have been like that.

At the end of the winter we returned to the Roggeveld, and I suppose Jakob came with us to help with the trek, but he must have gone back shortly afterwards to fetch Sofie. They probably got married in Worcester, but none of us was there, though I know of no reason for it, only that they were already married when they came to us and that he led her into our circle as his wife. Anyway, it was still spring when she came, that bleak, treacherous spring with its changeable winds and its constant threat of cold and frost, the veld fleetingly bejewelled with colour and the dams glittering like lakes and marshes in the sun. We must have been expecting them earlier, for I remember that to me as a child it had seemed an endless wait, and when the dogs began to bark and we heard the horses outside, it was already dark, so that Dulsie stooped to pick up a burning branch from the hearth when we went outside to welcome them. That is how I saw her for the second time, just as she had appeared to me the first time, the oval of her face lit up for a moment by the flickering of a flame, before Jakob lifted her off the wagon-chest: that is how Sofie came to us.

A rich man's daughter – who said that? It was at a wedding or a funeral, as usual, where the voices flowed together as I moved among the people without anyone noticing me or realising that I overheard their words, gathering information and collecting splinters to piece together a pattern. Father's funeral, and the men discussing Maans – whose voice had it been? I can no longer identify it, nor put a face to it, it is only the words that I still remember: "But after all, she was also a rich man's daughter"; for by that time both Maans's grandfathers were dead, and he had inherited from them both. Yes, it must have been true, for it was clear that in the house where she had grown up, there had not been that painstaking effort to make ends meet that we were used to, and that everything she had needed had been supplied readily and generously, and in her conduct there was also a certain delicacy and refinement rarely found among people in our part of the world. Perhaps these things would not have been immediately apparent, but to us who shared a home with her they became clear enough, and I remember Mother, when she was annoyed, commenting to Father on the new daughter-in-law's dainty little manners and whims. More money, more servants, more comforts, the few months she had spent at a boarding-school in Worcester and the satin dress and ruby necklace she had brought along in her trunk when she got married, all these things distinguished Sofie's world from ours.

Was that why Mother, no matter how annoyed she sometimes became, still hesitated before Sofie, withdrawing at last in sullen silence without even trying to take her on. If there had to be conflict between the two of them, it seemed inevitable that Mother would be victorious, and since when had she ever shown reluctance to impose her will and have her orders obeyed? Why then did she, otherwise so passionate, so forceful, so domineering, hesitate before this girl and grant Sofie a measure of freedom never bestowed on her own children? It was not out of affection or respect, for Mother was fond of no one except Jakob; nor was it out of love, for Maans was the only one for whom Mother had ever felt love. At best Sofie was tolerated in our household, never accepted or even looked on with approval – no, it is not my imagination, though I can offer no proof of my opinion; I know I was no more than a child, but how could I not have been aware of such things in that house where our family lived together in five rooms and we women worked side by side day after day while the men were out? Why she had this almost privileged position among us, that I do not know, however, and only hesitantly can I try to explain it. Groping through the past, step by step along the invisible road, I remember the house in the Karoo where we arrived that evening and Sofie on the threshhold, the candle in her hand, Sofie in her satin dress on the dance floor, Sofie who had gone to school in Worcester and could read and write, and I remember Oom Ruben with his wretched wife and half-wild children and their strange submissiveness and animosity even towards those who were their kin. I struggle to form the thought, I find it difficult to say the words, and how could one ever associate a word like fear with Mother, she who remained fearless right up until that bitter and silent deathbed? But once again I wonder if this had not been what had remained concealed behind all Mother's passion and ambition after all, and if this might not also have been the reason for her inexplicable indulgence towards Sofie: the sudden fear and uncertainty of a barefoot girl from a migrant family in the presence of the wealthy farming people on whose goodwill and mercy she and her family had been dependent all their lives? No one will ever know.

What am I saying? Words keep running through my mind, and alone in the dark I am stringing together words I was not even aware I knew, and running off sentences in a way my slow tongue could never have managed before. But to what end, to what end?

Words are no longer of any use now, and the past is beyond redemption; if the girl on the cot at my feet should wake, she would distinguish no sound in the dark nor hear any movement, if she should get up to set the night-light burning once again, she would see nothing in the dim glow but the familiar room and the old woman in the bed, motionless against the stacked pillows, wide-eyed and awake. She sleeps unhindered, however, her breathing regular, and the darkness is on fire as Sofie dances before my eyes, flickering like a flame, radiant in her satin dress, black on black, veiled by the golden haze of the candlelight and the powdery dust, to the beat of fiddle and accordion, to the rhythm of stamping feet on the clay floor, like a relentless, insistent pulse. Sofie slender and straight in her black dress, and Pieter, my brother, facing her in the candlelight in the dark, the two of them together, flickering shadows black on black in the dark. The girl on the cot remains motionless.

We never entertained and we seldom visited the neighbouring farms when I was a child, but that New Year after Jakob's wedding my parents held a dance on our farm, for with his marriage many things began to change even though the transformation did not last long; it was only many years later, when Maans came of age, that there was dancing on our farm again. When Jakob got married, however, a dance was given to celebrate the wedding and to welcome the new daughter-in-law and, I suppose, also to show the neighbours, look, this we have, so far have we come by scrimping and saving and planning, silently and resolutely, and now we can breathe more easily at last and look up, without having to defer to anyone, without having to rely on anyone, and inferior to no one; come and see. Am I doing you wrong, Mother? But you never said anything yourself, you were never prepared to explain, nor did you ever acknowledge the least obligation to explain or justify. Now it is too late and only I have remained to piece my bits and fragments together to discover for myself the pattern that emerges.

Thus at New Year there was dancing on our farm, as I have said, and for days, for weeks, our house was filled with bustle and something I might even describe as exhilaration, though perhaps I am thinking mostly of Sofie when I say this, for she was as exuberant as a child at the thought of merriment and people and music after the first months of isolation and silence she had experienced with us, laughing and gay in the dark house where we lived side by side in silence, dancing through the darkness like a flame, so that, in spite of my own shyness and reserve, I, too, was touched by her happiness. The musicians had already arrived and were exchanging banter with the servants in the kitchen, and now and again one of them played a quick tune, a fragment of a waltz or seties on the fiddle or accordion, that echoed through the shadowy house provocatively and defiantly; outside Pieter called out that the first guests were arriving. The sun had not yet gone down, but inside the bedroom a candle had to be lit, and Sofie turned to me from the small looking-glass over which she had stooped to pin up her hair; out of the gloom, out of the shadows, out of the dark she rose up towards me like a swimmer from the dark waters of a pool, entangled in the heavy, gleaming folds of her black satin gown, her wedding gown, that she was wearing here with us for the first time tonight, and she reached out to me with both hands. "Sussie, you have to help me," she whispered, her eyes shining with excitement, as if she wanted to share a secret with me, but she only wanted me to fasten the beads around her neck, beads as black as her dress, unexpectedly radiating faint colours when I held them up to the candlelight. "These are rubies," she told me, still whispering as if it were a secret we were sharing, and my hands were trembling so much that I struggled to fasten the tiny hook. Silently I touched the dark, shiny gemstones and the dark, smooth fabric of her gown, for such things I had never seen before, and I looked at the rest of her finery, the narrow gold bracelet and the little gold ring with the heart. Sofie's dark head bent over the candle-flame and the pulsing of the restless music through the house and Gert calling outside and Pieter who came running across the yard, laughing with excitement, and the vast, open land out there, widespread, basking in the last rays of the sun, though here inside the house it had long been dark, the rolling veld with the shrubs and rocky ridges aflame in the late light and in the distance the dust of the vehicles on their way here.

We did not have many neighbours we could invite, here along the edge of the plateau in the sparsely populated Roggeveld with its scattered homesteads, but neighbourliness was neighbourliness, and those who were able to ride over, did so, amazed, uncertain and inquisitive about this sudden hospitality on our side; from Kanolfontein and Driefontein and Jakkalsfontein and Gunsfontein the people came, and their carts stood outspanned against the kraal wall. The house was filled with people and noise and activity, the golden glow of candlelight filled it; the women with their tiny glasses of sweet wine took their places on chairs against the walls of the voorhuis and outside in the dark one could hear the laughter of the men where they gathered around the brandy cask.

I remember Mother that evening, with shining eyes and a rare blush on her cheek-bones, rigid, tense and watchful, as if the arrival of the strangers posed a threat to her, and this rare show of friendship exposed her to danger, but nevertheless also proud of her home and the hospitality it could offer, so proud that, with all her strenuous efforts to be gracious and friendly, she was almost defiant towards her guests. I remember Mother, and Sofie in her glistening black gown, the focal point of that entire gathering, obscured for a moment as the candle-flames flickered in the draught or people moved past the light, but then glowing before my eyes once more in the diffused light. I noticed the mistrustful neighbours lined up against the wall studying her, and the jealousy of the country girls, huddling together shyly in their Sunday clothes; I saw the eyes of the men weighing her, though I did not recognise or understand that expression, and no matter how incomprehensible it has remained to me after all the years, I have seen it often enough since to know the words people use to describe it: wonder, admiration, lust and desire.

Jakob could not or would not dance, Blink Jakob, thickset, muscular and awkward – his thick neck I remember, and the broadcloth jacket stretched tight across his shoulders. Thus Jakob soon disappeared among the men around the brandy cask in the dark, and the young fellows were free to compete with each other for Sofie's favour: the bashful, reticent farm lads, ill at ease in their Sunday best, the swaggering young men in their stiff collars and embroidered waistcoats, the unassuming and the bolder ones, the confident and the hesitant ones of our small world were crowding around her in the voorhuis. I sat on the floor in a corner, outside the circle of the candlelight, among the

guests' children in whom I took no interest and who, after their initial
efforts to make friends had proved fruitless, had soon forgotten all
about me. Gradually they became weary, however, and fell over where
they were sitting or lying, but I stayed awake and observed, sleepless
in the shadows, and heard the remarks the married women along the
wall made amongst each other when Mother was not near, and the
whispers of the girls crowding around the looking-glass in the bedroom by candlelight.

Without taking the least notice of Jakob's absence, apparently even
unaware of it, Sofie danced the night away, and as the other dancers
grew tired and dropped out or went outside to where the brandy was,
more and more often it was my brother Pieter who was her dancing
partner, just as tireless as she was. I believe the farm lads of our district never really knew what to make of Pieter, but he was popular
among the girls, with his quick tongue and nimble feet, his teasing
manner, his agility and grace. Where, among us, had he ever got the
opportunity to learn how to dance, I wonder now; but he could certainly dance, and well too, and all night long you saw his slender body
moving among the dancers as if he could find no rest; later he took
off his jacket and danced in his shirtsleeves, and more and more often
it was Sofie that he chose as his partner. And why not? After all, they
were the best dancers there. Pieter in his shirtsleeves and Sofie in her
glistening gown of black satin, together in the fine haze of the dust
stirred up by the feet of the dancers on the dung floor, in the golden
glow of the tallow candles that lit up the room hazily, together, as in
a dream, with the child in the corner watching and remembering, listening and remembering: the envy, the disapproval, the resentment,
the spite, the desire that surrounded them, and the two young people
together, as in a dream.

In the end I, too, fell asleep among the other children on the floor, and someone must have picked me up there and carried me to my room, for when I awoke I was lying on the little cot underneath the window, covered with a patchwork quilt, and strange children were sleeping in my own bed. It was the noise of gunshots that had awakened me, for it was dawn and outside the young men were welcoming the new year: I knelt on the cot, resting my elbows on the high window-sill, and looked out at the silver-grey morning, chilly and still as a pool. The shouting and shooting were distant and came from somewhere at the front of the house, but inside it had become silent, only the sound of a single violin lingered somewhere, persistent, languid and melancholy, as if the fiddler no longer knew how to finish the tune, and so just kept on playing in the dim light of dawn. He must have been sitting at the hearth in the kitchen with the servants, seeking out a little warmth against the chill of the morning; and in the empty yard Gert and Jacomyn were dancing together in the silver daylight to the rhythm of the thin, dreamy waltz.

Jacomyn – yes, I have not mentioned Jacomyn at all; but she came to us from the Karoo with Sofie; she followed Sofie as she climbed from the wagon when Jakob brought her to us as his bride, and Mother told Dulsie to take her to the kitchen. She was no more than a girl, only a few years older than Sofie herself, and her mother had been a slave in Sofie's family in the old days, for Oom Wessel and his family were wealthy people, as I have said, who owned slaves just like Ouma's people in the Bokkeveld; Jacomyn herself had still been born into slavery, and when the slaves were set free, she became Sofie's personal maid and she came with her to the Roggeveld voluntarily when Sofie got married. She slept in the kitchen with old Dulsie, or sometimes on the rug before Sofie's bed, and Mother kept her distance from her, just as she did from Sofie herself, while she, on the other hand, treated us with aloofness and was usually withdrawn and sullen in our company. Only towards Gert did she show a certain ambivalence, and after her arrival he hung around the kitchen far more often, so that Mother had to chase him away and even Father had to admonish him on occasion. With Jacomyn, a further element of division of which I became increasingly aware during that time was introduced into our already divided little world, for Dulsie reacted to the intruder with immediate animosity, complained endlessly to Mother about her doings, referred to her scornfully as a Slamaaiermeid and maintained she practised magic, while Jacomyn berated her as a Hotnot, and treated her with insolent indifference.

What was the cause of the division in our family, in our home, on our farm – brother against brother, parent against child, master against servant and servants among themselves; whence came the animosity, dissension and spite? We lived together in the same house, shared the same yard, worked together on the same land, met with the same predicaments and faced the same threats and dangers, inescapably dependent upon each other on those barren heights, inextricably connected in our isolation, and nonetheless irrevocably divided, with no hope that the rift would ever be healed. Nine people in the same house and on the same farm, bending over the same task, working together shoulder to shoulder, and yet we never really got to know each other, or made any real effort to get closer, but just brushed past each other in our daily lives, and gradually the abrasions developed into festering wounds. Only in the evenings during family worship did we all come together to unite in the apparent solidarity of a common activity; or at least we gathered in the same room, family members around the large table in the voorhuis and servants to one side in the corner by the kitchen door while Father read aloud from the Bible and led us in prayer. Together – yes, only apparently so, for were we united even within the walls of that single room? How much did Father understand of that text he followed with his finger, word for word, head inclined towards the candle-flame, those words of admonition or judgement, of love or absolution, trivialised into a mere low-pitched monotone; how much of it did any of us hear, understand, take in? While he was praying I studied the people around me from behind my entwined fingers, my own family around the table in the uncertain light of the candle, Father, Mother, Jakob, Pieter and Sofie, and in the floating, fluid shadows along the wall the vaguer outlines of the servants, Dulsie, Jacomyn and Gert.

Who followed the prayer and submitted to it, except, perhaps, Father himself in his devotion? Wide-eyed I watched them at that moment when they thought they were unobserved, all busy with their own troubles, dreams or ambitions, eyes shut, heads bowed, hands raised, frozen in the routine gestures of supplication and worship, yet with their thoughts far away. From behind the protection of my folded hands I saw the glance wandering absently, the eyes filled with desire, tenderness or malice that for a single unguarded moment rested on another, eyes searching out eyes and for a single unguarded moment finding each other over the bowed heads of the others. What I saw there, I could not name or recognise at the time either, yet I was already aware of something stirring and changing, like the veld when the clouds sweep past swiftly and the landscape of stone and shrub loses its starkness for a moment to drift away in changing patterns of shadow and light. It was just a moment in the uncertain circle of the candlelight, and then the prayer was over, the chairs scraped across the floor, the candles were lit and we withdrew for the night: the family to their rooms, Dulsie and Jacomyn to their beds on the kitchen floor, Pieter to the outside bedroom where he had been sleeping since Jakob's marriage, and Gert to his sleeping place in the shed or behind the kraal. The circle of our worship had been broken once more, each got up and turned away from the others, and if you woke during the night, you would hear in the great silence of the house only the heavy breathing of the sleepers. Perhaps someone would cry out in his sleep, groan or sigh, an unintelligible sound in the darkness which you might interpret as you wished if you heard it, and then there would be silence once more, sleeper separated from sleeper in the palpable silence and darkness.

Did winter come early that year, or had our customary departure for the Karoo been delayed for some reason? We left home in cold and billowing mist that cloaked the escarpment, and we descended down Vloksberg Pass into depths we could not see. Our small procession of wagons, riders and sheep flocks descended almost blindly, following the rocky track along the edge of the cliffs, as if we were disappearing into the churning white waters of a drift, never to reappear again. How do I know it was that winter, the winter after Jakob's marriage; what gives me the right to be so certain? It could just as well have been any other winter of my youth, with the straggling trek moving down the pass to the Karoo while I stayed behind for a moment, my shawl wrapped tightly around me against the cold and wind, watching for a sign that the mist might be opening somewhere, that in our descent we had moved far enough down the mountain to catch a glimpse through an opening in the mist of the Karoo landscape in the golden sunlight down below. The last lagging sheep had already been chased ahead, the last herdsman had disappeared ahead of me down the track, the last sound, that otherwise would have echoed so clearly here in the cliffs, had been muffled by the billowing clouds; for a moment I was alone, and suddenly I was fearful, aware of the baboons on the cliffs and the wild cats in the ravines, aware of every other invisible threat that might be lurking in the fog, and I turned around. My foot caught on a stone and I heard it roll away and dislodge other stones until the rattle of falling rocks was absorbed by the muffling fog; and I fled, stumbling over the loose stones and rocky ledges, down the slope, following the direction in which the wagons had disappeared, blindly through the fog along the edge of the invisible abyss, until the rear end of our trek became dimly visible ahead of me, the wagons slowly feeling their way through the mist. I can remember no other anxiety from my childhood quite like that unexpected moment during our trek to the Karoo, that first winter after Sofie had come to us as a bride.

In the little school that Sofie had attended at Worcester, she had learnt different kinds of needlework and embroidery, and I think Mother expected her to teach me now as well, but Sofie was not really interested, nor did she have the patience, and even Mother had to acknowledge my awkwardness with the needle, so that nothing ever came of the plan. She had also had some piano instruction, but who had a piano in those parts, and so that, too, was of no use, though sometimes when she was busy on her own she sang some of the songs she had learned at school.

Thus all that remained of her education was the few books she had brought along in her trunk and sometimes took out to read, seated against the wall near the window because of the poor light. When she saw I was interested in her books and could even read from them a little, she laughed and asked who had taught me: "Pieter," I answered timidly, for even to Sofie I did not want to speak of Meester, and in a way it was true, after all, for Pieter had helped me too. After that, Sofie began to read with me from her books and, though Mother regarded the books with suspicion and did not approve of Sofie's reading, so that she was quick to interrupt it with some instruction or other, she did realise that it was useful, and so my occasional lessons with Sofie began. In usefulness I myself was not interested, but to be involved with her in this activity, shoulder to shoulder and heads bowed over the pages together in the feeble light, that was good for me and, anyway, the books she had brought along were story books that I could understand better and enjoy more than those I had read with Meester. Later she also gave me writing lessons: there must have been a lot she did not know, though she did know a little Dutch and a little English, but nevertheless her knowledge was greater than mine and she helped me as far as she could. In the monotony and isolation of her life with us, the lessons must have seemed a welcome respite to her, even almost like a little game with a girl only a few years her junior: I can remember that there was sometimes a great deal of laughter where we sat together with our heads bowed over the pages. It often happened then that Pieter would be attracted by our high spirits too and, in spite of his duties on the farm, he would manage to be somewhere in the vicinity when I had my lessons and he would be drawn in until Mother discovered him inside the house.

It was after we had returned from the Karoo that these lessons in the dimly-lit voorhuis began, during Sofie's first spring with us: the slate-grey land had regained some colour in the warmth of the sun, the dams in the marshlands glittered in the sunlight and the rocky ridges were fleetingly suffused with the brightness of flowers. The remoteness, the distance, the sunlight and the glittering of the water beckoned to us all day where we were busy inside the house, visible in fragments through the small windows set deep in the walls, and sometimes when Mother was not near to see it and forbid it, Sofie would call Jacomyn and pull me along by the hand, and then we would leave the books or the sewing and slip out into the sunshine of the day. Far off in the distance I can still see us in the wideness of that spring landscape, the two women, the glitter of the water behind them, and

Sofie unbuttoning her bodice in the heat, laughing and breathless, and Jacomyn, her headscarf tied around the wild flowers we had picked, her dark hair gleaming in the sun. Sofie and I together at one end of the table in the voorhuis where I was busy with my writing exercises, the front door left ajar to let in the light and the brightness of the landscape outside, with Pieter facing us, sprawled lazily, elbows on the table, teasing, or trying to distract us, cutting a quill pen and passing it to Sofie across the table. The water glitters in the sun and for a moment my eyes, accustomed to the dark house, are dazzled. Never had I experienced a spring as beautiful as that one, I must admit here at the end of my life, that spring before Maans was born.

Of the books Sofie and I read together like that, I understood very little at first, but Pieter borrowed them from her, and it was a secret between the three of us that had to be kept from Mother. She never caught him reading, for she would have taken the book from him and she might even have given him a thrashing, grown-up as he was, but she did know about it, just as she knew about everything else. "He's lying about somewhere outside again, reading," she exploded towards Father when some or other chore had been neglected or overlooked, and the words were also a reproach aimed at Sofie whom she never accused directly. "You must speak, husband, you must speak!" she cried out with her usual vehemence, but Father just smiled and stroked his beard defensively as was his habit. When the two boys got into an argument, Jakob sneered at Pieter's book-learning and his preference for the women's company, but Pieter only retreated into an unwonted silence and made no reply.

Sofie and Pieter and I at the voorhuis table, Pieter's blonde head bent over the quill pen he was carving for her; Pieter handing it across the table, and Sofie reaching out her hand to take it from him, while I glanced up from my seat beside her and noticed it: a gesture like so many others among people who live in the same house and share the same life, passing the knife, the bowl, the leather thong, the candle, and accepting it without a further thought. Why then do I remember the passing of the pen rather than that of knife or bowl, candlestick or thong? Outside the dams were blinding in the sun, for the fountains were running strongly after the winter's snowfall and the pools were full; among the bulrushes and the reeds the water caught the light and the hollows were sodden. Sometimes Sofie and Jacomyn would disappear together and leave me alone inside the house with Mother and her silent but unmistakable disapproval, and only at dusk would they return. Or was there only that one occasion, that evening when they arrived home agitated and afraid after the candle had already been lit in the voorhuis? They had gone for a walk to pick flowers and some children had thrown stones at them – was that the way it happened? I must have been half-asleep by that time and I only remember the agitated voices; they must have stumbled on the shelter of one of our herdsman families in some remote part, and the children they came upon were unused to strangers, or took fright at the white woman, and threw stones at them. I remember how angry and upset Mother was and how furious Jakob became, while Father tried to soothe and appease. Were they raging at the children, or was it Sofie who had infuriated them with her irresponsible behaviour? I still remember Jakob's dark face and how he struck the table with his fist and threatened to chase the people at Bastersfontein away once and for all so that they would never return; but is that really the way it happened, was it Bastersfontein he mentioned that evening in the candlelight, or are there other memories that have become entwined with what I recall of that evening? Was that the evening when the chair fell over and the door was slammed shut? Out of cobwebs and shadows my imagination weaves illusions in an attempt to find something I can understand.

Dimly, dimly, across the years, through the dreams, through the drowsiness of the child who once heard it all through a haze of sleep I remember the clamour of the angry voices by candlelight, the chair, the door; I remember the thatched roof collapsed over the walls of the house and the dried-up fountain where no mud retained a print any more.

How rich the Roggeveld always was for a few weeks after the end of winter, when the wild flowers appeared in the bright light and cold wind of the tentative spring, the only wealth that meagre land ever knew. I remember the spekbos radiant-white like a snowfall along the rocky ridges, large patches of yellow katstert, blazing like candles, and the fields of kraaitulpe like fire, the gous-blomme and botterblomme and perdeuintjies, and when the scattered clouds swept past the sun, the entire bright veld creased and furrowed like water, and the people moving across it were like swimmers on the surface of a dam, rolling on the waves of shadow and light. As the women approached, laughing, their hands filled with flowers, their feet were tangled in the shadows; Pieter stumbles as he runs towards us and for a moment he is carried forward by the surge, his golden hair gleaming in the sun. How did Pieter manage to extricate himself from his work and slip away to come with us? Laughing, he reaches out with his hands to break his fall, laughing, he struggles against the swell and for a moment remains afloat on the heaving surface where he is caught by the sunlight, and then the dark water washes over him and obscures him from my view. The women's voices waft away on the wind so that I can no longer hear Sofie and Jacomyn calling my name; I start, and see Sofie standing before me, her dress flapping in the wind, and the flowers she has picked fall from the careless posy she holds out to me and are blown away by the wind. Impatiently she presses the flowers into my hand and turns around, turns away from me, and disappears into the tide of sliding, shifting shadows and light; laughing, she runs after Pieter, while Jacomyn remains standing beside me, following them with her eyes.

It was during the spring after Sofie's arrival, that spring and summer, I presume, because I am bewildered by the succession of bright days and I can no longer distinguish one from another; but that summer she was already pregnant with Maans and everything was different, not only because the birth of the child would determine the date of our usual departure for the Karoo or because Sofie was more often indisposed as her pregnancy progressed, but because of the high expectations the birth of Jakob's son raised in Mother, so that Sofie was treated with a newfound attentiveness and consideration, and the pregnancy and approaching confinement were increasingly allowed to influence even the most important arrangements and routines of our daily lives. This was the child of the eldest son, the first grandchild and the future heir, and from the way Mother was preparing for his birth, I must conclude as I look back now that she had begun to amass his inheritance much earlier, even though the process was evident only occasionally, as with Basterfontein and Kliprug.

That summer Sofie was pregnant, and when I think of that summer my first memory is of Jakob and Pieter and Gert harvesting corn in our field, and of Pieter's pale body as he stood on the wagon, laughing in the sunshine. By this time Sofie was walking with difficulty and had to lean on me over the uneven surface of the track; yes, now I remember how it was, and it becomes clear again how those memories fit together. Gert had come back home to fetch the wagon, and Sofie came running to where I was busy in the voorhuis. "Come, Sussie, let's go along to the corn-field!" she whispered as if it were a secret that no one else should know, and we slipped out through the kitchen and disappeared around the corner of the outside room quickly before anyone could see us from the house. We followed behind the wagon, trying to catch up with it, Sofie's hand on my shoulder as she leaned on me heavily over the uneven rocky track across the veld; but though she moved with difficulty and was soon out of breath, she was laughing like a child, driven by an excitement which swept me along though I did not understand. Laughing and out of breath, we caught up with the wagon and climbed aboard, and so we reached the cornfield where Jakob and Pieter were harvesting together. To me it was just an adventure and it was only when we arrived there that I realised from Jakob's outburst how much I did not understand yet. What was the reason for his anger? Sixty years later I still cannot understand it. Jakob had never shown any consideration, neither had he ever been particularly attentive to Sofie as far as I can remember; could it have been Mother's disapproval and reprimand he feared, or did he in some way not quite clear even to himself sense that his authority as Sofie's husband was at risk, did he already begin to sense he was losing her and she was slipping away from him in the golden haze of candle-light and dust, into the dark depths of the shadowy water? Jakob had always been a strange man with his silences and his outbursts, and who could say what was hidden behind them? To this day I struggle to find an explanation or an answer, so what can one expect from the child in the cornfield sixty years ago? Mystified, I knelt on the ground and watched them as they stood there, Jakob and Sofie and Pieter, in the summer sun in the field where the sheaves were stacked, and I realised they were grown-ups whose lives I did not understand: I remember the heat and the silence and Jakob's fury, and how the tap of the water barrel beside me was dripping and had formed a moist, dark patch in the soil. I poured a little water into a bowl to drink and to splash on my burning face, and then Sofie sat down beside me on the ground and I poured her some water too, while the men began to stack the sheaves on the wagon, Jakob and Gert handing them to Pieter, who stood on the wagon, so that the load was stacked higher and higher until they had to throw the sheaves up to him with pitchforks.

I knelt next to the water barrel and watched their shirts turn dark with perspiration, and Jakob's muscles bunch together as he continued rhythmically and relentlessly in order to finish and reach home before sunset, as if his irrational passion and fury had been translated into labour, while the other two men strained to keep up without showing that they were tiring. And when the last sheaves had been thrown aloft, Pieter took off his shirt as he stood above them on the wagon and wiped his face with it, and I remember his lean, slender body and how he stood there on the stacked sheaves, laughing and taunting the other two, Pieter with his quick tongue and his banter, and Jakob with his relentless silence: how clearly I remember my two brothers as they stood there in the cornfield. And Sofie, where was she? I do not see her, I cannot remember her; I can only presume she was still sitting there beside me on the ground and, like me, was watching Pieter on the wagon and Jakob down below. All I remember is her voice reaching me, without being able to say where it came from. "Come, Sussie," she said, "let's go", and when I looked up, she was already walking away from us across the veld, so that I had to run after her. As we were leaving, we heard Jakob call after us, and after a while Pieter also began to shout at us to come back and ride home on the wagon, but Sofie gave no sign of hearing them, neither did Jakob make any attempt to follow us. We walked straight across the veld in the direction of the house, while the men on the wagon had to follow the track, and arrived only after us, but it was a long way for us to walk, and over the last stretch Sofie began to lean more heavily on my shoulder again.

Was I thrashed by Mother because I had disappeared from the

house without permission? I do not know, because by that time I had learned to distance myself from Mother's anger and her punishment. I do not remember whether anything more was said – the faces around the table and the angry voices could just as well have belonged to that evening as to any other; the chair falling over, the door being slammed – but it was our last excursion of that kind and Sofie's last escape from the house, for very soon her condition became more of an impediment, confining her to the house increasingly. I know that she tried to occupy herself with sewing where she sat near the window in the voorhuis, but she had very little patience and she often pricked her fingers with the needle so that the item she was stitching was flecked with blood, and sooner or later she would let it fall, on to her lap or to the floor, and just sit staring through the window. Our lessons did not continue for long either, and later I would just sit down on the floor beside her with one of my books and try to read to myself as well as I could manage in the available light, my back resting against her chair: motionless she would sit there with her swollen body and her swollen feet and often she would cry to herself, tears streaming soundlessly down her cheeks. Why? Sofie at the window with Mother's foot-stove under her feet, and Jakob leaning across the table, both hands resting on the tabletop, and the bitterness of their accusations and reproaches, so that Mother came from the kitchen to intercede – do I remember this, can I really remember it, did it really happen? Cobwebs, shadows, illusions; I shall never know, only that the separation and estrangement between them were real, however it may have been expressed, and that I knew about it and can still remember it to this day.

The baby was expected early in winter and it was out of the question that Sofie could go down to the Karoo with us: it was thus decided that, for the time being, only the men would go with the sheep, and that Pieter would return with the wagon and a load of firewood and would take us, together with the household effects, as soon as Sofie felt up to the tiring journey. It was the first winter I ever spent in the Roggeveld and that alone is reason to make it stand out in my memory. The men had left, the herdsmen and their families had gone, and only us women were left behind at home, Sofie with her shawl wrapped around her in the voorhuis where the fire-pan now burned all day, Dulsie and Jacomyn in front of the fire in the kitchen, and Mother and I. Dulsie was disgruntled because she would have to endure part of the winter here, but otherwise we co-existed mostly in silence, and silently we moved past each other, briefly united only for evening prayers, where Sofie read aloud from the Bible and Mother strung familiar phrases together into a prayer. After a while Pieter came back from the Karoo with the wagon and he occupied himself around the house, chopping wood for the kitchen and tending the oxen, but there was very little for him to do, and actually we were all just waiting for the child to come so that we could join Father in the Karoo. As I remember it, Pieter was mostly inside, and he often sat with us in the voorhuis, listening as I read aloud, or talking to Sofie.

How long did that waiting period last? I no longer know. I remember it as a lengthy, vacant, translucent time, cold and clear as glass, the violence of the wind against the locked doors and shutters, the sombre horizon with its leaden ridges and the low sky threatening snow, the intensifying cold, and the silence in which we waited. The night deepens, and only the tabletop and the small glass panes of the wall-cupboards deep in the twilight of the voorhuis still catch the light, until even these reflections grow dim and only the coals in the pan on the floor still glow in the dusk.

On one of those bitter grey days, as I was helping Sofie to her room, I discovered she was holding, hidden in the palm of her hand, the wilted red bell-shaped flowers of a plakkie, though it was long past the flowering season. "Boetie gave them to me," she answered distractedly when I asked her, and he must have come upon them somewhere in the veld on one of those occasions when he disappeared from the house without telling anyone where he was going and without anyone even bothering to ask. Had she always called him "Boetie", for that was my name for my younger brother; or was it only because she was speaking to me?

Sofie did not have an easy delivery: I know I was woken during the night by her screams and could not fall asleep again. Encapsuled in the dark of the room and the comforting warmth of feather mattress and skin-blankets, I lay listening to the regular recurrence of those screams, and towards daybreak I finally dozed off again from sheer exhaustion. All of the next day the screaming in the front room continued, and I could not escape or evade it, for I had to stay inside, though none of the women had time to take any notice of me. Rigid with fear and confusion, I withdrew into a corner of the kitchen beside the hearth, not so much for the warmth as that it was simply the farthest I could escape from Sofie's room and her screams. What had my life been thus far? Grim, austere, sparse, even, without much tenderness, not to mention love, yet only periodically and partially had I been alarmed by things I did not understand, and only on that single occasion in the fog on the mountain pass had I experienced fear or terror without being able to supply a reason for it. Without the friendly cloak of the mist to hide the abyss from me, I now stared down into the darkness and vaguely realised I would have to choose before it was too late, that I should turn around and turn away and find my own way along the steep, rocky precipice. Was there truly a choice, had there ever been a choice? Considering my life, one would scarcely think so; but still, without being able to explain what I mean, I want to say that if ever I had the privilege to choose, it was at that moment as I sat alone in the corner of the dark kitchen, determining my own future blindly and unwittingly.

And Pieter? Men do not cope well with reality, and Pieter least of all: it was always Jakob or Gert who slaughtered for us and Jakob who took the lead when the men went hunting for red jackal or wild cat, and that day Pieter fled the house and did not come back inside in spite of the bitter cold but, wrapped in a jackal-skin kaross, he paced up and down in the distance, far enough so that he could no longer hear Sofie screaming. At twilight her screams at last became fainter, intermingled with feeble squawks and the voices of the women attending the birth, and Mother entered the kitchen to fetch a candle, and told me that Sofie had a boy. In the pale grey twilight of the winter evening I ran out to tell Pieter so that he could come inside and I remember the razor-sharp cold on my face and the swirling silver snow in the air, the fine white shimmer of snow on Pieter's hair and on the jackal-skin around his shoulders as he came inside to the candlelight and the fire.

Thus Jakob had a son, that squawking little creature in the crib beside Sofie's bed. That winter in the Karoo he was christened Hermanus after his grandfather, and he was called Maans; but he would be the only grandchild, and there was never any heir other than he.

After the confinement Sofie was eager to get to the Karoo, and Mother, too, probably wanted to escape from the Roggeveld as soon as possible before winter really set in and we were snowed in. Thus, as soon as it became possible for Sofie to travel, Pieter took us down in the wagon, with Sofie and her baby cocooned in down quilts and pillows as we jolted from one rocky ledge to the next, along the edge of the cliff.

Nearly every year of my youth and most years afterwards I travelled to the Karoo with my family in that way, at first down the slopes of Vloksberg Pass, and later, when the road had been built, by way of

Verlatekloof, initially with Maans as a newborn baby in Jacomyn's arms, and later with the little boy running behind the wagon, or as a young man, helping to herd the sheep, or as an adult, taking responsibility for the trek himself. Why then do I remember this particular trek as the last one, while in truth it was one of the earliest in a long sequence through my entire life? Down the pass with Pieter and Sofie and her baby, over rocks wet with rain, fine, blustering hail lashing our faces, to the Karoo where birds twitter in the winter sunshine and streams surge down cliffs and crevices, heralding the rains that have fallen on the heights above, where waterfalls cascade from one ledge to the next and the day is filled with the rushing of water and the grinding and milling of the pebbles in its course.

It was late afternoon when the small trek arrived at our winter quarters in the Karoo, and I jumped from the wagon as it halted and saw Jakob walking slowly towards us through the veld, rhythmically beating his horsewhip against his leg. Pieter lifted Sofie from the wagon in his arms, while Jacomyn followed with the child, but Jakob did not approach to greet his wife or to look at his child, and we remained waiting beside the wagon as if we had arrived among strangers where the reception was uncertain and the welcome dubious. Where could Mother, who had come with us, have been and why was Father not there to welcome us? I remember the Karoo scent of herbs and bushes and grass, the twittering of the birds, and the rumble of milling rocks churned up by the floodwaters. What was the nature of the change that had taken place, so that nothing was the same after this? According to what pattern, or rules, the memory decides what to retain and what to discard, I cannot say: I remember Jacomyn climbing down from the wagon on our arrival in the Karoo with the baby on her arm, the way she ducked her head with the gleaming black hair from which the scarf had slipped from under the tented hood and with one hand lifted her dress before her feet; after all the years I still remember that insignificant, incidental gesture and I see clearly before my eyes a woman who is long dead, but what I want to know now remains hidden from me, and I can only feel around in the darkness of the past for the splinters that may help me restore the pattern.

The last trek to the Karoo I called it, even though forty or fifty others followed in years to come, and so it was, for that winter something ended, and on our return to the Roggeveld in spring everything was different. Sofie spent only two springtimes with us, the spring after her wedding and the one when Maans was a baby, but in my memory they have remained distinct, though it would be difficult for me to describe the difference between them. That she had new responsibilities and duties was not the reason, for I do not believe she took much notice of the child, and she never seemed to be bothered by the way Mother took charge of him: she never showed the least inclination to resist Mother's possessiveness, and otherwise he was left in Jacomyn's care, and Jacomyn had very few duties in the house other than to look after him. Mother and Jacomyn and old Dulsie fought silently and wordlessly over the possession of that squealing little bundle who now formed part of our family, and each was determined to stake her own claim and to stand upon her rights, while Sofie held herself aloof from the battle. It was Jacomyn, however, who raised Maans as a baby, and later I; for a few years it was as if he were my child, until Mother appropriated him completely and he finally married the woman she had selected for him. Thus that victory was Mother's too.

That spring, I might say, it was already as if Sofie was no longer one of us. What had happened that winter in the Karoo? Nothing that I can remember, nothing I ever knew about, and perhaps no more than the usual visits back and forth of neighbours and acquaintances, the music and the dancing. Sofie's family and friends were also there, of course, and for a few months she was back in the world she knew. I remember the luxurious warmth and the rush of the swollen fountains and streams, the boisterous and excited shouting and the music from beyond the thorn trees – it could have been that year or just as well any other, because that was the way the winters in the Karoo usually passed. To us, however, it was never more than a delay and an interruption, and the annual return to the Roggeveld was a homecoming every time, so predictable that, when we delayed, the sheep found their own way to the familiar heights without waiting for us: upward through the narrow shadow of the kloof to the pale undulations of the plateau with its constant threat of unseasonable frost or snow, the glittering of the water in the dams, and the dark house with its sturdy walls. For us the return was a homecoming after every absence but for Sofie, could it ever have been anything but exile?

It was late that year before spring finally arrived, and long after our return there was still frost. Sofie usually stayed inside, as she had done during the last days of her pregnancy, and our lessons were resumed, with the exception that I had suddenly been seized by a burning desire to unravel the secrets of the letters and to master the contents of the books, and to be able, in my childish eyes, to read and write as fluently as Pieter and she. Perhaps in my own way I also had something of Mother's burning ambition, or perhaps I cherished the idle hope of having my progress rewarded with her approval. Or perhaps I merely hoped to be able to enter Sofie and Pieter's world in that way, and to participate in what they shared, and from which I was excluded, something I could only associate with the reading and writing in the voorhuis, as I could find no other explanation for it. As usual, Pieter was often there when I had my lessons, teasing or distracting us, or arguing playfully with Sofie about the pronunciation, the meaning or the spelling of a word, until she herself began to laugh. Frowning and determined, with ink stains on my fingers, I bent over the stained paper, and when I looked up I saw them as they sat teasing each other across the table or conferring over a book. Heads close together, they spelt out the foreign text and followed the words with fingers accidentally touching, in the dimly-lit room where there was no observer but me, a child bent over her task, too busy to take notice and too young to understand.

The chair is overturned violently or falls over as someone jumps up from the table, and I awake from my dream; the door is slammed thunderously. What has happened, and whose voices are arguing so fiercely in the other room? Only once or more often, I do not know, but it must have been more than once in that divided house in which we lived, for strife and anger were nothing strange during my childhood years. Jakob's scorn at my sudden quest for learning, Jakob's increasing animosity towards Pieter, brother against brother, and Pieter's insidious, relentless badgering, Sofie's restlessness and her impatient outbursts against her husband, and in the kitchen the continuing feud between Dulsie and Jacomyn, and Dulsie's squabbling with Gert. Spring arrived too late and too hesitantly that year, and in the renewed winter that followed our return from the Karoo, we were forced together inside the walls of the house too often, together in the voorhuis and kitchen with all our discontent and unrest. I still remember the glittering of snow on Pieter's hair and on the jackal-skin around his shoulders; but no, that was earlier. What glittering do I remember then, blinding in the sunlight, and where did Pieter stand like that in the drifting snow, across which snowfield did he come walking out of the distance?

It snowed – after our return that spring it was still snowing, I remember now, and in the voorhuis we sat around the fire-pan together. What else? And Pieter then, walking towards me across that glittering expanse, across all the years between? We had been waiting, and in the early morning Pieter came walking towards us across the glittering snowfield with the jackal-skin kaross around his shoulders; but no, not like that. What had we been waiting for in silence, and where did he come from when he returned to us, the time I recall now? Let me try to remember.

Spring was late, and after our return from the Karoo it remained cold for a long time, and it snowed heavily at least once, that is how it was. I see us women around the fire-pan in the voorhuis, and carefully I feel my way, afraid to move too fast or to disturb, by a thoughtless movement, the delicate fretwork of the memory, for there is something here that is important. We are sitting in a small, silent circle, but it is not the customary closeness of cold evenings, for only the women are together, and I am aware of tension and distress, of the coming and going of men in the kitchen and someone stamping his feet on the clay floor of the kitchen to shake the snow from his shoes. On a low stool in our circle sits Jacomyn with the baby on her lap, and the child is crying plaintively, so that she rocks him to and fro to soothe him, but Sofie pays no attention to his whining. Sofie sits very straight in her chair, and where I sit beside her, pressed up against her as is my habit, I can see the white knuckles of the hand clutching the shawl around her shoulders. And that was how it was. And now – where to now? I hesitate for a moment, and then, suddenly, I know.

When the weather came up, Father sent Pieter to help bring a flock of sheep that had been grazing near the edge of the mountain to the kraal, and before he could return, it began to snow, so heavily that it was impossible to go out to help the herdsman and him. Later that night, when the snowfall was over, a big fire was lit on the ridge behind the house to serve as a beacon in the dark, and the following day Father and Jakob and Gert went out to search for them; but though nothing was said, I do not believe anyone expected them to have survived the heavy snowfall on the exposed mountainside. So the morning passed with us waiting for news at home, and later I was standing in the doorway, gazing out over the glittering white world stretching away, so that it was I who saw the man in the distance walking towards the house across the snow, and across the distance and with eyes blinded by the reflected light I recognised Pieter and called out, and the women came running from the house. They had been trapped by the snowstorm on the edge of the escarpment when they had only just begun herding the sheep together, so that they were forced to take shelter in a hollow under an overhanging cliff, where they spent the night: at first light Pieter made his way through the heavy snow on the slopes to let us at home know that they were still alive, while the herdsman stayed behind to search for the scattered sheep. It was a long time before they could herd together the survivors from the crevices and caves into which they had fled before the storm and where they could sometimes be trapped for days before the snow began to melt.

Thus Pieter survived and returned to us, and I remember a rare celebration in which we all took part, even in that divided household, for as I have said, while our jealousy, spite and resentment forced us apart, in our isolation we were always driven together again by the struggle for survival in that harsh world where we were inescapably dependent on each other's help to face the dangers and hardships of daily life, like the white man and the Bushman, the master's son and the servant, who survived the long dark of the winter's night together in their shelter, at last to see daylight again. I remember Father pouring sweet wine at the table that evening of Pieter's return and even I was allowed a mouthful. However, even here, in this festive moment, with the family gathered around the table, discord and unity were intertwined. What malicious remark did Jakob make about the wine poured for Pieter in such an unaccustomed way? That I do not remember any more, only Father's answer: "For this thy brother was dead, and is alive again; and was lost, and is found." Jakob was about to reply, his face dark in the candlelight, but at that moment we heard a rustling sound and Sofie came to us from the shadows of her room, dressed in the rustling black wedding gown that she had put on as if it were truly a celebration we were partaking in here. I still remember that, whatever else I may have forgotten or may have tried to forget, the silence at the table as she took her place among us, Father pushing her glass of wine across the table and Mother, after a moment's silence, remarking in an undertone, "We do not dress up like that here," as if it were a reproach. I remember Sofie in her black dress, her eyes glittering, and Jakob's dark face as he sat reluctantly sipping his wine, and the single candle next to Father's chair that left most of the large room in darkness. The chair overturns, the chair is knocked over, the candle-flame flares fiercely as if the wind has suddenly blown open the shutters, and the candle topples and falls over the edge of the table, its faint glow extinguished. On our knees in the dark we feel around on the floor, we stumble over the table and chairs now unfamiliar to us, we search in the dark for the tinder-box, and call to Dulsie in the kitchen to bring a glowing ember from the fire to illuminate the sudden and complete darkness – that evening or some other evening, or perhaps never. I can only tell what I remember.

That year spring did not bring the abundant flowers of the previous season, even though the spekbos stood white along the ridges. The sky softened and the light brightened and the landscape fleetingly took on a green radiance, but in hidden places along the escarpment, in crevices and rocky outcrops, patches of snow remained until late.

With the arrival of warmer days Sofie resumed her walks in the veld, and she often took Jacomyn and the baby along; Mother and Dulsie had much to say about these walks, and about the child being taken outdoors like that, but as far as I know no one tried to forbid it. Sometimes she would ask me along too and, if I had no work to do, Mother silently and disapprovingly allowed me to go. I can still see our little group on that grey expanse, Jacomyn with the baby in her arms, and the wind of the escarpment plucking at the women's frocks and at Sofie's hair; I see Sofie with hair billowing around her head, laughing and clapping her hands, suddenly appearing as young and as carefree as a child again.

The landscape surges in patterns of light and shade as the wind comes rolling over the ridges, and Sofie and Pieter laugh and call out to each other in words blown away by the wind – yes, Pieter, for Pieter was there too; how clearly I remember that. I am sitting on the ground beside Jacomyn, watching the baby asleep on the shawl she has spread out for him. "Where is Sofie?" I ask. "Never mind," she answers distractedly, without raising her eyes. "Never mind, they are coming, they are coming." I smell the air around us, sweet with the scent of wilde anys, and I notice the shrubs that have taken root in the clefts and the swaying white blooms of the spekbos on the ridges, that pale spring of grey and silver and white under a faded blue sky, with the water in the distant vlei glittering for a moment before growing dull once more as the entire landscape darkens under the billowing shadows that obscure the sun. That spring – yes, it was during that spring, the second spring, when Maans had already been born; I was mistaken. They are coming, they are coming. The wind shakes the branches of the renosterbos, the harpuisbos and the white blooms of the spekbos, and I get bored where I sit waiting with Jacomyn. For whom, for what? I have forgotten, for years I forgot, but now I am slowly beginning to remember again. They are coming. Pieter, my brother, in his shirtsleeves, laughing among the shrubs and bushes of the veld, and Sofie, laughing, her hair billowing around her head – it was during that spring that I saw them running through the drifting, rolling landscape, stumbling along the treacherous shadows, stumbling, falling and disappearing under the dark surface of the shadows. Did he come with us? But that is unlikely. Did he meet up with us somewhere, was he waiting for us; could it have been prearranged, and if so, how and where and when? They are coming, they are coming, Jacomyn says quietly, her head averted as she plays with pebbles and gravel where she sits waiting, and the air is sweet with the scent of wilde anys. There is so much I have forgotten, only to remember again now, to try and understand, so much I will never remember any more, so much I will never understand.

I jump up, I stumble through bushes and trip over rough, gnarled trunks, scraping my knees on rocks, shouting into the wind, groping, lost among the thickets and clefts of the dried-up fountains. Perhaps it is better not to remember it all, perhaps we are unable to endure the full burden of our memories. They slip, they slide and are lost to me. Under the ripples of shifting light and shadow they disappear, a bright wall of water separating them from me; uncomprehending, I stare down from the edge and see Sofie with her face upturned and her hair floating wide as she sinks down, see the brightness of Pieter's white shirt in the intensifying darkness as he sinks down with arms outstretched to where my eye can no longer follow them. Their bodies, now weightless, are carried by the water into the depths, borne along the invisible stream. For a moment they turn towards each other in the swell – the pale faces with dilated eyes, the streaming hair, the outstretched arms; the surging water forces them together as in an embrace, as if in search of rescue, before they disappear together and, screaming, I jump up in my bed and recognise by the dim glow of the oil lamp my familiar room with the shutters closed against the night and Dulsie who has fallen asleep on the rug beside the bed where she is watching over me.

It is quiet, no sound can be heard in the emptiness of the night. Silence, darkness; wait for the cocks to start crowing in the dark, wait for the first greyness to become visible through the shutters, for the girl to wake up and stir and feel around to light the candle. Nothing.

That summer – I remember nothing; silence and darkness. The eagle's feather in the sky, the vulture's feather, the feather motionless in the sky. The jackal on the ridge, the wild cats emerging from the rocky clefts at night to attack the sheep flocks. The whitened bones of some animal on the rocks in the narrow ravine, or the sudden brightness of blood on a rock. Who heard the cry?

What more? I do not remember anything more about that summer, it is dark before my eyes, silence is all around me after the stream of memories that has engulfed me. The shot echoing among the cliffs, startling the chattering baboons, thundering back and forth among the cliffs, just about to die away when the boom of another rifle from an adjacent kloof starts up the echoes anew. In the house the women jump up from where they are sitting in the voorhuis and run outside, and I see the white knuckles of Sofie's hand. But no, that was another time, and the hunters firing their rifles miles away in the kloof were out of earshot. There had been no shot anyway, it was that he had lost his footing, his foot on the rock, his head against the rock. I cannot remember any more; I do not know any more. I do not want to remember any more.

Wait; wait without thinking or forcing, hear the silence without listening, and stare wide-eyed into the dark. The night will pass; perhaps the night will pass without the need to remember. Wait.

Sofie's hand, the knuckles white; Sofie raising her hand to touch the blood on her face; Sofie, her long hair screening her face from the candlelight. Did he strike her? How do I know this, and was there no one to intervene?

Do not try to remember. What do I know? Simple facts that may be accounted for simply, without trying to establish pattern, meaning or coherence, without searching for more, but even that is too much.

She was not happy with us or with Jakob, of course not, but how much did I ever really know about that, except for the chair overturning, the door being slammed or the angry voices in the other room, and who can say whether these things concerned Sofie and Jakob? I can still picture Sofie clearly with the blood on her face, but is it memory or imagination? The fields of spring flowers I remember, but there were many springtimes, and can I still distinguish between one year and another? That they fell, stumbled and sank down into the dark water, of course I never saw anything of the sort, but how can I distinguish between memory and imagination when one image is as clear to me as the other? Simple facts are no longer simple; every word, every image is loaded with further memories or deeper insights from which they can no longer be disentangled. If I have to remember then, if I am forced to give this account, where should I begin, and what should I mention, what omit? But I must begin.

Summer came and the land regained its usual greyness, the sunlight was brighter; of that summer I remember heat and dust, and in the vlei the clear water surrounded by reeds and bulrushes began to dwindle, leaving at first a ring of mud, trampled by the sheep that came to drink there, then drying up, gradually cracking and crumbling. It might have been any other summer, but I remember it because Sofie's baby was still very young and his whining forms part of my memories:

the plaintive wailing of the sickly child, and Jacomyn's voice in the bedroom, hushing him, and the sound of her bare feet on the dung floor as she paced up and down. That year the lynxes were troublesome in the gorges, and one of the herdsmen brought a dead lamb that had fallen prey to one of them to the house to show Father, and then Father told Jakob and Pieter and Gert to take their rifles and go and shoot the creature, for his health was showing signs of failing, and he began to leave most of the work on the farm up to Jakob. They rode out that morning before daybreak, before I was up, and Father stayed at home. The sewing and the shiny needle in my hand, the wailing of the baby and the shuffling of Jacomyn's feet, and the white knuckles of Sofie's hand – but no, that was the winter when Pieter came walking back to the house alone across the snowfield, back from the dead. I am confused, and if my memory can deceive me like this, how can I trust it? Better to remain silent and wait, for the cock to crow, for daybreak. But I must remember.

Thus the three men rode out with their rifles and, as usual, the women stayed at home and that evening towards sunset, as I was playing outside the house on my own, I looked up, and in the haziness of the late afternoon sun I saw distant riders approaching through that drifting golden light, two riders with three horses, and when they came nearer, I saw that it was Pieter and Gert and that they were leading Jakob's horse, and I went to call Father.

Let me just tell it as it happened; or, in any case, let me repeat the account that was given, and not try to explain or clarify or understand, for sometimes the very least said is already too much. They hobbled the horses that morning at the top end of Kalantskloof, they said, and Jakob said he would go down the kloof himself while they were to search the adjacent kloofs; and then Pieter and Gert went down Baviaanskloof together and shot a reebok there. The two of them stayed together, they said, and heard no shots from any other kloof and saw no sign of Jakob, and in the late afternoon, when they returned to the place where they had left the horses, he was not there, neither did he return, though they waited until late. They shouted, they said, and fired their rifles, but heard no answering shot, and so they decided to return home and fetch help before dark. Stuttering slightly, as he sometimes did when he was excited, Pieter told the story to Father where the two of them stood in front of the house with the horses, and at the front door Mother and Sofie were listening. The reebok they had shot lay sideways across Jakob's horse, its eyes dim and the blood dried around its stiffened jaw.

They all went out to look for Jakob then: messages were sent to the nearest neighbours and, however little contact there may have been, and even though there could be no real question of neighbourliness, not to mention friendship, it went without saying that they would come over to help. The men and the voices and the horses and the flickering light of lanterns or torches in the yard lasted for several days and several nights, I know, for they searched for him in Kalantskloof for days, and they explored all the adjacent kloofs where a man on foot could get lost in the course of a morning, and all the cliffs and ledges from which he might have fallen, the crevices into which he might have disappeared, the hollows where he might have found shelter from the heat of the sun; but every evening they had to return to report that they had found nothing, not even his hat or his rifle. The women came over with their husbands to keep us company, and sat in the voorhuis: the subdued voices, the tales of sickness and sudden death, the bowls of coffee that were served all day long, and the wailing of the sickly child, the white knuckles of Sofie's hand – but no, why does that image keep returning? It does not belong here where it is constantly intruding. The neighbours helped search for him and found nothing and at last they had to give up and return to their own tasks, and we remained behind in the silent house, not knowing, or even able to guess what had happened.

For the first few days Father still rode out with them, but now he sent Pieter and Gert back to Kalantskloof to shout and fire their rifles and to explore the kloof, as if he believed it was still possible to find something, and the herdsmen were also instructed to let the sheep graze in the vicinity of Kalantskloof and the adjacent kloofs, so that they could look there for tracks or signs. And so it was a Bushman herdsman who arrived at the house one morning to report that he had been trying to reach a sheep that had slid down into a cleft in the rockface, and among the shrubs and branches blown together there, he had seen the crumpled dark fabric of a man's jacket. Then Father had the wagon inspanned and rode out to the kloof with Pieter and Gert, and he waited on the wagon – for he was unable to clamber down those cliffs – while Pieter and Gert went to search in the crevice and brought Jakob back. It must have been quite a while after his disappearance, for the body had begun to decompose, but there was no doubt it was he: he had probably lost his footing on the slope, slid down the smooth rockface where he could find no handhold, and been trapped in the narrow cleft where the searchers could not see him in the dark among the shrubs and grass collected there; during his fall his head had struck a rock, so that his skull was shattered and his face hardly recognisable, and his rifle, which the herdsman also found in the crevice later, had snapped and was irreparably damaged, as if he had gripped it more firmly as he fell. They wrapped the body in an oxhide and laid it behind the shed, for they could not bring it inside; it was nearly dark when they arrived here, and Mother and Dulsie took basins of water and clean cloths and tallow candles and went to the shed to wash him and lay him out, but Sofie did not go. How do I know all this; how do I know it was an oxhide in which they wrapped him? But that is how it was.

The field-cornet came over to examine the body, and then Jakob was buried in the graveyard beyond the ridge, beyond the pear trees. All the neighbours came over again for the funeral – there must have been twenty or thirty people, including the children – and I remember their subdued conversations and how they fell silent when they noticed a member of the family. After the ceremony at the graveside I served bowls of coffee in the voorhuis and, because I was only a child, they did not take much notice of me. It cannot be right for a wife to stand at her husband's graveside with dry eyes, they remarked deprecatingly, and spoke of Jakob's fall and what he could have been doing in the kloof where his body was found, so far from the place where he had last been seen. That was when I discovered for the first time how much you could see and hear if you remained silent and withdrew, if you watched and listened and did not allow a single word or gesture to escape you; it was then, as I moved unnoticed among the funeral-goers with the coffee, that, without realising it, I learned how to live the rest of my life. But the carts and wagons were inspanned again and they left, and on Jakob's grave stones were stacked, with upright stones at the head and foot. We heard nothing more from the field-cornet. I can still picture Sofie among the guests on the day of the funeral, Sofie in the black satin dress in which she was married; but in all that time I did not see her with anything but dry eyes either.

After Jakob's death it would probably have been possible for Sofie to return to her own people in the Karoo, but she stayed on with us and was treated with greater consideration and acceptance than when he was still alive, for if she left, she would take her child with her. That, I suppose, was how Mother and Father saw it, but I knew more than they, and when I think back now I realise only too well that Jakob's child never really concerned her, and her decision to stay was not determined by him, one way or another.

I remember us together in that silent house in our black dresses, Mother and Sofie, Jacomyn with the baby, Dulsie in the kitchen, and I. Now that Jakob was no longer there to help Father, Pieter necessarily had to shoulder a heavier load, and I also remember how sullen and obdurate he often was, so that even Father at times lost patience with his indifference and his carelessness, and in the kitchen where only the servants could hear him, he mentioned that he wanted to leave. "It's time he got married," Mother remarked brusquely one day. She was sewing, and bit through the thread as she spoke; the four of us were in the voorhuis together, Father and Mother and Sofie and I, and I can still see that decisive gesture, and Sofie beside me in her black mourning dress. Pieter was no farmer and would never be one, but what other possibilities were there for him? He had a quick tongue and he was smart, he could read and write a little, he could dance well and play the violin, but actually that was all. Somewhere beyond the mountains, somewhere in a world where we never went, and in which we had no part, in the Boland or at the Cape, possibilities may have existed for him, but not here with us.

I forgot that he could play the violin, but now I hear again that plaintive, lilting melody coming from the kitchen where the servants sat in front of the fire in the evenings. I remember Mother glancing up at the sound, frowning, for she probably found it improper so shortly after Jakob's death, but as far as I know she never mentioned it, and neither did Father; us women in the voorhuis in our black dresses around the single candle burning on the table, with Father who had fallen asleep in his armchair, groaning now and then with the gout, and that doleful music in the kitchen. As I remember, Pieter seldom joined us in the evenings, preferring the company of the servants in the kitchen or disappearing to his room outside, and during this time I also liked to slip away to the kitchen whenever I could, to the smouldering fire and the idle chatter and gossip of Pieter and the servants, the insinuations I could not understand and the sudden outbursts of pent-up emotion that I found equally incomprehensible, Pieter and Gert – no, it was Jakob and Gert between whom there was ongoing animosity and jealousy, and yet it is Pieter and Gert that I suddenly remember, their hands at each other's throats, throttling each other, with old Dulsie seated at the hearth, laughing at the spectacle. What happened and who separated them? Jakob or Pieter? Jakob, I say, and yet my memory insists on seeing Pieter there. "Hotnot, take back what you have said!" – "White man, take your hands off me!" They were arguing about a rifle, for Gert had used Pieter's rifle without permission and Pieter accused him of breaking the cocking-piece, and all evening they sat in the firelight, provoking each other with accusations and reproaches: "Who was the one that broke Jakob's rifle?" one finally snarled at the other. Jakob's rifle that Father had bought in Worcester for his confirmation, the rifle that was found snapped and broken where he had fallen on the rock and plunged into the crevice: yes, it was indeed Pieter and Gert who sat talking together that evening in the kitchen, but who spoke the words that set them at each other's throats, and what did they mean? By that time Jakob was already dead.

Sometimes Sofie still walked in the veld and sometimes Jacomyn went along with the baby; Sofie with the bodice of her black mourning dress unbuttoned so that her pale neck showed. I am mistaken, I am still mistaken, trying to force the wrong splinters together to form a pattern: it was during this time, after Jakob's death, how else would I remember it like that, with Sofie's pale skin against the blackness of the mourning attire, and Jacomyn with her face averted from me. "Where is Sofie?" "Never mind, they are coming, they are coming."

It was not the spring, it was the summer after Jakob's death that I remember, with Sofie in her black dress, lost in the swells of the shifting shadows over the veld, sinking down into the depths with streaming hair, and vanishing into the dark where only Pieter's white shirt still flashes for a moment. But the flowers that I remember just as clearly? Summer and spring flow together and one year passes into another, and no certainty remains.

Sofie's face, veiled by her hair, Pieter's face upturned for a moment to the surface to catch the light; their expressions are grim and they are not laughing any more, their faces set. That I remember, disjointed, drifting images that cannot be captured between the fingers or linked in any way. The dams flashing in the spring sunlight, the brightness of the veld like a gleaming silver lake, and the silver moonlight in which the wide landscape lies undisturbed. I am confused again and I hesitate, uncertain. What is it that struggles to be released from my memory? Sofie's face veiled by her long hair in the candlelight, a deeper and more motionless silence and the flame of the candle-stub burning motionlessly in the bowl before it is suddenly extinguished and silver moonlight spills over the floor. Voices in another room, the words inaudible, or perhaps kept low on purpose so as not to be heard.

I do not wish to remember any more

Silence. If only I could sleep, if I could die, but neither is possible: this is dying, but not yet death; I lie awake and waiting in the sleeping house, defenceless against thoughts and memories and the inexorable obligation to report and to remember. Who would ever have thought it possible that I could remember so much, that, unwillingly and under protest, I could recall so much in a single night?

Here, in this room where I am lying now, I also slept as a child; it has been my room all my life, except during the years when I lived in the town house, first with Mother and later on my own; until Maans built the new house with its wooden floors and fireplaces and wall-paper and we all moved there, Stienie's house where I never felt at home, not even in my own room. This is my room; strange how it turned out that I was carried from the new house to be brought back here to die. I still remember the heavy silence within the shelter of the thatched roof and the thick walls and the uneven dung floor: over there is the window with its shutter closed against the night, and there the door to the voorhuis; on the other side of this wall Mother and Father are asleep in the big old four-poster, and in the kitchen Dulsie has spread her bedding in front of the hearth. Nothing in this sheltering dark is uncertain, and when I awake during the night, I am aware of that; drowsily I lie for a moment, cherishing the feeling of safety, and then I doze off again quickly and effortlessly. The small, secret night noises are barely discernible, the rustling of a mouse behind a chest, or a bat in the loft, and the call of some nocturnal animal far away in the ridges, the sudden frightened bleating of a lamb caught by a jackal, or a steenbok surprised by a lynx. In the shadows of the ridges the lynx pounces on its prey, and far away in the night a scream has died away even before I can turn over and fall asleep again, the carefree, deep sleep of a child. Are you asleep, Sussie? I do not know any more, scarcely aware of the whispered question, of the rustle of a woman's dress. A hinge creaks, someone stumbles on the uneven floor, and for a moment nothing stirs – was that what woke me, or was it the flickering of a candle-flame against my eyelids?

It was Sofie's voice here in my room, but what was she doing here? That it was here, I know for certain, for there was the door to the voorhuis and there the window overlooking the yard and the outbuildings. Sofie untied her hair as if preparing for bed, and the long, dark hair tumbled down around her face like a veil as she bent over the candle to blow it out. Are you asleep, Sussie? The house is quiet: behind the chests, between the rafters, in the thatch of the roof nothing is astir now; no nocturnal creature is calling on the ridges. I turn over and sink back into sleep.

Why would I imagine this, or with what could I possibly be confusing it? She blows out the candle, and I turn over in the dark, I sink back into sleep, and am called back by the light on my eyelids; bewildered and only partly aware of my surroundings, I perceive the brightness of the moonlight falling into the room and spilling over the floor where the shutter has been opened. Why would I imagine something like that? She blows out the candle and darkness shrouds the room, darkness shrouds the sleeping house; the shutter swings open on its hinges almost soundlessly, and the moonlight slips over the window-sill and spills over the dung floor of my room. The moon is full, and it is a brightness like daylight that makes me stir uneasily in my sleep without awakening fully. I see the bright square of the window and a dark figure appearing outside, etched against the light, and I see him hoisting himself up over the window-sill and swinging himself over swiftly, before the shutter is closed and everything is dark once more; I hear the intruder dropping down lightly and the rustle of Sofie's dress, but I know there is no reason for anxiety or concern, even if I do not understand what is happening, for in that moment when the shutter was open, dazed and sleepily, through eyes half-shut, I recognised Pieter.

I am dreaming; I dreamed, it is a delirious dream from those long weeks of my illness when feverish images recurred endlessly, soundlessly, unexplained and inexplicable, Pieter hoisting himself over the window-sill and landing inside, as nimble and silent as a wild cat, as soundless as a dream, while old Dulsie has fallen asleep where she watches beside my bed. She has forgotten to snuff out the wick of the night-light, and the candle flickers fitfully, so that restless images dance over the uneven surfaces of floor and walls, here in the room where I am lying now. What did Sofie want here with me, she who had her own room in the house where the baby's crib stood and Jacomyn slept on the rug in front of her bed; why would Pieter enter the house here, through my window? I must have been dreaming.

I lie awake in the night and try to remember; motionless I lie against the stacked pillows in the room where, as a child, I slept so blithely, and can find no refuge in sleep any more, powerless even to turn away from what I would rather avoid. The rustling of clothes or the whispering of people speaking with heads close together, lips held to ears, scarcely audible, part of a sleeping child's dream.

Strange to think back and remember a time when, as a child, I felt completely carefree, with no knowledge of any lurking danger that could affect me: the house, the yard, the veld stretched out before me and I took that freedom for granted, I ran through the streaming light and shadows of the veld and reached out to grab the flowers in spring-time. From what distant place does that memory suddenly return? I must have been very young when one day old Dulsie took me along to the farthest orchard to look for apples on the trees that had been left to grow wild. I was running ahead when a yellow cobra suddenly raised itself from the bushes in front of me, and I remember the glistening body drenched with sunlight and the smoothness of that rapid move-ment when I chased him up from his lair, just for a moment, before old Dulsie saw what was happening and stooped to search for a stone. She was too slow, however, for the very moment she bent down, he drew back and slithered into the renosterbos, glistening golden and unharmed; and afterwards I never ran quite as freely through the veld again without taking care where I put my feet.

Strange to think that there was once a time when I could wake up at night without asking, wondering or remembering, and fall asleep again, unhindered, reassured by the vast darkness, the shelter of the house and the presence of the people around me, asleep in the other rooms. How long ago it seems now, that time when I learned to mistrust the silence, startled from my sleep by a rustle in a wall or in the thatch of the roof, startled from my dreams by that distant scream in the ridges, to lie awake, like now, in a darkness filled with unease and memories: the rustle of a dress, the whispering voices of two people, their lips close together; Pieter, my brother, hoisting himself over the window-sill, fleetingly visible in the brightness of the moonlit night, and Sofie's face veiled by her hair as she bends over the candle-stub to blow it out. For a while she slept in my room when I was in bed with some children's disease, and held a cold compress to my brow, dosing me with medicine and the infusions brewed by Dulsie to make me sleep. These are things I remember and not my imagination.

In the morning I used to dress and go to Sofie's room to say good morning and I stayed with her until Mother called me away to come and help in the house. Because I had been ill, for a time I was allowed to remain in bed a while longer, and that morning I overslept, for when I got up, her bed had already been made and the room had been tidied, and only Jacomyn was there with the baby. "Where is Sofie?" I asked, but that morning she was sullen and tight-lipped, as was often the case, and she did not answer; the door to Father and Mother's bedroom was closed, and in the kitchen Dulsie was banging the pots at the hearth and took no notice of me. Sofie was nowhere to be seen. "Where is Sofie?" I asked Dulsie, but she would not answer me either. "Go play outside," she said impatiently. "Why are you always inside?" Everything was different, and I could not say what had changed so suddenly, and at last I went outside and wandered about alone in the cold bright autumn morning until Mother called me for family prayers.

"It is you who wanted it like that," I heard Father say when I entered the voorhuis, but nothing more was said. He sat at the table with the Bible in both hands, ready to read to us; he spoke softly as was his wont, but deliberately, and Mother grew pale and turned away, and his hands were trembling.

We said our prayers and I ate in silence with Father and Mother, just the three of us, and I did not ask where Pieter and Sofie were; and after we had eaten, Gert saddled Father's horse and brought it to the door, and I realised he was going away when I saw Mother packing provisions and a few items of clothing into his saddle-bags. He had stopped riding long ago but with Gert's help he mounted slowly and painfully. As he was standing there with his hand on Gert's shoulder, about to put his foot into the stirrup, he suddenly remembered me, and he turned to look for me, and called me to him. There, in front of the house, he embraced me and took leave of me, took leave of me for good, and then, with Gert's help, he mounted and turned the horse around and rode away in the direction of Vloksberg Pass and the Karoo. Mother stood looking after his departing figure for another moment before she went back into the house and called for me to continue with my work. The child had to be weaned and for a while he needed all the women's attention, so that they took little notice of me.

Why do I say "for good"? Father returned from the trip; but he was away for a long time, a matter of weeks rather than mere days. Is it possible that Mother and I lived together during all that time without saying a word? I am probably exaggerating when I ask this, but I know she never used to say much, and the mysterious events were never explained to me, not by her or anyone else. It is as a time of utter silence that I now remember the weeks of this waiting period, except for the evenings when I had to read from the Bible for the two of us, as well as I could manage by candlelight, struggling with the syllables, and stringing into a prayer Father's familiar phrases about mercy and compassion. Where is Sofie? I wanted to ask her. Where is Pieter? Where has Father gone? But the questions died away on my lips and I continued to endure my bafflement in silence. Only once did I push open the door of Pieter's outside bedroom tentatively and look inside as if I were hoping to find an answer to my questions there, at the same time fearing the shape it might take. There was nothing to fear, however, only the low cot on which he had slept, the burnt-out stub of a candle on the shelf beside the bed and the horns on the walls from which he had hung his belongings. His clothes and his saddle and bridle had disappeared with him, and when I saw the dark, empty room, I realised he was gone, beyond my reach.

While I was standing there, Gert came around the corner of the shed and laughed when he saw me on the threshhold. "Are you looking for your brother, little girl?" he teased as he walked past me, but he spoke softly, so that he might not be heard from the house. "You are searching in the wrong place. You need a horse to get where your brother is."

He walked on to the stable and forgot about me, but I followed him and stood watching for a long time where he was dressing a leather thong, whistling, paying no attention to me. "Where is Sofie?" I asked after a while, and I know I spoke very softly and found it even more difficult than usual to say the words; but he heard me, for he was startled and stopped whistling. "As far as a horse can go in an hour," he said at last, smiling, not looking at me, and then he began to croon softly to himself.

> "*The black horse and the grey,*
> *o they have run away*
> *I seek them in the mountains,*
> *But they are in the vlei . . ."*

He is teasing me, I thought, though he did not chase me away impatiently like Jacomyn or Dulsie, and his voice was not unkind. He said no more, however, though I waited for a long time, and only when I turned to go back to the house, did I hear him again, singing softly.

> *"The sorrow and the pain,*
> *o the sorrow and the pain.*
> *The herb to cure it grows beside*
> *The foundation, not the plain."*

I stood listening as if I expected him to say more, but it was just one of the songs and rhymes that Gert was always making up as he worked, and as I crossed the yard back to the house, I could still hear him singing softly. During this time, with Jakob dead, Pieter gone and Father absent, it fell to Gert to manage most of the work on the farm and so he was often in the yard and in the kitchen without fear of being chased away by Mother. Perhaps his new standing had gone to his head, for I remember him being more high-spirited than usual, and whenever he was in the vicinity, he could be heard singing or humming to himself. Once I came upon him and Jacomyn behind the kraal wall, standing close together in intimate conversation, Jacomyn with her glistening black hair combed up high and her bright floral shawl with the long fringes wrapped around her shoulders as if it were a festive occasion. When they saw me, they seemed alarmed, but only until they recognised me, for I was only a child and held no threat to them; neither did I ever tell anyone about finding them there.

During this time of silence and solitude I sought the company of the servants more and more often. Where else could I turn? Sofie was gone, Pieter was gone, and even Father with whom I sometimes spent time, had said farewell wordlessly and left. Thus, whenever possible, I crawled into a corner of the kitchen, where Dulsie put up with my presence. As I have said, Gert was often indoors during this time and when the child was asleep, Jacomyn joined the others in front of the fire and, forced together like that by loneliness, their individual grudges and grievances were often forgotten for a while and they would talk and tease and scold, without noticing me. "When the master comes back," Dulsie sometimes mumbled to herself, unhappy about something that had gone wrong on the farm, or the winter trek to the Karoo that had been delayed too long; and once, "When Pieter comes back", so that I looked up at the mention of that name I had not heard since he disappeared so inexplicably from our midst. Then Gert laughed where he was drinking his coffee in front of the fire. "That will not happen soon, old woman," he said. "The riem has not yet been cut that is long enough to catch those two." "I don't know about that," Dulsie answered peevishly, drawing at her pipe. "Sometimes I feel I could reach them in an afternoon if my knees were not so stiff." I sat in the shadows in the corner of the hearth, and Jacomyn, who was kneeling in front of me to warm the child's milk, suddenly looked up as if she had been startled by something. For a moment it was quiet in the kitchen. "Then you'll have to go quickly if you still want to catch them, old woman," Gert said quietly, "and be careful that you don't step into a porcupine-burrow and break your neck". "I won't be the first one to break my neck," she snapped, and he swore and took his hat and went out to his sleeping place: the ceasefire here was never more than conditional, and at any moment it might break down into attack and defense. Which two, I wondered, when they had been talking about Pieter? But after that when I thought of Pieter and Sofie, I always saw them together, two horses galloping away through the vlei where the light flashed on the glittering water among the reeds, galloping away from us across the veld, together.

And then one day – it must have been weeks later – Father came back, alone, and Gert came running to hold his horse and to help him dismount and Mother came out of the house to support him. He greeted us, but said nothing, and he and Mother went into the bedroom and closed the door and it was a long time before Mother called Dulsie to bring him some coffee and wash his feet. Usually when he had been away, he had something for me on his return, acid drops or a handful of raisins or nuts, but this time he did not bring anything, as if he had forgotten about me. We continued to live together like that, Father and Mother and I, and he never spoke about that long absence or mentioned it at all. What I do know about it, rather than suspect, infer or guess – what I do know, whether true or untrue, reliable or not, I overheard incidentally much later, when old Dulsie was shouting abuse at the family of a herdsman who had briefly been in our service earlier, before being dismissed by Father. "Basterfontein's band of drunk Basters who lied to the master and made him ride all the way to the Boland in search of Pieter!" That is all.

So we continued to live like that, Father, Mother and I, together around the table for breakfast and supper, together around the table for family prayers before going to bed at night. Father was forced again to take on much of the farm work that he had left to Jakob and Pieter before, and from time to time, with Gert's help, he mounted his horse painfully and rode out to inspect the sheep. I never heard him complain, however; and after his long absence he seemed quieter and even more withdrawn. Did nobody speak any more, was the silence that descended on our home absolute? Anyhow, that is how I remember it now.

Only two events from the time after Pieter and Sofie's disappearance and Father's return from his journey stand out in my memory.

One of them – when was it, when could it have been? Jacomyn went out with the child as she did every day, and when she had left the house, Mother went to the bedroom, the front room where Jakob and Sofie had slept, and suddenly I heard something crack and splinter, shattering in pieces as it broke. Frightened by the noise where I was standing in the kitchen, I did not immediately understand what was happening, and then I realised that Mother had smashed Sofie's framed looking-glass against the wall. It must have been very soon after Sofie's disappearance, when the grudge and bitterness over her flight was still intense – could it even have been on the day of Father's return, while he was asleep after the long journey? Every trace of Sofie had to be obliterated: Dulsie came and swept up the shards, quickly and submissively, asking no questions, as experience had taught her, and in the oven outside Mother wordlessly burnt the rest of Sofie's belongings. What they were, I do not know, for I did not dare try and find out, even from a distance; neither do I know what Sofie had taken with her or how much it had been possible for her to take along. Her books must have been left behind, and those Mother would have torn apart with great satisfaction before stuffing them into the back of the oven. And her black satin dress, her wedding gown, did she leave it behind, and did Mother with brute force tear the heavy, gleaming fabric along the seams to burn it, looking on as it smouldered slowly? I do not know, only that nothing remained, that Mother stayed outside at the oven until everything had been destroyed, reduced to ashes in the cold oven, powdery ashes that were blown across the yard. Only the child remained to remind us of Sofie's short stay, and Jacomyn who looked after him; but the child, after all, belonged to Jakob, the heir.

And after this, one afternoon very soon afterwards it seems to me now, Mother told me to fetch the writing materials. Father was away once again, though I no longer remember where he was, and Jacomyn had gone out with the child, while Dulsie was collecting harpuisbos twigs for the fire; that I remember very well, that the two of us were in the house alone that afternoon. I fetched the ink-well and the pen and brought them to the big table in the voorhuis, and Mother placed the family Bible in front of me. "Write," she ordered, and I saw that she had turned to the page where the dates of our births and deaths were recorded and she was pointing at the last inscription, that of Jakob's death in Father's scarcely legible hand, with above it the birthdate of his child, and above that his wedding date, his and Sofie's. "Write there," she ordered, and prompted, "Died . . ." It was Sofie's name she was pointing at and, bewildered, I turned and looked up into her face, for no one had told me that Sofie was dead, but it was clear that she would not stand for any questions or objections, and so I bent over the book and wrote what she told me to, while she stood beside me grimly. Did she leave us to die then, I wondered, or did she die suddenly during that mysterious journey, and why were we not informed when Father returned, why did I have to write it into the Bible while Mother and I were in the house alone, and why did he not do it himself as he usually did? But it was untrue and the date was false, it was the date of Sofie's disappearance or perhaps that of Father's return after his long search, that Mother made me write into the Bible on her own authority, as if the mere inscription would instantly render it true; and I had to do it because she herself did not know how to write and probably could not even read well enough to make out where Sofie's name was written.

Years later, when Maans was a young man and he opened the Bible to record Father's death, he read through all the entries. "But this is your handwriting," he said to me. "Why did you write in the Bible when Mammie died?"

It was a rainy day and it was even darker than usual in the voorhuis: Mother sat close to the window with her back to us, and I did not know whether she had heard the question. "Oupa was often ill during that time," I said at last, and in the silence I heard the rain dripping through the thatched roof on to the floor-boards of the loft; and it was true that he was frequently ill in the time after Sofie and Pieter left us, even confined to his bed at times, but that was not why he had not entered the date into the Bible himself. He had probably never even seen the inscription, for the next entry in the family tree was his own death, so he had had no reason ever to look it up.

How long did that silence last? Father immersed in his pain and Mother in her bitterness, Jacomyn distant and waiting in the house where she was merely tolerated, and Dulsie gradually becoming old and grumpy, and the only sound the wind outside, the whirling dust against the shutters, and the wailing of the baby as Jacomyn paced up and down with him, shuffling across the floor on bare feet. How long could it have lasted? Oh, long, very long; months passed and eventually became years, seasons of blustering snow and uncertain springs drifted across the veld, and the only sound was the wind against the shutters. My only company was the servants as I sat unnoticed in the corner of the kitchen in the evenings, the silent listener in the corner, and sometimes entire days passed during which no one thought to address me except to give me an order or to scold me for some oversight. It was autumn and the wind whipped the dust across the veld, so that the shutters were closed and we lived in the dark with only the fire in the kitchen glowing in the hearth; the darkness and the silence, the rattling of the doors and shutters in the wind and the grating noise as the wind swept along dust and fine pebbles and branches, and the child crying, and Jacomyn's bare feet across the dung floor. I was often alone, and in my childhood years loneliness gradually became second nature to me. Sometimes I wandered far from home without knowing what I was looking for, driven farther and farther, gazing at the faded, flat landscape from every ridge, as if I were searching for something. But what did I expect to see? Dassies slipping away among the rocks when they saw me, or a jackal buzzard rising from its prey to hover in the air on outstretched wings, the sheep flocks grazing among the bushes or the wispy smoke of a herdsman's lonely fire at his shelter miles away, or at most a lone rider, unrecognisable across the distance, or the white tent of a wagon on the distant mountain pass, strangers passing by our isolated homestead without even considering turning off and paying us a visit in our isolation. I did not expect company, however, neither did I desire the arrival of strangers in our midst; I turned from the distant road and chose places where not even the sheep went, and I walked farther and farther as if I were heading for some distant destination. I saw the low hills darken and the renoster-bos glow with a bluish tinge as the thin silver sunlight faded at the end of the day, and in my fervour to reach that mysterious distant goal, I began to run, stumbling along the plateau on the crest of the mountain at the end of the world. The silver light streamed away before my eyes and I lost my footing on the uneven ground.

One of the herdsmen apparently found me there in the veld. Whether they had been searching for me and whether they had been anxious or worried about my disappearance, or for how long I had lain there before he found me, I have no idea. I fell, I suppose – what does it matter now, except for the scar on my forehead, and I learned to live with that a long time ago. Near the edge of the escarpment he found me, far from home, but that is all I know. When I regained consciousness, it was night, and by the light of the oil lamp I could make out among the flickering shadows in the room old Dulsie where she sat sleeping on a chair beside my bed; and then it was dark again.

Of course it could not have been so very long, those months of emptiness and silence in the empty, silent house; it was autumn when Pieter
and Sofie left and not yet winter when they found me in the veld, near
the end of autumn it must have been, for my illness had once again
prevented Mother from going down to the Karoo with Father, and
we had to stay behind in the Roggeveld. I suppose Gert went with
Father, and perhaps Jacomyn and the child as well, and Dulsie must
have stayed behind to help Mother. Or did Mother go with Father after
all, leaving me behind with Dulsie? I was sick all winter and uncon-
scious or delirious most of the time, so that my memories of those
months are vague and confused, but I do not remember Mother being
there, only that Dulsie was always beside me with a kaross around
her shoulders against the cold and her feet on a stove, or curled up
on the floor in front of the bed at night; Dulsie holding me, trying to
make me drink from a bowl, Dulsie throwing open the shutters that
had been closed against the cold and letting the first pale daylight of
spring into the room.

Why do I not remember Mother? The more anxiously, the more
deeply I delve into my confused memories, the more they slip and slide
away, but not for a moment can I find her face anywhere. There is no
one I might ask about it any more, and yet I realise that sixty years
later it is still important to me, I still want to know whether Mother
left me or stayed with me and whether she showed any sign of anxiety
or concern during my long illness. How dearly I would like to discover
her among the fragments of my memories, bending over my bed for a
moment, her hand on my brow, her arm around my shoulders; but it
is only Dulsie I see before me. Who helped her then? Sofie I remember, bending over the flickering light, her face recognisable for just a
moment, and then her dark hair like a veil, hiding it from view, obscuring her features; Sofie – but no, that was a different time, it is an older

memory, and if I had seen her during this time, bending over my bed in the candlelight, an inscrutable look in her dark eyes, if I had seen her, then it must have been an illusion, a shadow, a distortion created by the darkness on the walls of the room where I lay.

Dulsie's head sinks forward in her vigil beside the bed, she nods for a moment as she dozes off, then sits up abruptly, bewildered, looking around her, uncertain of her whereabouts. Then slowly, mumbling to herself, she gets up and arranges her bed on the floor, and against the wall her distorted shadow joins the other shadows, lengthening and shrinking, extending and flowing together in fluid patterns. The dancing light of the flame, flickering for a moment in the wind, and the smell of the kraal and the veld, the smell of fire made with bushes and dung, of dung fire and smoke and herbs. Why do I remember that smell, and how did it find its way into my room where the shutters were closed against the cold and where we lived in eternal half-light and candlelight and darkness? The smell of smoke and bushes, the smell of boegoe and soil and dust, and a hand on my forehead that was not Dulsie's. Could it perhaps have been Mother, Mother after all? But no, a strange hand, and strange voices murmuring in the dark. Who was that stranger – the wife of a herdsman who had slept in the house with Dulsie during that long winter? I do not remember any-one who resembled her, however, neither was she like the Basters or Hottentots of our parts. On some of the farms in the Roggeveld there were still Bushmen from the days of the raids and battles before my birth, when the men were killed and the surviving women and children herded together and put to work by the white farmers, and it seems as if it could be an old Bushman woman that I remember; but we never had any of these people in our employ except as herdsmen, and they would never have been allowed inside the house. It is possible that it was an illusion, one more illusion among the many that merge with the shadows, and yet I know it was not my imagination, and that I saw her here in my bedroom, beside my bed, with her hand on my brow, and I remember the muttering of strange voices and the smell of bushes and herbs and kraal fires.

That, however, is all I remember of those weeks and months, for the winter passed without my being aware of it, and it was spring, and the sheep returned from the Karoo: I opened my eyes in my bed and saw the bright silver light streaming inside where Dulsie had thrown open the shutters, and the pale blue of the sky outside, and I was aware of the delicate, hesitant warmth and the smell of the veld after the rains. Outside the sheep were bleating at the kraal and I heard Father shouting at the herdsmen and Gert's voice calling; inside the house I could hear Mother in the kitchen. I lay there like someone who had returned after a long absence, trying to make sense of the sounds. Like someone searching for words in a long-forgotten language, I recalled their names one by one. I averted my face from the bright window, exhausted by the effort, and fell asleep again.

I survived, though apparently no one had expected it. While I was ill, they had ordered boards from the Boland and a coffin had been made for me that I saw unexpectedly years later when it was taken from the rafters in the shed for the funeral of one of the neighbours' children. Maans said it was a child's coffin, and it took a while before I realised it was mine and I could picture my own shape in the dimensions of that child's coffin, the thin girl who had turned around at death's door after months, to arise from her sickbed. Yes, as if I had returned from another country and spoke a different language, and for a while they did not know how to behave towards me and where I fitted into their circle. Were they grateful, were they glad? No one showed any gratitude or joy, except perhaps Father. Because there was no mirror in the house, it was only much later that I saw myself with the scar on my forehead where my head had struck a rock as I fell, but I could feel it with my fingers, and I must have been a peculiar sight, for during my illness my hair had been shaved, and it took long before it began to grow out again.

That spring with the wild flowers and Sofie laughing in the veld, the flowers whipped from her hands as she held them out to me; that spring of the shifting light and shadows when Sofie and Pieter sank down into the shadowy pools and were lost to me; and finally that long spring of my return – how much had changed within two years and how different that season was when, carefully and hesitantly, I learned to move through the house again. A time of delicate, drifting, silver daylight and the gleam of the water in the dams below the house, and across the pale green fields of spring the two horses galloped away noiselessly to vanish over the horizon. The day was quiet and the house empty and for some reason I was alone, alone with the sudden knowledge, relentless and unavoidable, that I would always be as alone as I was at that moment. I was a mere child and did not understand, but I turned my face from the silver light and did not want to know, not yet. Always. I could clearly feel the scar with my fingers and when, much later, I stood in front of a mirror again, it did not show me anything I did not already know.

How much later it was, I do not know exactly, but it must have been towards the end of that spring that we were awakened one morning by old Dulsie's shouts, and learned with dismay that Jacomyn and Gert were also missing. By that time so many people had left, however, that this fresh disappearance did not really affect me, though it must have been difficult for Mother, because Dulsie had aged and could not do much in the house any more, while Father was practically helpless and had been depending on Gert more and more. I still remember waking at daybreak to hear Dulsie shouting in the voorhuis, and sleeping on fitfully, vaguely aware of something I did not understand. What became of them? Gert took his own horses and the saddles and bridles and rifle that belonged to him, and Jacomyn her few pieces of clothing and trinkets and the floral shawl with the long tassels, and they disappeared from our world, over the edge of the mountains into the abyss. Much later, when Dulsie had become confused, in one of her incoherent fits of scolding and self-pity she railed against one of the Baster women who had helped us in the kitchen: "So insolent," she muttered to herself, "just like that Malay meid who left here with Gert to go to the Boland." Did she know, or suspect, or guess, or was she merely rattling on without knowing what she was saying? It was possible that they had indeed gone to seek their fortune in the Boland, for what other refuge could there have been for them with their horses and saddles and rifle, their bundle of clothing and trinkets? We neither saw nor heard from them ever again.

Did they love each other? I wonder suddenly, though the question has never occurred to me before and even now I hesitate to ask, for we never thought of our workers in those terms, and it never crossed our minds that our servants could fall in love or love each other, as seemed possible for us. But what is the use of wondering or asking, for I shall never know. Did they simply see a chance to escape, and conspire to outwit their masters, encouraged by the example of Pieter and Sofie before them? Or might there have been something like love, Gert and Jacomyn alone at the kraal wall, her black hair shining in the sun and the floral shawl around her shoulders? I shall never know.

I drew the blanket over my face against the pale daylight and turned over, turned away, and something brushed against my cheek, against my lips, and slid from the pillow and came to rest under the bedcovers, in the hollow of my neck, an unfamiliar weight of which I remained aware in my sleep, as I was aware of the voices in the voorhuis. I slept on fitfullly until at last I awoke, and there, against my neck, I found a small cloth bundle which I unwrapped dazedly to discover a tiny ring. Not yet completely awake, I stared at it, trying to remember where I had seen it before, and then I realised it was Sofie's ring with the little heart that she had worn the night of the New Year's dance, and I realised that Sofie was back, that she had returned to us from afar, and I jumped up and ran barefoot through the voorhuis to her room to welcome her. But Sofie was not there: Father had gone out to the kraal, as there was no one else to do it, and in the kitchen Mother and Dulsie were feeding the baby, so that it took a while before someone noticed me, and Mother told me to get dressed and come and help with the chores. I returned to my room, returned to myself, returned to my silence, still holding in the palm of my hand the tiny ring with the heart that had gone unnoticed, and I hid it under the mattress where it would not be found readily. No more was said about those who had left, except sometimes by old Dulsie muttering to herself in the kitchen, and it was as if they were all dead and their deaths might as well have been entered in the Bible.

One day soon afterwards when no one was near to see what I was doing, I went outside. It was the first time I had left the house since the day of my flight, the day I was picked up in the veld, and I remember hesitating at the corner of the kitchen, my hand on the familiar roughness of the stone wall for support, overwhelmed by the wideness of the yard in front of me, by the sudden expanse of the veld and the blinding brightness of the silver light streaming from the lofty sky. I did not hesitate long, however, fearful of being caught at any moment. Slowly and resolutely I crossed the yard, light-headed and weak after my lengthy illness, Sofie's ring in the palm of my hand. Straining against the spring breeze that threatened to unbalance me, I finally reached the graveyard beyond the ridge, and there I hid the ring in the place between two stones where I had also secreted Meester's little cross many years before, and I left it there where it would be safe. She had left it for me with Jacomyn, and when the time came for Jacomyn's own departure, she came to my bedroom at night, barefoot in the dark, and left it on my pillow where I would discover it in the morning: I never found another explanation and if one existed, I prefer not to know about it, even now at the end of my life, but rather to keep believing that Sofie had let me have this gift months after her departure in the place of the farewell that was never said.

3

....

Gradually I recovered and adapted to the routine of the house and farm once more. For a while my reticence was still tolerated, but not for long, and one day I was sitting in the voorhuis when Dulsie pressed the baby into my arms impatiently. "There, take the child, he's yours," she snapped, and that is how I was given custody of Maans. He was just beginning to walk and he was a lively child, but he was never really naughty or disobedient and, as for me, I had all the time and patience in the world. We were good company for each other, for even when he began to talk, it was some time before he learned to understand or wonder or ask, and so it was possible for me simply to carry on at first, without having to think or remember. Moreover, he was a beautiful child, with Jakob's dark eyes; of course Sofie had dark eyes too, but Maans was Jakob's child, entirely his, or so I always thought. I came to love that child who had been given into my care so unexpectedly; yes, I loved him, until he grew up and outgrew me, and now there is almost nothing left of that closeness. He was in the house with me all day, either in my arms or on my lap, and later I took him out for short walks in the veld, until eventually I was no longer afraid of the space and the light; later it was good for me to have an excuse to escape from the quiet, gloomy house and sit in the veld with Maans playing near me. Dreamily, I turned my face to the sun again, unaware of what I was doing. I discovered anew the daylight and the day, and the familiar world revealed itself to me once more. They are coming, they are coming; but I could no longer remember who, and I tried to keep the remaining memories at bay while I gazed mindlessly at the distant glitter of the dams in the light, until Maans became impatient because I did not listen or reply, and playfully tugged at my clothing or pulled my hair until it came undone and billowed around my head and across my face. As a child I went along with others without asking where we were going, others led me, carefree, by the hand; now I took this child out for walks and decided on our destination myself.

Father tried to find someone to work for him in Gert's place, but none of the Basters he hired was as clever or trustworthy as Gert, and after a while some omission or oversight was always discovered, or there were complaints and objections, and the man bundled up his few possessions and left with his family; or otherwise the wives came to help in the house and quarrelled with old Dulsie, or Mother lost her temper and flew into them with a bundle of harpuisbos twigs as was her wont, and then the woman shouted angrily that she would not stay here a moment longer and urged her husband to claim his wages and leave. It became more and more difficult to find suitable workers, for it was during this time that the Basters in the Roggeveld were being forced from the land they owned or inhabited amongst us, and later no outspan or winter quarters or grazing was available to them, so that one by one they moved away from our region with their rickety wagons and their handful of sheep; it was probably also during those years that Father made the first of his land purchases, though as a child I knew nothing about it, neither did I have any interest in it. Thus, of all the families that worked for us briefly after Gert's departure, I no longer remember individual names or faces, only a few anonymous voices, scraps of conversation at the back door or in the kitchen, jokes, shouts, curses or rhymes that still sound in my ears, swirling around me in the dark, entwined and entangled after all the years, forming new patterns in which I can no longer recognise the familiar threads. They are dead and gone, every last one of them, leaving me without a name or a face, buried outside the wall encircling the white people's graveyard, or somewhere along the road in the Karoo, or farther north in the interior where their journey had taken them, near Groot River, and the stones that were stacked over them have been scattered and washed away; their children and grandchildren have died too, somewhere on a plain, in a kloof or beside a campfire, and the last memory of their existence has been wiped out. Only their voices still sound in my ears here where I lie awake in the night.

Someone puts a karee log on the fire in the hearth, someone throws a handful of harpuisbos twigs on the fire, so that it crackles and flares, and I hear Dulsie's voice as she coughs over her clay pipe, and then the others join the circle one by one; but the faces, fleetingly visible in the dancing firelight at the hearth, have become obscure to me. "The mountain big and blue, O how will I get through . . ." Who sang or hummed that song? "I seek them in the mountains . . ." – but that was Gert, that was earlier. Rhymes, verses, songs, like the ones Gert always used to make up.

> *"Cain and Abel had a fight*
> *Who had the pretty maid in sight?*
> *Rode away into the night,*
> *Never more to see the light . . ."*

But who was it? It is not Gert's voice sounding in my ears, though I still remember the words clearly.

> *"Abel was murdered by his brother,*
> *Was seen by another . . ."*

Words I did not understand as I sat listening in the dark; furtive laughter I did not understand and a sudden hush when someone approached, Mother on the threshhold of the kitchen . . . "Jakob's voice and Esau's hands", and the women's screams as the group scattered. Jakob's voice and Esau's hands, and how angry Mother had been, how relentlessly she had thrashed about with the stick she had grabbed, with pale, stony face and burning eyes, and the women in the kitchen scattering to escape, fleeing from the house. Esau's hands . . . What had infuriated her so? The next day the woman who had said it left with her husband and her children and their few goats, and from the yard she shrieked imprecations in the direction of the house while Mother slammed the kitchen door and turned away, pale and trembling with silent fury. It was during that time, I am certain, for Gert had already left and Jakob lay in the graveyard under the stones that had been stacked over his grave, so I knew they could not have been talking about him. Or could it have been he – Jakob, who had slipped and fallen into the dark crevice on the mountainside, hands out-stretched against the rock?

Now I remember again: suddenly the thread running through the design becomes clearly visible in the dark. The women were saying what a beautiful child Maans was. Pieter had also been such a spindly little thing when he was small, Dulsie went on; Jakob was never like that. Yes, one of the women added, it is Jakob's voice but Esau's hands, and the people sitting at the hearth in the dark burst out laughing as if they understood the words, just as Mother entered the kitchen and overheard them. I did not understand, or perhaps I simply chose not to understand, just as I always did when a choice was possible for me; but in the end understanding was inevitable as the stories did the rounds, stories repeated with unexpected acrimony or slipping out before the speaker could help it, stories repeated because no one realised I was present or because they thought I could not hear; warp and woof woven together over the years into a tapestry in which I can finally make out the pattern. Could Maans have been Pieter's child? In later years, when it became possible for me to ponder and to question, many years later, when I was growing older and Pieter himself was approaching the end of his life, I often reflected on this matter, and at times Maans must have wondered why I was gazing at him so quizzically, as if I were searching for something in his features. I never found anything, however, no, I never did believe that Maans could be Pieter's child; but that must have been what people in those parts believed or wanted to believe and what they told each other, until even I became aware of it, until it became an accepted fact that no one questioned any more and in its own way the rumour became more important than anything that might actually have occurred. But who still remains that knew Jakob and Sofie, or cares about Pieter's memory; who still speaks of these matters? Who remembers?

At the time we must have been the subject of a great deal of gossip, and what else could be expected, with Jakob's death and Pieter and Sofie's disappearance, with Gert and Jacomyn's sudden and mysterious departure and, finally, my long illness as well; what else could be expected in our small, isolated world where everyone ended up knowing everything about everyone else, that miserable handful of white and coloured people in the boundless desolation at the edge of the mountains? Perhaps they tried to help, as people will in times of affliction or need, and perhaps they made offers of goodwill. I remember the people who helped search for Jakob and the neighbours who attended his funeral, lined up silently along the walls of the voorhuis, but I know that as a child I did not see their presence as a sign of sympathy, but rather as an intrusion. Oh, when I was a child it was just too rare for us to receive visitors, and possibly I was simply unused to it and the curiosity and distrust I remember were no more than imagination on my part. But the unspoken words that I remember just as clearly, the questions and the speculations that I overheard incidentally? Where did a group of men once talk about that day, and someone wondered who had searched for Jakob in the kloof without finding his body where it had been lying all the time? The details I no longer recall, but I remember overhearing the question and waiting for an answer that was never supplied. Those men all knew the answer, and the question and the silence that followed were an accusation, even though it was never uttered. Who searched in that kloof, and how did Jakob lose his footing and, with mangled face, fall down into the narrow cleft between the rocks? I shall never know; neither do I wish to know. It is better so.

Did the neighbours begin to avoid us again after these events, or were they simply discouraged from coming to our home? When visitors arrived, Father was always glad to see them, they were welcomed and coffee was served, or sweet wine or brandy but, just as they remained intruders to me, so they did to Mother as well, and even more so in the time after Jakob's death and Pieter's disappearance. People inevitably noticed that there was no welcome in her stiff hospitality and sparse words and gradually they stopped coming again. At last the only visitors who still came, were a neighbour in search of an absconded apprentice or a lost sheep, or a servant sent to borrow an awl or a bag of horseshoe-nails.

Only the small, familiar sounds of the house still filled the silvery days, and the howling of the wind around the corners of the building, against the shutters or in the thatch when I awoke at night and could not fall asleep again. Father still mounted his horse painfully and attended auctions to buy sheep or land; later he bought a black Cape cart in which he set off to attend funerals in the district, but I do not recall Mother often accompanying him, for it was as if she were more withdrawn than ever during those years, though the passion and the zeal and the sudden, unpredictable flashes of temper had intensified. No, actually I cannot remember Mother ever leaving the house in the years after Jakob's death, except when the minister came from Worcester and there were church meetings on neighbouring farms.

Those meetings and the long journey to Worcester for Nagmaal I remember because they became an ever greater ordeal for me as I grew older. I felt strange and ill at ease among the children of my own age, and awkwardly I hovered at the fringe of their company until it was possible to escape. Once I was standing behind an outspanned cart when I heard a girl ask where I was, and someone said something I could not make out in a cold, disdainful tone. "Oh, that mad creature," an older woman remarked; and that must have been how I appeared to them, the thin, shy, lisping girl with the scar on her forehead who fled from the people, the tents, the outspanned carts and wagons, to escape from the friendly interaction, shy as a deer in the ridges, dashing away from the people, the voices, the greetings and laughter and jesting, the nicknames, the whispering in corners and the incomprehensible jokes and innuendo, the girls with their arms around each other and the boys to one side with their impertinent glances and their nervous excitement, the approval and disapproval of the older women lined up against the wall, the entire united community of other people into which Mother and Father were briefly assimilated, but in which I could play no part. I turned and fled to the servants' fire beyond the outspan, and I warmed myself and shared their coffee when it was offered to me, and soon enough they forgot about my presence and continued as if I were not there.

That winter after my illness we all went down to the Karoo as usual and when we returned that spring, Miss Le Roux came with us. Someone had probably brought her from Worcester and Father must have fetched her halfway with the cart, I do not know, for I was told nothing, and even Dulsie spoke only vaguely of the stranger who was coming. However, she came from Worcester to join us in the Karoo before we returned to the Roggeveld, for I was standing in front of our reed house with Maans on my hip when the cart came to a halt and Miss Le Roux climbed down slowly in her black dress. Mother's formal welcome and my own mystified silence could not have put her at ease and, in fact, she probably never felt at home with us: as strange as she seemed on her arrival at our outspan in the Karoo that afternoon, so she remained to us, in spite of living in our house for two years. I soon found out all about her, but only because I was her sole companion in her loneliness, for I certainly never questioned her, nor did I show the slightest interest.

She had grown up in Worcester: her parents were both dead and of the six daughters the eldest was married, while the youngest lived with her to help with the children; two lived in town and worked as seamstresses, and the remaining two became governesses, and that was how Miss Le Roux came to us in her dusty black dress, with her travelling-case and her trunk, recommended to Father by old Dominee himself, as she often stated emphatically, as if it gave her special standing. She could not have been much older than twenty, a stout, giggling young woman in a black mourning frock, with her effusiveness and excitability and her hiccuping laugh, with her nerves and swoons and sudden tears, her eau de cologne and her vial of smelling salts.

She returned to the Roggeveld with us and the big bed in my room was given to her, while I shared the narrow cot in the corner with Maans; she unpacked her things and hung her black dresses, her black caps and her black cape on the nails in the wall. We spent all day together, she and I, and at night in the dark I listened to her regular breathing in the big bed. She brought along writing paper and quill pens and a knife to sharpen the points and readers in Dutch and English: I knew how to read and write after a fashion, but she made me practise anew and taught me to spell, she read me poems and made me recite them, I learned arithmetic and she told me Bible stories – it was probably all she knew, but it was more than most people in our parts did in those days. I was a quick learner, she said in generous moments, and assured Father that I was a clever girl. Only with sewing and other needlecraft she had no success, in spite of her patience and perseverance, for I was an awkward child and no matter how often she made me unpick the uneven stitches and start over, it only resulted in the cloth becoming even more crumpled. I learned what she could teach me and listened to the lengthy accounts about her sisters and the house where she grew up, and at night I listened to her regular breathing in the dark, but she remained a stranger whose presence I endured silently as she hovered over me, gushing and breathless.

Of course she must have been lonely. Had anyone warned her of the remoteness of the Roggeveld; could she have guessed how isolated our lives were? But even if she had been warned, what alternative did she have? Her parents were dead and somehow she had to make a living, and she was probably only too grateful for the old Dominee's recommendation. Father was kind, as he was to everyone, but it was Mother who determined the course of events in the house, and to Mother Miss Le Roux was a hireling who had to remain aware of her inferior station and her dependency. Could this young woman's education have unsettled her, and was that why she treated her so dismissively? Who will ever know what went on in Mother's thoughts? Mother reacted to the long stories, the nerves and the fainting spells with a disdainful silence, and it was only Miss Le Roux's skill with the needle that gave her a certain status. Thus, after our lessons she hemmed the innumerable sheets and pillowcases that would be used by our family for many years to come, on the farm as well as later in the town house: Mother died in a bed made up with sheets Miss Le Roux had sewed and after Maans got married, Stienie still used that linen for a long time. In the kist where our linen was stored, the bedding piled up without explanation, just as the land and the sheep flocks were accumulated silently and steadily during those years, in preparation for an unknown yet alluring future.

How could she have been happy with us? On a board across her knees she wrote long letters to her family in the Boland, but how often could she send off those letters? I do not know. And what passerby ever brought along a reply? But sometimes a letter did arrive somehow, and I remember the tears and the excitement, and the long stories she told me about this one or that one, and about the births and deaths in the distant world beyond the mountains where she came from. When a rare visitor arrived, she was always excited too and, giggling and breathless, she presented herself in the voorhuis uninvited, to join the company. It was usually a young man from one of the neighbouring farms who had ridden over with notice of a funeral or a visit from the Dominee, and the way she hovered and fussed made him uncomfortable, and long after the visitor had left, after the sound of the horse's hoofs had died away and the familiar silence had taken hold of the farm once more, she remained restless and agitated. The young men in our parts were unfamiliar with the Boland girls and their ways; she frightened them away with her unbecoming eagerness when they called on us, and when we attended church services in the district, it was clear that they were avoiding her. But what other future was there for her?

I see that emptiness now, I recognise that loneliness, though I still do not quite understand it, but at the time I was only aware that she was making herself ridiculous with her fluttering and her airs in the company of the young men who were invited into the house for a bowl of coffee, and with all her questions and insinuations after their departure. Over the untidy, irregular stitches of my sewing, I studied her in silence, as deprecating and scornful of her weakness as Mother herself, and I decided that I would never behave like that; that I would never be like her.

What did I mean by that resolution, the silent disapproval of a mere child who knew nothing about other people or about life? Even today I am not quite sure. I would never be as dependent as she, I thought – on her brother-in-law, on the Dominee, on Mother's good-will and Father's wages, on the favour of any random young man; I would never deliver myself into the power of others the way she did, fluttering around an embarrassed young caller in the voorhuis who was trying his best to escape. I was already learning to be silent and to hide my feelings; in due course I learned not to feel at all, and with practice and experience my skills improved. I was a quick and intelligent girl, and I learned fast.

For a year life continued in this way. Perhaps Miss Le Roux had been hired for a year, or perhaps there was simply no chance for her to leave the Roggeveld until the end of autumn when we moved down to the Karoo again. When the time came, she was very excitable and high-spirited for a while and she spoke of the Boland and her people and her friends more than ever, while preparing and packing for her departure. Down in the Karoo she embraced me tearfully and told me never to forget her, and I stood there with Maans's hand in mine and watched as she and Father left in the cart for the place where she would be fetched. It was over, I thought impassively; but it was not. One day before the end of winter Father fetched her again and Miss Le Roux returned to us with her trunk and her travelling-case; she came back to the Roggeveld with us, and unpacked her things again in the room she had left a few months earlier, and hung her black dresses on the nails in the wall. She was quieter and more subdued, the moments of excitement rarer, and after each outburst she withdrew into herself again; she did not speak of the Boland as often as before and did not write so many letters. Our lessons were resumed where we had left off and nothing was said, only Mother was cooler and more distant than ever. She was not free to choose what she wanted to do with her life, and it probably turned out to be the only possibility for her, to return for another year to the solitary farm, the lonely house, and the company, all day long, of a silent, critical girl and a toddler.

She did her work thoroughly and dutifully, I must admit, and however restless and moody she may have been at times, in her lessons she was painfully precise: what she taught me I retained, and remember to this day. "Remember, your late father paid dearly for your education!" old Oom Flippie Marais chided once, years later when I was a grown woman, in the hallway of our town house one late afternoon shortly after Father's death. "He paid a lot of money for your education," he snapped, "with governesses from the Boland and what not! Who else in these parts had as much?" He must have come to visit Mother that afternoon, for he was an elder in the church and they lived in town, but what was the reprimand about, and why was the old man so upset, a spiteful, envious old man who came upon me in the half-light of the hallway where I was not expecting him? But he was right: who among the people of that generation was as educated as I, a mere girl? Father paid her in gold coins, I remember, and she locked away the money in a tin box in her trunk; and what she taught me I retained all my life, everything except the sewing and the handicrafts.

The mourning period for her parents had long passed, and when she was in the Boland some family member gave her a brightly-coloured frock – why do I suddenly see it so clearly, the grey material with the small, regular pattern of purple flowers? She planned to remake it for herself, and from time to time she would suddenly throw herself into the task resolutely and work at it until late, using fine, strong, tiny stitches, her head close to the candle-stub, oblivious to all else in the world. A stiff, glossy fabric with a pattern of stripes and flowers, round and round, and she mentioned a white collar she wanted to make. Why did she rush so to finish it? For what occasion and for whose benefit did she want to wear it? But the next minute it was as if she had lost interest or hope, and for weeks the unfinished frock would lie folded in her trunk once again. I never saw her wear it: I suppose she first had to wear out her black mourning outfits. It must have been at this time, during the second year Miss Le Roux spent with us, that I went to our bedroom one evening to fetch something. It was twilight but not yet dark, so that I did not take a candle, and in the half-light I saw her: motionless at the window with the dress on her lap, needle in hand. She was startled when I entered so unexpectedly and averted her head quickly and brushed her hand across her face. I was scared and shy and pretended not to see or understand; with my back to her I stooped to search for something in the chest in the corner, feeling around in the dark, not remembering what I had come to fetch, and again I promised myself, blindly and uncomprehendingly, with my face to the dark wall, unaware of what I wanted to avoid or how I would do so, that this would not happen to me.

Thus Miss Le Roux spent two years with us in all, and the next time we went down to the Karoo for the winter, she and Father left in the cart once more, after which we did not see her again. I must have been fourteen or fifteen by that time, for soon afterwards I was confirmed and considered fully educated: I could read fluently in Dutch and English, even the old-fashioned black letters in our family Bible, and give the meaning of most words I encountered, I could write evenly in round, open letters on unlined paper, with few spelling errors, and I could do arithmetic on paper as well as mentally, and calculate amounts in pounds, shillings and pence. I was the youngest in the confirmation class in Worcester and I knew more than any of the other young people, boys or girls, so that the old Dominee praised me in front of all the others and held up Father and Mother as an example to all parents in the Roggeveld. The other young people avoided me more than ever, however, as if I were a strange apparition, and it was almost as if they felt an animosity towards me that I could not understand. But what did I care about their antagonism? I had been confirmed and we returned to the farm and I would have nothing more to do with them.

When she left, Miss Le Roux left behind the books from which she had taught me, for Father had probably paid for them, and she counselled me not to forget what I had learned. The books remained in my room and I read in them regularly, without Mother ever commenting, though I know she was not fond of books or book-learning and never liked to see anyone read in our home. I helped her in the house and looked after Maans, and when he was about five or six, Mother said it was time for me to teach him what I knew, so that was added to my duties. I taught him to read and write and do arithmetic, everything I knew, and from time to time Father got in touch with a Dominee in Worcester and had a few more books or a case of pens and writing paper delivered. He was an easy-going child who tried his best and gave me no trouble, even though he did not learn very well, and I did not mind sharing my own knowledge with him. Personally I had never seen much use in my education, for it was more than was needed to be confirmed, and otherwise it only served to set me apart from the other young people at Nagmaal and church meetings, the boys staring at me awkwardly and the giggling girls with their arms around each other turning away from me.

Why do I relive all these things? Why do I remember how, in the late afternoon, towards evening, Maans and I would sit on a bench in front of the house, he spelling out the letters in his reading-book while I was busy with some task? The child bent over his work and the peace of the late afternoon, the wall of the house still warm behind my back with the precious heat of the day, the time when the cows came home to be milked and the shadows stretched across the yard – why do I remember this? The child asks me something so that I bend down to help him: I look up, and across his bowed head I see the veld stretched out in the evening light and the horizon changing colour, and I realise with sudden clarity that this is why they gave me an education, why Miss Le Roux was fetched from the Boland and paid in gold coins, why Father ordered the books and the cases of writing paper from the Cape: not for me, their daughter, but for the grandson and heir, so that when he was old enough I would be properly equipped to take on the task of his education.

What else did I expect then, and what reason did I have to be surprised at this insight? In some way I must have believed that it was for my own sake, their only daughter, their only remaining child, as a sign of affection that seldom found any other way of expression; but it was a foolish and reckless belief, for surely I had no right to expect more than the food, clothing and shelter that were granted to me? I still remember the desolate feeling that came over me as I sat beside the child on the bench in front of the house, staring at the veld stretching away to the horizon in the evening sun, wide and unbroken: the bench and the child beside me, the bowl on my lap – what was I doing? – and the emptiness before me in the evening light. Then I realised again how alone I really was.

For the next few years Father did his best to struggle along on the farm while his health declined rapidly, but during this time, with Maans beginning to grow up, Coenraad came to us. We did not receive many visitors, as I have mentioned, but sometimes a stranger would turn from the road or get lost and arrive at our door, usually on horseback, but sometimes on foot, like Coenraad. It was not customary for white people to travel on foot, and such visitors were not invited into the house, but were mostly given something to eat at the kitchen door and allowed to bed down in the outbuildings. When Coenraad arrived on the farm, however, we were without labourers yet again, so he did a few chores for Father and in the end he stayed on. I do not know much about him, only that he was a foreigner, and where he had been heading with his bundle of belongings I do not know either, I suppose for Beaufort or Colesberg, but he remained with us for as long as Maans was a boy. He worked diligently and conscientiously and never shirked his duties, not even when he had been drinking, and the only trouble Father ever had with him came from the farmhands, for they complained that he was a hard master and that he beat them. Father did not approve, and in the old days he used to reprimand Jakob when he treated our people too harshly, but by this time Father's word no longer carried much weight on the farm, and it was Mother and Coenraad who conferred and made decisions, for she trusted him and always took his side when there were differences of opinion. He slept behind a screen he had erected in the shed and joined us only at mealtimes, and I remember how strange I found it that he did not attend our family prayers, but as far as I know nothing was ever said about it.

Coenraad seldom entered the house except at mealtimes, but I remember him in the evenings at the table in the candlelight, conferring with Mother. Father sat with them, half-absently stroking his beard with one hand, not contributing to the conversation. Something gleams in the candlelight, there is a sound – is it Coenraad receiving his wages? Suddenly I remember the glint of metal, and Mother's face in the candlelight, her sharp eyes fixed on the money as she counts out the coins. Was it his wage that he received, or could he have been given money to buy sheep at auction because Father himself could no longer go? Sometimes he was indeed sent out alone, and he even had his own mount, and it must have been Mother and he who conferred and decided on the purchases, as he increasingly became the one to bargain with the people who came to buy sheep from us. Father counted out the gold coins from the pouch Mother had fetched in the bedroom and Coenraad rode off to carry out their instructions; but more and more often it was Mother who made the decisions and gave the instructions, more and more openly it was she, and we were prospering. Father was a good person, an honest and just person, but he had never actually been a farmer. It is good when a woman is the boss on a farm.

Who said that? Surely no one in our parts would have said anything like that, except in jest or scorn? Good or not good? It is not good . . . ?

I was spending most of my life indoors, at Mother's side or in her shadow; my duties, my timidity and our strange, isolated way of living bound me to the house increasingly, as if life were something I watched as it occurred outside in the brightness of day, in the yard beyond the threshhold, outlined by the doorframe. I was standing in the dim light of the house – who was in the doorway, visible against the light, and whose voice could I hear outside? Were we so frequently cursed, did so many people come to protest, threatening us with reprisal, or calling down heaven's vengeance upon us? Yes, they probably did, and most likely more often than I ever realised, for how else were those gold coins collected, the morgens of land accumulated and the sheep flocks increased? It is not good; it is not right . . . Who was it?

The daylight outside, and a voice. Father or Mother was standing on the threshhold, or both; both were standing there, and a herdsman had come to complain. It was not right.

Now I remember everything I had forgotten, including many things I have no desire to recall. A herdsman had come to complain to Father that Coenraad had thrashed his child, the man standing outside in the yard, while Father came to the kitchen doorway, leaning on his stick, Mother behind him as usual, just inside the door. Where could Coenraad have been that I do not remember him? But there was no need for Coenraad to worry about the labourers' complaints and tales, after all, for Mother always supported and defended him. In the end the man had no choice but to leave and look for other work: "It is not right!" he cried. "It is not good!" What had happened, exactly? I do not know, but once he got going, Coenraad beat the labourers mercilessly, and he spared neither woman nor child, that I remember well. "We are also human!" he shouted over his shoulder as he crossed the yard, and the woman's voice – yes, his wife had come with him, with the child who had been punished for some transgression or omission: "It is not good when a woman is the boss on a farm!" That was how it happened; that is what I remember. But, right or wrong, the man had to leave with his family and I suppose we found other workers yet again. It is not right – good or bad – how well I recall those words now. And the beams that have collapsed at Bastersfontein where the house stood empty, the thatch collapsed over the walls, and the fountain dried up.

It was during this time, when Coenraad was still with us, that I went to Bastersfontein, when the houses there stood empty because we could not find labourers, and when Maans was still at home; Maans was young and did not understand, laughing beside me as the wind plucked at my clothes, and my billowing hair blinded me momentarily; it was during this time, when the child was my sole companion during the day, and in the evenings when he was asleep, I withdrew to join old Dulsie at the hearth as she smoked and muttered to herself, increasingly unaware of my presence or of events around her. She had grown old and was probably tolerated in the house only through Father's intervention, for there was little she could still do and she lived mostly inside her own head, always talking about the past. Could this have been why I went to the kitchen in the evenings, sitting silently in a dark corner of the hearth, because it was the only place where I could hope to hear Pieter and Sofie's names? But if she knew anything, she never let on to me, cautious even in her withered old age, and the things she remembered and the long, rambling conversations she had with herself were seldom about subjects that interested me, except that one evening in late autumn shortly before we went down to the Karoo: a cold evening, with Dulsie muttering and mumbling, drawing at her pipe and shoving another branch into the fire. Perhaps Mother and Father were already asleep, for Father went to bed early, and I was lingering at the fire in the only moments of freedom I knew. One of the first cold evenings of frost or sudden snow in the Roggeveld when preparations for the trek had already begun, the fire dwindling in the hearth, and Dulsie talking to herself about Jakob and Gert once getting into an argument about a bay horse, and about a saddle and bridle that had belonged to someone or had been taken from him. I could not follow and was no longer listening when suddenly, as if woken from a dream, I was alerted by the sound of familiar names. "And Gert and that arrogant Malay meid stealing food here in the house, thinking I cannot see them, or hear them whispering here in the dark, and Gert riding over to Bastersfontein every night when Jakob and Sofie were hiding out there . . ."

In the dark corner I sat motionless: Jakob and Sofie, Jacomyn and Gert – what was she talking about? Something stirred, something rustled in the shadows beyond the last glow of the fire burning low in the hearth. Old Dulsie had forgotten what she was talking about, however, and said no more, and I dared not ask in case she spoke again. Something stirred in the dark; but it was nothing, only the wind driving the fine, sifting snow through the gap underneath the door. Then Dulsie laughed triumphantly. "And Gert lying so shamelessly and making the Oubaas ride all the way to the Boland to look for them, Gert with his smooth tongue who took Jakob's saddle and bridle for himself when he left . . ." Her thoughts travelled far; she drew on her pipe thoughtfully, suddenly cackling loudly. "Oh, how he fooled them," she crowed, rocking gleefully at the memory. "All the way to the Boland with Jakob's saddle and bridle, and the two of them sitting at Bastersfontein all the while, Jakob and Sofie, while Gert rides around with his saddle. Oh, how he fooled them, good, good!" she cried, rocking from side to side. I did not move, I did not breathe, too afraid to miss a word or to misunderstand, but the confused memories faded and the old woman dozed on her seat in front of the fire: I was rising cautiously to go to my room when she spoke again. "Back from the Boland empty-handed," she mumbled contentedly, and then she fell asleep and I covered the last glowing embers with ashes and went to bed myself.

I suppose I could have asked, there is no harm in asking, but I had learned long ago that you get no answers to your questions, and in her lucid moments Dulsie would never have discussed these things with me. I never discovered what train of thought had suddenly sparked off those comments that evening, and she never referred to anything like that again, no matter how carefully I listened to her musings: thus I had to be satisfied with the scant information I had come upon so inadvertently. Jakob and Sofie at Bastersfontein? – no, that could not be right. But Pieter and Sofie; and Gert riding over to Bastersfontein at night with food Jacomyn had stolen from the house, Gert who finally left us to seek his fortune elsewhere, with his horse and his rifle and the saddle and bridle belonging to the late Jakob who had been found dead in the kloof, Gert and Jacomyn . . . What had actually been behind Dulsie's gloating words, and whose side was she on: did she blame Gert for the way he had deceived Father, or revel in the success of his deceit? But she was on no one's side, dependent like all of us on the goodwill of any random person who could aid or protect her, equally inclined to disparage and insult her fellow-servants as to delight in the ruin of her masters, her loyalties permanently divided by the need for survival. Alone, I realised as I bent over the hearth to extinguish the fire and felt my way to my room through the dark house; alone, man turned against man in selfishness, discord and spite.

In all the years Bastersfontein had been no more than a name to me, an isolated place where Jan Baster and his people once lived and, in later years, our herdsmen and their families, and I had never been there myself; yet it was on our land, at the farthest limit of our farm, and there was no reason why I should not go there if I wished. I would have to wait, however, until spring when we returned from the Karoo: wait, I told myself while I helped Mother pack the crates and tie up the bundles for the trek downward; wait, I said as our trek began the descent down Vloksberg across the rocky ridges, and I looked back at the faded grey winter landscape of the plateau we were leaving behind, looked back at the clouds covering the distant horizon where I knew Bastersfontein lay; wait, I repeated during the months of our stay in the Karoo, and I yearned for the Roggeveld more strongly than ever. Why was it so important for me to go to Bastersfontein, and what did I expect to find there? I did not know that myself, and today I still do not know, only that the names that had emerged so suddenly from old Dulsie's incoherent mutterings in that time of silence and loss were to me the first firm evidence I could cling to, and the only promise that I might somehow discover what had happened to Pieter and Sofie. Wait, I said, and I did not mind waiting, for to be patient was another thing I had already begun to learn.

When spring arrived, we loaded the wagon once more and followed the sheep up the slopes where the flowers were appearing in the crevices, and once again we took possession of the empty house waiting for us just as we had left it behind months before, the doors closed but not locked. The cots and beds were reassembled, the feather mattresses spread out and the beds made; the fire was rekindled in the kitchen hearth; our lives continued. I had not forgotten my resolve, but I could not simply disappear without explanation for an entire day, and so I had to endure patiently, waiting for the rare occasion when Father and Mother would be away all day. At last, that same spring or early summer, it happened – it must have been a funeral, for that was the only reason why Father still left home in those years, and Mother had begun to accompany him so that he would not have to travel on his own; I do not remember anything else, for it was unimportant to me. I only recall the fact of my sudden freedom, and how I hurried to finish my chores, and then I tied a handful of dried pears in a handkerchief and told Maans to come, for today we were going for a long walk. To the end of the world? he asked, for Coenraad had once taken him on his horse to the edge of the plateau where he could look down on the Karoo. Yes, yes, I answered impatiently without listening, and took his hand and set off.

It was far that we had to walk, but not so far that we could not be back before Father and Mother returned, as long as we walked briskly and did not dawdle, and for most of the way Maans ran ahead of me, turning around, laughing, to ask if this was far enough, if we were almost there. Spring or early summer, radiant in the glow of the silvery sunshine, the wind blowing at us from the rim of the mountains, and in the shelter of the rocky ridges, in the hollows and on the sunbaked slopes we came upon fields of flowers illuminating the silver-grey veld with their brightness, spekbos, gousblom and botterblom like in earlier springs, but I took no notice and hurried Maans along when he wanted to linger to pick flowers. The farther we walked, the more anxious and impatient I became, as if it had become imperative that we reach our destination: perhaps, if we could only move fast enough, I argued irrationally as I stumbled over the uneven ground, if we could only get there in time, it might still be possible to find something, though I still did not know what I was looking for. The remains of a fire, perhaps, with the ashes still warm, bedding that had retained the impression of a body or bodies, the fresh tracks of horses? No, not really, I had never deceived myself so completely, but at last there was something within my reach, something tangible after all the secrecy and evasion, the rumours and suspicions on which I had survived for so long, perhaps incomprehensible in itself, but nonetheless comforting as a symbol of the things I could not understand, like the ring on my pillow in the early morning, or the cross between the stones in the wall. Eagerly and hopefully I pressed on, and time and again I over-took the child running ahead of me, and I communicated my excitement and anticipation to him, so that he insisted on knowing how far we still had to go and if we were there yet.

Blindly and instinctively I headed in the direction I knew Basters-fontein had to lie, never doubting that I would be able to find and recognise it. Maans had stopped again to rest, for he was beginning to tire from the long walk, and I reached the crest of a low ridge and saw a hollow ahead of me with reeds and water, a moist, fertile spot in the pale-bright spring landscape, and I knew it was Bastersfontein. I began to run, with Maans behind me, crowing with delight, not understanding what was happening at all; my hair had come undone as we were walking and I had not bothered to tie it up again, and it blew across my face so that I could not see where I was going, and I stumbled and fell to my knees, tears pouring down my cheeks, while Maans danced around me, laughing with joy at our unusual game, excited to find out what would happen next.

But that was all; that was Basterfontein, we had arrived there. A moist, fertile place nestled in the shelter of a low ridge, a few dilapidated hartbeeshuisies, the collapsed remains of a few old shelters or kraals of stacked branches, the fluttering of white butterflies and the small, shiny leaves of the harpuisbos reflecting the light – what more had I expected? I remained on my knees, and later Maans became bored and ran off while I knelt there still, tears pouring down my cheeks, crying for the first time in years with no one to see my tears, no one to know. Does Maans still know, does he remember?

After a while I wiped my face with my hands and tied up my hair, and I got up. So this was the place where Pieter and Sofie – but no, not even that: this was the place that a confused old woman, muttering in front of the fire in the late evening, had identified in passing as the place where Jakob and Sofie, or perhaps Pieter and Sofie, had hidden, or perhaps not. How could I tell how much of her tale was truth and how much imagination? Perhaps I had misunderstood completely, perhaps I had not even heard her correctly, yet it was all I could cling to. Here Pieter and Sofie had hidden for an indefinite period while people had been searching for them, here Gert had ridden over at night to bring them food stolen from the house, and from here they had finally continued on their journey, destined for somewhere I could not follow. I had to believe that, it must have been like that, for it was the closest I could ever get to them again. Gert and Jacomyn had known, even Dulsie had known, though she had not been let into the secret;

our herdsmen and their families must have known of the white people living at Bastersfontein, but nobody had said anything, nobody had given them away, silently united in the plot in which the fugitives were protected from the masters and were helped to escape. Father rode to the Boland in search of them without anyone enlightening him, and I struggled desperately to create from a few incidental words a story in which I myself could believe.

The hartbeeshuisies had stood empty for a long time; the mouldering thatch had disintegrated and the leather thongs securing the posts of the framework had given way, so that the entire structure had collapsed and it was no longer possible to enter. Here they must have slept together at the beginning of their long partnership; at this fountain they must have knelt to wash and drink the clear water from their cupped hands. Did they expect to be followed and tracked down, or did they not even consider the possibility, so that they spent the waiting period laughing together, with no fear that it would pass and that reality would set in? There was no sign left of their presence, the remains of their fire had long been obliterated by the rain and the soil held no footprint or hoofmark any more, but in the moist earth around the fountain there were the fresh hoofmarks of the klipspringertjies who had recently come to drink there. Even the herdsmen had not been there with their flocks since winter.

It was time to return, for we were far from home: as far as a horse could travel in an hour, I remembered dreamily, as far as old Dulsie could walk in an afternoon, and suddenly I recalled Gert's words. Could it have been more than banter on his part when he sang to himself as he was dressing the thong; could he have been telling me something without my realising it? That was probably the way it happened and I should accept it and stop thinking about it; in any case I was not disappointed, though I had to make up stories on the way back to make our long, unexplained journey seem worthwhile to Maans. I stood on the ridge for a moment, looking back, and I watched as light and shadow washed and surged over the wide landscape before the dark waters closed over everything, rendering all that had disappeared into the dark invisible for ever. I had lost them, across the wide, barren Roggeveld and beyond the undulating horizon, like the wind, like the fog, like the thin, swirling snow, down the narrow, steep cliffs and passes of the mountains – Ouberg, Vloksberg, Verlatekloof, Komsberg – down to the Bokkeveld or the Karoo, from the starkness of the interior to the Moordenaarskaroo, the Koup, the Nuweveld or the Hantam, lost in the desolation of Boesman-land and Namaqualand where no white people remained, to Groot River where the hopeful Basters had sought refuge, and over the distance in the quivering heat it was impossible to recognise them or to follow the rest of their journey, the last certainty obliterated by the heat's distortions.

We returned home and washed our feet and hastily I prepared the evening meal and laid the table, but when Father and Mother returned it was late, and no one asked what had happened during the day. When Maans spoke eagerly of the long walk we had taken, Father asked where we had gone, but he was tired and keen to go to bed and he scarcely listened to my answer. We walked to a place where we had taken out honey years ago, I said, for I wanted to see whether there were still bees, but there was nothing. We passed old shelters, I said, but we did not see any people; and then I got up to take Maans to his room, for he also had to go to bed. That was the first time I had ever lied to Father, but it was probably also something I had to learn, like the silence and the vigilance and the patience, and part of the skills I would need to survive. But in a way my story was not completely untrue, for while I was putting the child to bed I suddenly remembered that day when I was still very young and we all went along to take out the honey, Jakob and Pieter and Gert and I, and Gert removed the honeycomb from a cleft in the rock, and on our way back that evening one of them – I do not remember who – carried me on his shoulders for I was too exhausted to walk.

4

....

I do not believe Father ever had enemies, but it was during this time that we discovered just how fond people were of him and how highly regarded he had become in our district over the years, in spite of the secluded life we led on the farm; for as it became more and more difficult for him to move around among the people, it was they who started coming to him.

For as long as I can remember establishing our own congregation in the Roggeveld had been under discussion; that is to say, the men discussed it when we met for church services, for what concern was it of the women? During this time it was brought up again and began to receive more urgent attention, and it was specifically to learn Father's opinion and obtain his advice that people came to call on us. We were not used to visitors, not to mention the substantial groups arriving now: we had to take all the coffee bowls from the kist and the spittoons that had never been used were brought out as well, and later Coenraad hired a stable boy whose chief duty it was to look after the visitors' horses. Even Mother was surprised, though she would never have let it show, but there was a kind of agitation and nervousness in her behaviour as she welcomed the visitors, unlocked coffee and sugar and arranged for meals, and it was never clear to me exactly how welcome these uninvited guests were. In time, however, I believe she realised how the solemn gatherings of elders and deacons in our voorhuis flattered us and how those conferences dignified us, and somewhat unwillingly she began to go out of her way to welcome and entertain these visitors.

I had nothing to do with these meetings, of course, but as her daughter I remained in the kitchen to carry out Mother's instructions, for by this time old Dulsie was no longer capable of much. One day, however, I was summoned unexpectedly when the men were struggling with a letter that had to be written. It must have been Father's proposal, for I do not think any of those solemn old gentlemen would have considered such a possibility, but in the circumstances they could not offer much opposition. Thus I wrote the letter as it was dictated to me, head bowed over the paper, while from across the table they watched my skilfulness with silent disapproval. Afterwards I withdrew to the kitchen without any of those present expressing a single word of approval or appreciation, or even just thanking me. The letter must have been written well, however, or they were convinced of my skill anyhow, for after this I was often summoned to the voorhuis where the men sat with their pipes and their chewing tobacco, to put their letters and memorials and petitions in writing. When they discovered that I could not only write in an elegant, legible hand, but also had knowledge of words, they would allow me, somewhat stiffly and unwillingly, to express a thought they had been struggling with; sometimes they simply spoke, without taking notice of me, and allowed me to put down their thoughts in my own words. When I read aloud what I had written, they nodded slowly over their pipes, and that was the only thanks I ever got from any of them. "I must say, a daughter like this is worth as much to a man as a good team of trek oxen!" Oom Daantjie van Wyk once exclaimed, but he always liked to tease and everyone assumed he was only joking. Later they also discovered that I could read fluently, could decipher longhand writing and explain difficult words, and I was summoned to read the letters and documents that had arrived from Worcester and from the Cape.

I had never liked people, especially not the company of strangers, but to be called into the voorhuis like that by Father never bothered me, for it was the first time I realised there was something in the world I could do apart from helping Mother in the house and teaching Maans. Moreover, I began to realise that when I was called upon to read to the assembled people, I was not self-conscious and my slow tongue no longer encountered any obstacle. Later still, they found out I also knew some English, and then it was not only the deliberations about the new congregation I had to help with, but sometimes a neighbour rode over on his own with a letter from the magistrate or a newspaper from the Cape to ask Father whether his daughter might look at it for him. Father was proud of me then, that was clear, and it was actually the only chance he ever had to feel proud of me, for I was a shy, withdrawn child who did not normally attract any attention or elicit any approval.

I bent my head over the paper and wrote down the requests, objections or admonitions without considering what I was writing: the scratching sound of the quill pen, the men around the table in a haze of tobacco smoke, and their monotonous arguing voices interspersed with sudden outbursts of anger or indignation, "in order that they, the undersigned members of this congregation, want to make their wishes known to the designated authorities, in accordance with their humble request . . ." It was not only here in the Roggeveld that the establishment of a congregation was being considered, for during this time many changes were taking place in these parts, as I discovered from the men's conversations where I sat in the voorhuis, waiting to be told what to write. In the Bokkeveld, as well as the Hantam and the Nuweveld, towns were being founded, there was mention of churches being built, ministers being called and church councillors elected. Around us new congregations came into being and the boundaries of the old ones shifted; magistrates and schools and such matters came under discussion, hitherto no more than strange, distant phenomena to us, connected with Worcester and the Boland, on the outskirts of the world we knew. When I got up and withdrew from the voorhuis, I soon forgot all about these matters, however, just as I forgot about the letters or petitions I had drawn up, for these were the men's affairs and did not concern me.

I still taught Maans, but he was beginning to grow up and did not spend all his time with me like before. He often rode out to the sheep; at first Coenraad took him on his horse, but then he learned to ride and Father gave him his own horse, ordered from the Hantam. He was given more and more duties on the farm and, after he had been my responsibility for so many years, I lost him again, the baby I had held on my lap when I arose from my long sickbed. The beams had collapsed, the thatch had mouldered, and nothing remained. Sometimes the house seemed very big and quiet and empty as we lived together in silence, Mother and Dulsie in the kitchen and Father in his armchair in the voorhuis: when I had nothing to do, I would sit close to him with some item of sewing, but it would soon slip from my clumsy fingers and I would just sit there, not moving or having the least desire to speak, silently occupied with thoughts I was unable to express. The thatch had mouldered, the stones had been scattered, and in later years there was no sign that a house had stood there, that people had lived there, the imprint of their feet no longer visible in the moist earth of the fountain where they had fetched water. I had fallen to my knees, tears pouring over my cheeks, but that was long ago. In the voorhuis I wrote letters for others and read their letters, but I never had any reason to write a letter myself, and not once did I receive one. I was a young woman and no longer a child.

In time the men who called upon Father began to bring their wives and families along. Initially the women entered our voorhuis hesitantly, as though uncertain of their welcome, almost as if they did not feel quite safe with us, and Mother was nervous and sat up very straight and spoke a bit too shrilly, with red spots breaking out high on her cheekbones. I did not mind the men so much, but I was never happy to see their wives, with their quick eyes that took in everything and their whispering as soon as we left the room. I can still see them eyeing Maans when the boy came in to greet, the son of Jakob who had died so mysteriously, the child of Sofie who had disappeared so mysteriously: they studied him eagerly as if they hoped something in his mere appearance would supply answers to all the questions they so desperately wanted to ask. Those names, Jakob and Sofie and Pieter's names, were never mentioned openly, however, and the questions remained unasked. They sat lined up against the wall holding their bowls of coffee or glasses of sweet wine, eyes darting around surreptitiously but incessantly, and minds working steadily, filled with speculation and suspicion that would be aired in detail later. I received no more than a passing glance from them as I served the coffee, for I was only the girl with the scar on her brow on which their searching glances lingered for a moment, and they showed no further interest in me.

Of course Mother noticed their curiosity and knew how many questions remained unasked as the conversation rippled on about church services and women's ailments, but she did not let on that she was aware of anything. I understood that it had become increasingly important to Mother that people should come to us and that, after the lengthy interval, we should continue as if the events that had taken place had never occurred, without our silence becoming too disturbing or our peculiarities too noticeable. As time passed the relentlessness of the lies in which our past had become entangled abated and became more acceptable, and only the presence of Maans in our midst still created a slight uneasiness, reminding us of those names that were never mentioned. What had he been told? I could never ask him outright what he knew about his mother, but through incidental remarks I found out that he had been told she was dead, and that was probably what had been said to the neighbours too, though no one believed it. Once when he was still young he surprised me, however, by declaring that he would have headstones erected on his Mammie and Pappie's graves when he grew up and, smiling, as if it were a game, I asked him to show me the place. "There!" he said without hesitation, and pointed at Jakob's grave and the adjoining grave where Father's sister was buried who had died when she was a young girl who had just been confirmed. I did not ask Maans who had pointed out those two graves to him, but I remember when Jakob's grave was dug, Father had remarked that he would be lying next to Tannie Coba whose namesake he was.

That summer, before the cornerstone of our church was laid, Father's birthday was celebrated formally and guests were invited again as had last happened when Sofie came to us as a bride, and how long ago that was, for by this time Maans was already a grown boy. There was no dancing this time, but for days we slaughtered and baked, and casks of brandy and Pontac were ordered from the Boland: after all the years there were wagons and carts in the yard once again and the rooms were filled with voices and excited children and candlelight; but to me it was not the same and could never be the same again. Father was happy, for he liked entertaining and receiving guests, even though he seldom had the opportunity, and in her own way Mother was content, albeit tense, with shining eyes and a clear blush on her cheeks, while Maans was elated about the people and the excitement and the wine they allowed him to taste behind Father's back, and for days he talked about nothing else. To flee the house, I suddenly thought as I stood with the coffee pot, trapped among the guests, to venture so far into the veld that the dim glow of the candlelight in the windows fades behind me and the raucous voices can no longer be heard, to be surrounded by the rolling silver landscape under the stars; to flee to Bastersfontein, I thought, where the water of the fountain seeps soundlessly into the sand. A woman holding a candlestick pushed past me to check on her sleeping children in the bedroom, for I was obstructing the way of the guests who were filling the house with their excitement and their loud voices, and the melted candle wax dripped on my new frock. To flee to the sheltered place under the ridge where no one will ever look for me and to wake every morning at first light and see the klipspringers that have come to drink at the fountain.

Thus we got our own congregation: there was a great deal of conflict and disagreement, but the congregation was founded and the corner-stone of the church was laid and the land for a church village was sur-veyed at De List. Henceforth we gathered for Nagmaal in the new village and there was no further need to travel down the mountain to Worcester. Initially people stayed in their outspanned wagons on the square behind the church, or they pitched tents, but Father bought three plots and began to build a town house immediately. But no, I must get the story right, for it was not like that: I remember Father in our tent in his old armchair that had been brought from the farm on the wagon, and the people coming to greet him and consult with him, while Mother saw to the layout and building of the new house; Mother in her black dress pacing out the exterior walls of the build-ing, deciding on the size of the large rooms, watching the bricks being hauled and the mortar mixed. Mother, shielding her eyes against the sun, shouting to spur on the workers. When the people came to town for Nagmaal services they always came to view the foundations of that big house, and later they came to watch the walls going up.

Mother hurried the builders and the carpenters and the thatchers along and sent Coenraad to Worcester with the wagon to fetch door-frames and window-panes, and our house was one of the first in town to be completed, with a voorkamer large enough for all the visitors who came to consult with Father, large enough for consistorial meetings to be held there for the time being, and for all the guests Mother wished to entertain. She ordered coffee cups and saucers from Cape Town, four dozen, and the old bowls were used on the farm and later not even there any more. For a long time after the founding of the congregation and the completion of the church we remained without a minister, and for a long time it was Father, as the most senior elder, who stood in for the minister when decisions had to be made or advice given. When no minister arrived to conduct the service, he was often called upon to read a sermon, for though he read slowly and painstakingly, the people wished him to do it and he did not like to refuse, and I can still see him reading from the book on a stand in front of him, his head slightly tilted and the finger of his stiff hand following the letters.

The shuffling and coughing of the people, the smell of the fresh thatch and the moist earthen floor, and Mother seated in the front row among the elders' wives, Mother's straight back, stiff neck and angular shoulders. Mother's eyes never wandered in church as she sat rigidly in the place of honour that was her due, while Father faltered and stumbled over the words, and after the service she moved among the churchgoers like a shadow, erect and unyielding in her black dress with the new gold chain around her neck, and she paused to greet people without ever really joining in their conversations, lingered to ask and answer questions without revealing anything or making any concessions. Yes, it was during this time that Father gave her the gold chain as a gift, or perhaps she ordered it from Cape Town herself, Mother who never wore any jewellery except her wedding ring: a long chain of narrow gold links reaching to her waist, as was the fashion at the time.

What did people think of her when they spoke to her outside the church or when they called on her in the new house to satisfy their curiosity? I do not believe she had any true lady friends, not to mention confidantes, and neither did anyone who knew her love or respect her, and she knew this without actually caring in the least, for she desired neither affection nor respect. What did they say among each other as they watched her walk away, followed by Maans and me? She did not care about that either. Father's status in the congregation and his increasing wealth were important to her, the front seat in church, the new house, the coffee cups, the visiting ministers who stayed the night and the unspoken envy and spite of the other women – I had probably always realised this as I lived beside her, but only now can I find the words to express it, an old woman alone in the dark with no one to listen.

It was during this time that Maans was sent away to school, and I believe that this was Mother's wish as well, for the desire for every child to be educated was as much a part of the plan she followed blindly yet relentlessly as the new house or the coffee cups. Most young people in our parts were taught at home by school-masters hired by their parents, like my brothers with Meester, or they somehow picked up just enough reading and writing to be confirmed, but in those days no one had a private governess like Miss Le Roux, neither was anyone sent away to school in the Boland, and Maans was the first. Where did Mother get this idea and why was it so important to her? Was it that her instinctive wisdom and insight told her that money and education granted power and commanded respect? Moreover, Maans was her favourite, just as his father once had been, and with an indulgence never evident before, she even showed him some affection at times. Thus Maans was sent to school in Worcester with a small roll of gold coins wrapped in paper, and he was instructed to have a suit made there and to have himself photographed in town and send us the portrait, which Mother kept in her Bible. Maans strongly resembled his father, a big, dark, slow boy, but without his father's fierce temper, a good, willing child who never gave any trouble or caused any problems: he was excited about leaving home, but at school he did not fare very well. I had to read his infrequent notes with their mistakes and ink blots to Father and Mother, and then Mother took them from me and put them away in her bedroom. Thus the three of us were alone, Father and Mother and I, with old Dulsie in the kitchen, but by this time she had become so old and confused that she could hardly be reckoned any more. Father walked with great difficulty, and the responsibility of the farm fell mostly to Coenraad.

When Maans left it made no real difference to me, for I had lost him when he began to grow up, and I had learned long ago that nothing endured and no belonging could be considered permanent. All my worldly possessions I had obtained through Father and Mother's mercy and I used them without ever regarding them as my own: clothes to wear, a brush and comb, a sewing kit, a Bible and a hymn book. The only possessions that were truly mine remained a secret that no one else knew of: the little cross Meester had left me and the ring to remind me of Sofie, wrapped in a remnant of cloth and a piece of sheepskin, secreted among the stones of the wall. I never went there to look at them – why would I, for what would I do with them? – yet I was always aware that they were there, an undisclosed and undisclosable secret while Mother and I were curing meat in the kitchen or paring quinces for bottling, while I sat beside Father's chair with the pillowcase I had to hem, while I served coffee to the visitors, absent-mindedly enduring their questions and their curiosity.

The tiny parcel among the stones in the wall of which no one knew, the memories that I shared with no one, the brightness of the water at

Bastersfontein and the thatch and the beams collapsed over the ruins, Sofie in her glistening black frock among the dancers, Pieter with his pale body on the haystack, laughing in the sunshine, the moonlight across the floor and the mist rolling along the kloof, and the stone dislodged by my foot, rolling away, reverberating from one rocky ledge to the next and from one cliff to the next, lost in the vast, invisible depths of the abyss before me. Sometimes I woke at night gripped by an unexpected fear, and in the dark of the sleeping house I lay awake as I do now, surprised by that fear which I could neither explain nor understand. In this bed, in this room I lay in the same darkness, thirty, forty years ago and more; but now there is nothing left to fear, all that remains for me is to remember, and slowly begin to understand.

It was during this time that Pieter came back to us.

One morning, while I was busy in the kitchen, we heard the sound of a rider approaching, and an unknown coloured man announced that he had brought a letter and stubbornly insisted on handing it to Father personally, refusing to entrust it to anyone else. At last I took him into the voorhuis where Father was sitting and he delivered his letter and was so insistent that it was for Father's eyes only, that it appeared to be part of the instructions with which he had been dispatched. I usually read Father's letters to him, but this time he did not ask me; and so I continued with my work, and after a while Mother told us to make the man something to eat and closed the door to the voorhuis behind her.

I do not wish to remember any more.

When will the first greyness of dawn become visible behind the wooden shutters; when will the first cock crow in the dark so that I will know that this night is over, that this night, too, has ended? How often I lay awake in the dark like this as a child, in this very room, in this bed, fearing things I did not understand, and again now as an old woman, with the memories taking hold of my mind while I am powerless to defend myself against them, against everything I am forced to remember and would rather forget. I do not wish to remember.

The table where I stand with the knife in my hand, the maid kneeling in the kitchen, blowing on the smouldering fire, and old Dulsie in her usual corner at the hearth – it is enough, it is too much already. We listen to the man leading away his horse to be unsaddled and fed, to the clink of the harness and the clip-clop of the horse's hoofs, while I prepare his food and pour his coffee. It is too much already, like a shadow passing across the yard, a fleece cloud in front of the sun, like darkness moving over my hands as I am working, over the worn tabletop. It is too far already; too late already.

He sat down at the table to eat, and in a lucid moment old Dulsie realised that he was a stranger and tried to question him, but he was a surly man who did not want to talk. From beyond Hopetown he had come, he said, and his master had sent him with a letter, but he could not be induced to say more, and he refused to divulge even his master's name. I scarcely listened to their conversation, for Father's affairs did not concern me and what my parents were discussing behind closed doors in the voorhuis was no business of mine, unless they needed me to read the letter or to compose an answer. This time I was not called in, however, and some time later Mother told us to pack some provisions for Father and gave orders for the cart to be inspanned; that same morning he left with the strange coloured man, without us learning anything more about the visitor or the purpose of his visit; Father who never left the farm any more except to attend Nagmaal in town and who hardly even left the house to walk slowly across the yard to the kraal, leaning on his cane.

For days Dulsie muttered crossly about these events about which she remained in the dark but, as I have said, it was no concern of mine. To push the kettle over the fire for the water to boil, to turn the bread out of the pans and to feel whether the iron was hot enough, those were my duties in life, and they measured out my entire existence. Only sometimes would I look up, cloth, iron, or pan in hand, and through a window or an open door I would notice the wide world outside the walls of the house, or I would see from the yard the horizon beyond the last farm buildings and the glittering of the dams, and then I might forget for a moment what I had been doing; but only for a moment. I was a good daughter, a model daughter, the old ladies sometimes remarked when they called on Mother, a blessing in the house, especially now, with Father needing more and more help, and they glanced at me appraisingly and looked away and spoke of other things, for to them it was only too clear that there was little chance that I would ever marry. What did Mother reply? I do not know; if I ever heard her answer, I must have chosen to forget it. I turned away from the horizon, I walked back to the house with the eggs I had gathered or the washing that had been put out to bleach and, if for a moment my eyes were blinded by the brightness of the sun, it did not matter at all, for I knew my way blindly from one room to the next, where my duties took me. Earlier, when Maans was a small boy, I often took him for walks in the veld, but there was no longer any reason for me to wander outside. The flowers along the ridges in spring, the wind gusting along the rim of the mountains and the tracks of the buck in the mud beside the fountain – I turned away and went inside, I crossed the worn threshhold of the house where duty held me captive, while in the sudden twilight my eyes still retained for a moment those distant images. I was a good daughter, a blessing to Father and Mother in the house.

Mother, of course, provided no explanation, but one day she told us to make the bed in the outside room, the room where Pieter used to sleep, for since his departure no one had been allowed to use it, and Coenraad, as I have said, bedded down in the shed; and Pieter moved in there. Mother silently unpicked the seams of Father's old suit and cut the pieces smaller, and wordlessly she remade it for Pieter to wear, for Father had always been a sturdy man, and Pieter was thinner than ever. Thus he was given clothes to wear, and a few skin-blankets, a razor and an enamel basin, for he had brought nothing with him, and he joined us for meals as if he had never been away.

If I peer into the darkness long enough, if with my meager remaining strength I struggle up against the pillows, craning my neck, I can almost make out in the darkness the window outlined against the first grey light that filters through the chink between sash and shutter. The memory of first light and daybreak penetrates the dark and is burned into the retina, and amid the absolute silence of the surrounding night, amid the rush of blood in my ears and the slow rattling of my own breath, I imagine that I hear the distant crowing of a cock. The girl on the cot at the foot of my bed stirs sleepily, the first movement in the long stagnant night, and gropes on the floor for her shoes, searches for the matches to light the candle, and for a moment I am bewildered by the sudden brightness of the flame; I, who have learned to see in the dark, am blinded by the light. The long night which has held me captive is over, and I am delivered from the relentless thoughts I cannot control and the memories I cannot evade, relieved of the obligation to repeat what I do not want to remember and to relive what I have forced myself to forget. Pieter came back. Pieter is dead, that is all; that is enough. I hear the women chattering in the kitchen as they light the fire and boil water, they come and bend over my bed and, as I lie helpless in their hands, I continue to cling to their words, their gestures and their dutiful care that promise me deliverance. Pieter is dead and rests in the graveyard beyond the ridge and in a few months, a few weeks, who knows how soon, perhaps even tomorrow, I, too, will be borne there along the narrow, rocky footpath, and it will be over. I do not want to remember. If only I can hold out long enough, I shall be safe.

But not yet. The night preserves its darkness and in the silence beyond this room there is no sound: helpless I lie here, surrendered to the night, and I cannot evade the reckoning demanded of me. The bright light burns into the retina and I see the house with Mother waiting outside, her shadow under her feet, and the black cart, and Father being helped out carefully, painfully. That is how Pieter returned.

No, not like that, not quite like that; there is more that I remember and can tell, more that I must tell. The morning comes to life before my eyes and the brightness burns in the dark, and I hear Mother calling for help. Who held the horses, who supported Father as he dismounted? Our attention was focused on him, on helping and welcoming him and bringing him into the voorhuis; we had already begun to move towards the house, our shadows under our feet, when he made a half-turn as if to give a further instruction about the horses, and we paused and turned around too. That was how Pieter returned to us. With our hands shielding our eyes against the brilliance of the sun we looked around and noticed a passenger under the hood of the cart. "Come, Pieter," Father coaxed gently as if addressing a child, and the figure in the cart stirred, ducked his head and climbed out.

Why must I remember, why must I be forced to remember here at the end of my life? In the end it was good, the way my life continued all those years, the unmarried daughter, the spinster aunt, on the farm and in our town house, between Roggeveld and Karoo, always present in the background and always prepared to help and serve where necessary. It was good the way it was and good the way it ended after all those years; if a service should be held at the graveside, the minister would readily find appropriate words and texts to sum up my life, and if a headstone should be erected for me, the dates of birth and death would suffice to review the course of more than seventy years. I have forgotten the treachery and the loss, I have forgotten how Pieter left and came back. Why must I remember now?

In the shade under the hood a figure rose hesitantly and, blinded by the sun's glare, we shielded our eyes with our hands and saw the passenger who had been sitting next to Father climb down slowly and step into the light, and we did not realise at once that it was Pieter who had returned to us.

Pieter, yes. Mother might have been expecting him, but I had not known. Pieter, I say now, but at the same time I do not know why I should have thought that. A stranger stood next to the cart, a man with shabby, oversized clothing and worn shoes, head bowed and eyes fixed on the ground as though waiting for further instructions: it was only because Father had spoken that familiar name after all the years that I knew it had to be him and that he had returned, that he had returned at last. "This is your mother," Father told him in that same gentle voice, and Mother went to him and embraced him. He endured the embrace passively, showing no sign of recognition, but because Father was looking at me expectantly, I went up to the man too and put my arms around him briefly and kissed my brother, kissed Pieter. He was back. It is enough, more than this I need not remember.

What did they tell people? Some explanation must have been given, convincing or not, credible or not, true or not, but not in my presence; Father and Mother never mentioned Pieter's return to me, neither was the subject ever broached by others. Of course people talked, however, and the pretexts, the lies, the rumours and the speculation gave rise to a kind of legend which in time reached even my ears. Much later, when Father and Mother were both dead, the conversation once turned to the diamond diggings, and Herklaas Vlok mentioned something to Maans in passing about "your Uncle Pieter there at Barkly West". Later still, Stienie once mentioned poor Uncle Pieter who had suffered so much on the Diamond Fields. Perhaps that was what she had been told, and she had believed it to be the truth; only it was not true, and could not have been true, for diamonds were discovered at the Vaal River only after Pieter's return, around the time of Father's death, when Coenraad left for the diggings and Maans also spoke of going. When Pieter came back, there was no question of diamonds, and Coenraad was still with us and Maans was at school in Worcester. At the time of Stienie's remark, it had all happened so long ago that the legend must have gained credibility, but Herklaas Vlok was my age and should have known the sequence of events; why would he tell such a muddled tale? I often pondered on these matters and wondered how much was fact and how much fiction and on how much truth the legend was based, how far they had wandered into Bushmanland or Namaqualand in the direction of Groot River, before a stranger near Hopetown dispatched his servant to fetch Father; but long before Pieter's death I stopped puzzling about these things, for I realised there was no sense in it. What was important was that Pieter had come back; and he had come alone, and he had come like that.

After his return he moved into the outside room again where he used to sleep after Jakob's marriage. He took his meals with us and was present at family prayers, but he never entered the house otherwise, neither was he summoned when guests arrived; he was bashful when strangers joined us at mealtimes, and very soon we got into the habit of sending his food to his room on such occasions. When we went to town, he attended church services with us, but there he slept in the outside room as well and avoided the house when there were visitors.

The children sometimes shouted after him in the street, teasing him, but eventually people accepted him the way he was, for he bothered no one. When he was asked a question, an ordinary, everyday question about the things he knew, he answered readily, but for the rest it was often as if he did not quite understand what was being said, and he never initiated any conversation himself. Sometimes, however, it was as if he had completely forgotten where he was and he would just sit, staring dully into the distance, and then Father would touch him and speak to him gently. After Father's death Maans continued to do this, for Maans also had a great deal of patience with him, but by that time it no longer happened so often, for in time he became accustomed to us again and our routines were not so strange to him any more. He knew the members of our family and called us by our names, but there was never any recognition, nor did he ever show any awareness of the past he had left behind years ago; every day he seemed anew like a stranger, or a visitor arriving with us for the first time.

Maans was not faring well, for the boy was not happy at school. During the winters he spent with us in the Karoo he sometimes complained to me, and I tried to console him a little or encourage him, and help with his lessons, but he did not find it easy to talk and I never did find out exactly what the problem was. Father might still have given in, for I think he missed the child, but Mother was adamant, and so Maans was sent back to Worcester every time. Later he stopped complaining and I hoped things had improved, but it was only because he was growing up and began keeping things to himself, a grown young boy who had started to shave and was preparing to be confirmed – on that occasion he was given Jakob's gold watch that Father had kept for him all those years. And then one day there was a letter from Maans that I had to read to Father and Mother as usual, in which he told them he found it too hard to learn and did not want to continue at school, but wished to go to Cape Town to become a soldier; and then Coenraad was dispatched to Worcester in the cart to fetch him, and he returned to the farm.

It meant a lot to Father to have Maans home again, for he was the only grandchild, the namesake and heir, after all, while Coenraad after all the years was no more than a stranger and hireling, and Pieter was incapable of more than a few small, menial tasks. In his unassuming way Maans was a hard worker, however, perhaps a bit slow, but precise and dependable. Jakob and Sofie had both been as bright as mirrors reflecting the light, as sharp as shards of mirror glass on which you could cut your fingers, but Maans showed none of their brightness, the quicksilver surface dull, casting hardly any reflection; actually he mostly took after Father, and Father loved him dearly. He obeyed the instructions he was given and discharged his duties; when we travelled to town, he drove the cart or wagon and in winter he helped Coenraad arrange the trek to the Karoo, and what he really thought or felt, no one ever knew.

It was after Maans's return from Worcester that Mother ordered the glasses from Cape Town, two dozen crystal glasses and two decanters that were unpacked and put away in our town house, for we were entertaining more and more often when we were in town; twenty-four chairs were lined up against the walls of the big voorhuis, and the elders and deacons were invited over regularly with their wives, and served sweet wine. I remember how the old ladies would inspect the glasses and the decanters, the large sideboard and the new curtains, making an inventory to be discussed at length later. In later years I believe Father would have preferred to stay at home, but nonetheless we went to town regularly for Nagmaal and other services, and entertained the elders and deacons and their wives.

When Maans came of age, however, the entire district was invited to the farm and there was dancing like all those years ago before he was born, when his parents were newly-wed, only this time the festivities were on a larger scale, for much had changed in the meantime and there was greater wealth and a greater need to show it off. I now realise that it was as a tribute to Father, however, and to him alone, that the guests arrived in such large numbers, and not for Maans's sake – for they scarcely knew him after the years he had spent at school in the Boland – and even less for the sake of our family. If I had not realised before how little regard people in the district had for us, it became quite clear to me that evening where, almost unnoticed in the throng, I happened to intercept, as I always did, the incidental words and phrases, the disparaging glances, the dismissive shrug of the shoulders. Father had earned their respect, and they were willing to enjoy our hospitality and to drink to Maans's health with the wine we supplied, but this willingness did not imply that they accepted us or felt obliged to us in any way. We were not part of their tight little community with its intermarriages, quarrels, friendships and gossip, relentlessly separated from them by our own persistent arrogance and aloofness and by the rumours that surrounded our family, unmistakably excluded from the inner circle of their fellowship, just as I was excluded from the giggling circle of girls waiting to be invited for a dance, waiting to be asked for their hand in marriage.

The house seemed strange to me with all these people, and hot and stuffy with the tallow candles burning everywhere on the tables, chests and window-sills, and when young Jasper Esterhuysen suddenly appeared before me and asked me something, stuttering with embarrassment, I did not understand what he was saying, and he had to repeat himself before it dawned on me that the music had begun and he was inviting me to waltz. No, no, thank you, I muttered without realising what I was saying, I must take my brother his supper; panic-stricken, I fled to the kitchen and while I was making my way through the people, I saw him return to Tant Mietjie, his mother, who had sent him, to let her know that I did not wish to dance. I remained in the kitchen for a long time: there were only a few servants there who had come with the guests, and old Dulsie, who was being kept awake by the unaccustomed noise. What brother? I asked myself as I remembered the lie I had told Jasper. After all, Jakob was dead and Pieter had left, and I had only been looking for an excuse to escape from him.

For a while I fussed aimlessly at the hearth without listening to the music in the voorhuis, the shuffling of feet and the shouts of the dancers, the laughter of the servants crowded in the doorway. "Jakob fetched himself a wife in the Karoo," Dulsie suddenly muttered where she dozed in the corner, and I remembered how he had lifted Sofie from the wagon on her arrival, and how she had glowed like a dark flame among the dancers. At the time I had been no more than a child on the fringe of the grown-ups' company, excited about the guests and the bustle and the noise, about this whole new world I was discovering, but it was over; I would never be a part of it, I knew, never one of the giggling girls invited to dance, never one of the married women against the wall in the voorhuis. Only Jasper Esterhuysen would still totter across the voorhuis floor, hair plastered down with pomade and arranged in curls over his low forehead, and only because old Tant Mietjie had sent him. I was in my thirties, and any possibilities that might have existed for me had passed unnoticed and slipped out of my reach.

I must take Pieter something to eat, I thought, and with some cake and a glass of wine I walked across the yard, past the outspanned carts, to the outside room where he was sitting on his cot in the dark. "Thank you, Sussie," he said when I handed him the refreshments, for he had learned to address me by that name, but he made no move to take the food, so that I put it on the cot beside him, and after a while I sat down next to him, for I had no desire to return to the house. The door facing the house was open, and across the yard we could see the dimly-lit windows and hear the voices and the music. He sat watching and listening across the distance; did the music bring back memories; did he hear, did he remember, or did no thoughts or memories remain, and was he simply waiting for the time to pass so that he could go to bed? It was impossible to say: no one could still get through to him. In all the years since his return, however, the two of us had never been alone together like that, everyone having forgotten about us that evening, and never before had there been the possibility of intimacy or confidentiality, the possibility of a gesture or a question. What happened? I wanted to ask him; where is Sofie? I wanted to ask, but it was impossible to speak. Thus we sat together in silence for a long time, until the sound of shots being fired and voices cheering outside made me start up, and I realised Mother would be looking for me. When I rose from the cot, Pieter did not look up and when I wished him goodnight, he did not answer immediately, as if he first had to consider my words and return from afar to reply.

On my way back to the light-filled windows and the music I kept close to the wall of the outbuilding to avoid the outspanned carts; I remember stumbling over a shaft and grabbing at the splashboard of a cart to keep my balance, and then hearing voices in the darkness of the shed where Coenraad slept, the deep voice of a man and a woman's laughter. Why do I suddenly remember this as if it were important? The darkness and the music and the candlelit windows and I, stumbling and falling to my knees on the shaft, the edge of the splashboard smooth and even under my fingers. In the darkness something stirred, and someone came out and walked past the cart without noticing me, and stood for a moment, etched against the dim light coming from the house, a woman swiftly smoothing her hair, smoothing her dress, before crossing the yard to the house; and when she ducked her head under the lintel of the kitchen door, I saw by the glow of the candle on the kitchen table that it was Oom Thys Breedt's young wife. This was a strange world in which I played no part, however, and it was not for me to wonder at what I had incidentally witnessed; I waited a while, motionless in the dark, but inside the shed all was quiet, and then I slipped across the yard and ducked my head as I crossed the kitchen threshhold. On the table the candle burnt motionlessly, and in her corner old Dulsie had fallen asleep.

It was late and some of the guests were getting ready to depart, but in the voorhuis they were still dancing. Mother looked up from her seat among the other women, straight-shouldered in her new black dress, and I knew that I had been right and that she had been look-ing for me. "I took Pieter some wine, Mammie," I said; "All right, my child," she answered with unaccustomed kindness in the presence of all these people who had come to celebrate her grandchild's coming of age, and old Tant Mietjie Esterhuysen nodded approvingly and smiled where she sat beside her. "See if your father wants anything, my child," she said in the same gentle tone, and I went out to where Father and a few other men sat smoking in front of the house. Old Oom Thys Breedt of Fisantkraal was among the group, in the midst of one of his long tales to which no one was listening any more, and Father just smiled at me, so that I turned to leave without noticing Oom Thys's crutches propped against his chair, and stumbled over them. Where can his wife be? I suddenly wondered as I stooped to pick them up and put them back, and I returned to the house and searched in all the rooms, among all the faces in the flickering candlelight and the dust, until I found her sitting among the younger women, smoothing her hair with a swift gesture. Why did I want to find her? I no longer know, if ever I did; I only remember the straight, smooth edge of the splashboard under my fingers, and the way she sat there, smiling, among the younger women.

Why do I remember that evening of Maans's coming of age in so much detail, young Jasper Esterhuysen and old Tant Mietjie and the darkness of Pieter's room, Dulsie by the fire in the kitchen and the outspanned carts in the yard? Everyone is long dead, the evening forgotten, but I still remember it all while I can no longer say how Maans and Stienie's wedding was celebrated, and all the New Year's dances and birthdays and weddings of later years have been wiped out of my memory. That New Year's Eve after Jakob brought Sofie to us as his bride, and the evening of Maans's coming of age, with Helena Breedt ducking her head as she entered the house while I watched through the fine haze of candlelight and dust as she smilingly smoothed her hair, made me realise anew that I would never belong with these people or have any part in their lives.

The boisterous young men made Maans drink too much that evening so that, being unaccustomed to liquor, he was very sick and in the end had to be carried to the shed and laid down on Coenraad's bed, for the house was filled with people. Where Coenraad was I do not know, for I did not see him that night. I stayed with Maans in case he should need anything, and I must have fallen asleep in the chair beside his bed, because I recall being awakened at daybreak by the sounds of vehicles being inspanned and the last guests departing; for a moment I was bewildered, and when I looked through the window I half-expected to see Gert and Jacomyn dancing together in the early dawn to the rhythm of the violin, but there was no one. I went out into the bright morning, and I saw the carts departing, and I knew I was safe again, safe at last.

That winter, just before people started leaving for their winter quarters, Jasper Esterhuysen rode over one more time with something old Tant Mietjie had sent Mother, and he stayed for lunch and lingered for a while. I did not say much to him but when he left, he took my hand in his own small, slack hand and said he hoped to see me in the Karoo that winter. No, I replied, we were not going to the Karoo this year because of Father's ill health, Maans would be going alone with the sheep; and I gave it no further thought.

That year we got our own minister at last, and in the spring he was ordained. We went to town for the occasion, Father too, though he had to lie across the back seat of the cart, supported by pillows; perhaps he felt he could not be absent now, after we had been waiting for so many years, or perhaps it was only because the visiting clergy would be staying with us in town and he wanted to be there himself to welcome them. I still remember the consuming zeal with which Mother prepared for the reception of these important guests, and how the servants suffered, the sudden outbursts in the kitchen and the screaming and slamming of doors, the hurling of utensils, like in the years of my youth, long ago. When the guests began to arrive, none of this was evident, however, and long afterwards people still spoke of the way they had been entertained by us. I only remember those sudden outbursts in the kitchen, and Father being too ill to attend the services: the people had to come to him, and there was an endless stream of visitors to our home.

When it was all over and the excitement had abated, it became clear even to Mother that the end was near and that Father would not be able to return to the farm; but he went anyway. Maans was sent to the farm to fetch the wagon, and we loaded him on his mattress, and so he was carefully and painfully brought home, for he said he wanted to die in his own house on the farm, not in the strange new house in town, and this time Mother bowed her will to his in an unusual and uncharacteristic way. Thus he died in his own bed in his own room, in the bed where he was born, in the house built by his father, and Mother and I took turns to keep watch at his bedside. I cannot say I grieved for him, for his death was a release from the pain he had endured so patiently and for so long; but as I sat beside his bed one night, alone in the sleeping house with the tallow candle burning low in the candlestick, I suddenly realised he was the only person who had ever showed me any love or affection, except for Pieter long ago when I was young, and Sofie, and all that belonged to the past now. In the distance I heard an eagle owl hooting, and I experienced the same feeling as on that cold silvery morning when I stepped out of the outside room and saw the guests departing and leaving us behind, the feeling that something had ended for good.

We buried Father in the graveyard beyond the ridge, and Maans inherited the farm. It was during this time that diamonds were discovered in the interior, and shortly after the funeral Coenraad left for the diggings: I still recall that he left on foot the way he had come, with all his possessions in a grain-bag over his shoulder. There was great excitement about the diamonds, and after the funeral it was the main topic of conversation; Attie Keuler left for the diggings overnight with a few young men from the Fraserburg district, and Maans also spoke of going, but Mother made no reply when he mentioned the possibility one evening at supper, and in the end he stayed and continued on the farm. It was also during this time that old Oom Wessel, his other grandfather, died, and he inherited from him as well, money, as was said in later years, and farms in the Bokkeveld and the Ceres-Karoo, so that more responsibilities fell to him, and he had to go to Worcester several times to consult with the attorneys.

After a year or two Coenraad came back without any visible evidence of being either richer or poorer, but he did not return to us. Oom Thys Breedt had died a short while before, and he married Helena and went to farm on Fisantkraal where he prospered, for he worked hard, and their children are well-respected people today, but people say Helena was never very happy. Jasper Esterhuysen married Danie du Plessis's widow and they lived with old Tant Mietjie on the farm. She had always been known as a miserly old woman, and they themselves lived frugally and carefully, so that people often made fun of them. They had no children, however, and when they died, everything they had accumulated so painstakingly was sold.

What Father's death meant to Mother, I do not know, for even during those last years of her life no familiarity ever developed between us. Perhaps she mourned the death of the man with whom she had shared fifty years of her life in her own way, without realising it herself, so unfamiliar the emotion must have been to her. However, after his death she gradually laid down her responsibilities on the farm, and though she still kept an eye on things, made decisions and gave orders, she left most of the work to me.

She began to grow old, one might say, and if I hesitate to speak that word, it is because of the weakness and degeneration it suggests. With the years a certain mellowness and tolerance set in that had never been in evidence before; she shrunk a little as well and became a little smaller and quieter, and perhaps it was also during this time that she noticed the first signs of her disease, without giving in to it or mentioning a word about it. There was no weakening or flagging, however, no sign of grey in her dark hair, and her back remained as stiff as ever. If I think about it now, I realise with amazement that she must have been close to seventy, but the fire, the passion, the relentlessness and the sudden fury, those were unabated. Nevertheless, after Father's death she seemed to withdraw from us, losing interest in the house and the farm; on the other hand the new town house was claiming more of her attention, so that she stayed there more often, sometimes even for a few weeks at a time. There was a minister now, she said, and she could attend church every Sunday; but were the church services really so important to her? It was the battle about her seat which claimed most of her time and attention during those first months after Father's death and which called for her presence in town, for she insisted on keeping her place in the front row among the wives of the officiating and resting elders: it upset quite a few people in the congregation, especially the wives, and there were people in the district who never set foot in our house again as a result of those events, but finally the minister and the church council gave in, and Mother retained her seat.

The town house became the focal point of Mother's life, I noticed, as if the farmhouse represented to her the difficult years of which she no longer wished to be reminded. Presumably she was a wealthy woman, or so people believed anyway, and she herself also gave that impression. I remember the tea cups she ordered for the town house from Worcester the year after Father's death, white cups with gold rims that had to be washed in the wooden tub in her presence, just like the crystal glasses and decanters and the coffee cups, before being locked away in the sideboard. When she was in town she liked to entertain, and there were always visitors and overnight guests in the house: the minister called on us regularly and often stayed for dinner, for he was unmarried, and Mother befriended old Mrs Aling who had come to live with her son for a while, so that there were many visits between our house and the parsonage farther along the back street, and notes were delivered by the servants, or gifts of butter or eggs or jam.

Sometimes the two old ladies fell silent when I entered the room and sometimes when the minister came for dinner there would be a sudden hush in the large dining-room, and I would become aware of the evening chill and the glow of the lamplight on the white cloth that was always spread over the table, and the sound of our knives and forks on the plates, and I would feel threatened without knowing why. He was a very dedicated man, Mother sometimes asserted, as if defending him against blame or criticism, he was devoted to his mother, and then I saw him the way she did: the broadcloth suit, the gown with the velvet straps and the starched white bands, the soft hands and the slight lisp that set him apart from other men, the wealthy family in the Boland, the studies abroad, the gabled house on the corner where he lived, the gifts of sheep and flour from the congregation, the education and the status. One day the ladies having coffee with Mother were discussing his health and how he lived so alone, and they hinted at the possibility that he might marry. "He's twenty-five already," old Tant Gesina Nel remarked, and cast a speculative eye on me where I sat to one side. "Let met see, how old are you now?" All the women seated in a semicircle with folded hands suddenly looked at me calculatingly, the way they inspected the crystal decanters and the gold-rimmed cups, so that I could see them working out how many years I was his senior and if I were too old for him, and I experienced the same momentary panic as that evening when old Tant Mietjie had sent Jasper to me across the dance floor. He was a quiet, pale, sickly young man who put me off with his soft voice and his soft hands, his sudden preoccupations and inexplicable silences. What had Mother been hoping for? For a while there were visits back and forth, and notes and invitations were exchanged, for a while he was a regular visitor, but his health deteriorated and eventually gave out, and after a few years he received his demission and returned to the Boland: he never served elsewhere and never married, and Mother never mentioned him again. She nonetheless continued with her efforts to decorate the town house, and in the voorhuis and dining-room we had paraffin lamps on brass stands at a time when only the church and parsonage were illuminated with paraffin lamps.

The women examined me critically for a moment, but it was only too clear that I found no favour in their eyes and the possibilities they had briefly foreseen received no further consideration: I was evidently unsuitable, even for Mr Aling. I was the unmarried daughter who assisted Mother, and after Mr Aling's departure it never again occurred to anyone that life could hold anything more for me. Sometimes some old man or farmer from the district still came to me with a document to decipher or a letter to read or write, but with the arrival of the minister and later the magistrate, it happened less often. In church I sat alone while Mother took her place among the wives of the elders. There were no further prospects for my life, and any plans or hopes for the future were for Maans's sake: there had still been the passing possibility of Mr Aling as a suitable husband for me, but it was of minor importance, and the chief goal that was being pursued with the gold-rimmed cups and paraffin lamps, with the hospitality in town and the large gatherings now taking place on the farm regularly, was to find Maans a bride who would befit his dignity and meet the high standards set by Mother herself.

In these years I began to notice how often Maans's name cropped up in Mother's conversations as she entertained guests: "Maans," she always said with slight emphasis, or to people who did not know him, "my grandson", with the same almost acquisitive emphasis, and when she spoke of him it was with a certain complacency they must have found strange, for there was no apparent reason for it. "Well, won't it be a lucky girl who gets her hands on Maans," old Oom Andries Nel chuckled one Sunday morning as the congregation stood talking after church, and the bystanders laughed in agreement. Overhearing it, I did not immediately understand the words or the reaction, as was often the case, but later I began to understand why the parents of grown daughters were calling on Mother, why their visits were fraught with so much pent-up tension as she inspected and evaluated the girls, and why she sometimes reacted with unwarranted vehemence when the name of a particular girl was mentioned, because it was someone branded as an outcast who would never find favour in her eyes. In my innocence I had seen Maans only as my brother's son, the hardworking and dutiful young farmer who did not drink, and only now did I see him through the eyes of the community as the unmarried grandson who had inherited richly from both grandfathers and who would be a good match for any girl who could win Mother's approval. I do not believe Maans himself had any say in the matter, and if he had any wishes or dreams himself, he did not express them. I knew he once wanted to be a soldier because I read his letter to Father and Mother, I knew he wanted to go to the diggings because I was present when he mentioned it to Mother, but he never spoke like that again, a friendly, smiling, agreeable but reticent young man who shared his thoughts with no one. He tended to walk with downcast eyes; when he looked up, he made no eye contact and when he did meet your eyes, his own eyes were veiled, as if he were unwilling to give anything away. But that was when he was a young man, and over the years that changed too.

Could there have been someone for whose sake Maans would have straightened his shoulders and whose eyes he would have met, someone in whose company, hesitant and stuttering, he could have found the words to express what he really felt inside? I know so little of him, actually, for in those years Mother and I were often in town, and even on the farm I did not see much of him, for he was usually busy, and in Mother's presence he always played the role of the caring grandson. Did he have friends whose company he sought out after church services or meetings, with whom he went for walks after Nagmaal in town, in the twilight, along the long straight street, with the water glistening in the furrows?

I remember standing in the garden, watching the water running in the furrow. What else, what more is there to remember? One spring, it must have been a year or two after Father's death, when Maans had brought us in for Nagmaal; it must have been that evening that I remember now. There was a vegetable patch alongside the house, and in front of the stoep I had planted a few flowers that I was trying to keep alive, and I remember standing in the garden with the water running in the irrigation furrow. Why do I suddenly remember that evening of which I have not thought for forty years? A spring evening at twilight, the chill air of the Roggeveld briefly tempered, the starkness of the new village and the surrounding ridges softened by the evening light, the greyness fleetingly tinged with colour; the white tents and tented hoods gathered around the church and the market square, where the Nagmaal-goers were outspanned, and the glow of their evening fires in the distance beyond the scattered houses, the smoke hanging over the roofs; voices of people and of youngsters suddenly bringing life to the accustomed silence, the laughter of young people so seldom heard in town. What feelings arose in me as I lingered alone outside in the garden instead of entering the house and closing the door behind me? I no longer know; it is too long ago, and I do not remember in such detail. Perhaps something like restlessness or yearning – but no, I doubt it, for if I had ever been bothered by restless feelings, that time had long passed. Perhaps something like resignation to the peace of the evening and my own solitude; perhaps I already had a vague realisation of my own freedom as I stood there alone in the garden, listening to the laughter of the young people in the distance.

I stood there until Mother came out on the stoep to see where

I was, and asked me where Maans was, and I did not know: some-where among the other young people, I thought, among the voices and shadowy figures in the growing darkness. The chattering young people strolled past the house on their way back to the outspan and they greeted us in passing, Mother on the stoep and me in the garden, and we noticed Maans, who was walking more slowly and had fallen behind, and the dim glow of a girl's white dress in the dusk; we saw them pause for a moment, their companions forgotten, before the girl broke away and ran after the other young people who had walked on. It was quite late and I began to think of going in, but Mother remained on the stoep, leaning over the handrail to stare after the white dress disappearing into the darkening twilight: Nellie Vlok, a modest, friendly girl, whose father worked a piece of land for the Nels of Elandsvlei and had a handful of sheep grazing there. I remember Maans standing in the street in front of the house, and the brightness of the sky, pomegranate-red beyond the church, the ridges etched in black, and the water still running in the furrow, invisible in the dark. Then Mother called Maans inside, and the next day we returned to the farm, though we had planned to stay in town longer.

And so it became Stienie.

Rumour had it that her father was a rich man, though there was no outward sign of it. He had served on the church council for years, but he was an unattractive little man who never had much to say for him-self. His wife had died early, just after the birth of their baby daugh-ter, and he never remarried, but filled his house with unmarried and widowed sisters, aunts and cousins, who raised his child and took care of his household. With the founding of the congregation, many of these old ladies took part in church affairs and fluttered around the minister, and they also called on Mother regularly when we were in town – "old ladies" I say now, though most of them were probably my age; but to me they were always Mother's guests, no matter how old they were. It was during this time that Stienie suddenly began to accompany her relatives when they came to visit Mother, though I should have thought it quite boring for a girl like her among the older women. She was reserved, however, a plump, dark girl who did not say much and was always most polite to older people, always ready to pass on, pick up, or fetch something. To me it was as if she were trying a bit too hard, and she always made me feel uneasy, for she seemed unnatural to me; but it must have been the way she had been raised in that house full of women. Mother approved of her and remarked complacently that it was evident the girl had had a proper upbringing.

Of course no one asked my opinion, and why should they, for it was of no consequence, and if the thought should ever have occurred to them, what could I have told them except that the girl left me uneasy with her affectionate behaviour and polite manners? That moment in the voorhuis, a sudden glimpse of something I had never suspected – no, how could I ever have expressed it in words or made anyone understand its significance? But I remember, and I believe it is the first clear memory I have of Stienie; I remember how one day I sat in the voorhuis with the women who had come to call on Mother and, glancing up from the sewing with which I was occupying myself after a fashion, I saw Stienie opposite me, unaware of my gaze. What were they discussing? It must have been marriages and deaths and inheritances, as usual, but I do not know, for my attention was focused on my pitiful sewing or on other things, not on the conversation, and for all I know Stienie had not been listening either, and what I saw had nothing to do with the conversation. I remember her pale, round face with the plump cheeks and the darting eyes, and how something suddenly moved across it like lightning, something that I could not describe, but that surprised me in this quiet, agreeable girl. "Yearning"

I might call it in the light of my experience over the years, if I have to find a name for it, but nevertheless I would be unable to explain what I mean: "yearning", "greed", "avarice", these are words that automatically come to mind, and I am at a loss how to find more accurate terms. What did she yearn for then, and did she ever find it? Was it what she has now – the money, the possessions, the privileges and status that still leave her unsatisfied, the hunger unsated? But in that single unguarded moment, unnoticed by any of the older women gathered in the voorhuis, in that moment I saw the tenacity and wilfulness hidden behind the easy-going and affectionate behaviour, and I knew she would pursue the fulfilment of her own desires with a passion and ambition that would in their own way be as narrow and unwavering as Mother's.

So it became Stienie, Stienie who turned up at our house more and more often when we came to town – for the cousins and the aunts were more often in town than on the farm – who came knocking at the kitchen door with a note or a message or a bowl of quinces, and sat down on the bench beside Mother's chair spontaneously to talk. Usually Maans was also present, for he always brought us in to town and took us out to the farm again, and sometimes he had to wait in town for days while Mother delayed her return, and then Maans was told to walk Stienie back to their town house across the street from the church, to carry the bowl she was taking back or the coffee grinder she had come to borrow, or simply because it was getting late and Mother felt she should not be walking back on her own. When they left, the house was suddenly very quiet: Mother stooped to light the candle and I began to draw the curtains. Outside it was so dark that I could no longer see Stienie and Maans. The child I had raised had been lost to me for a long time.

So it became Stienie, and she and Maans were married in the church in town, and afterwards the wedding guests were received in the town house, not on the farm as might have been expected. It was probably Mother who had arranged it like that, in order to show off the elegance of the town house, but it might also have been Stienie's own choice, for during the engagement she gradually began expressing wishes and making demands, regardless of how lovingly and meekly they were made. What Maans desired no one asked, and he fetched what was needed from the farm and endured the formalities and festivities, as he endured the uncomfortable tailcoat and white gloves, or the mocking and teasing of the young men against which he had no defense.

So it was Stienie. Why do I not remember anything about their engagement or their wedding? Is it by chance that one remembers or forgets, or does the memory have its own unfathomable rules? That it was a large and stylish wedding, that I know, even if only because it was discussed in the district for such a long time afterwards, but the only memory I have retained is of the shabby silk slippers Stienie gave to one of the maidservants years later with the passing remark that those were the shoes she had worn on her wedding day, almost as if she did not care. And yet other things, seemingly insignificant, stand out in my memory so clearly after all the years; like that quick, hungry look in Stienie's eyes and the over-eager motion with which she stooped to pick up the handkerchief Mother had dropped, the glistening of the water in the furrow at twilight, and the coldness of the window-pane against my fingertips as I stood looking out into the darkness before drawing the curtain. And the first Sunday they accompanied us to church after the wedding, Stienie in a rustling dress in mauve and green stripes that had been ordered from Cape Town, a small hat with ostrich feathers and ribbons perched on her forehead – yes, that was the fashion that year, but those colours and that little hat with its feathers were just too elegant for our village. She must have realised it herself, and she wore her clothes defiantly, as if she wanted to notify the entire congregation formally of her new status and wealth; she acknowledged no one as she followed me to our pew; nonetheless she was aware that every head in church was turning to stare after her. Was that what she had yearned for, to make her entrance in our modest, thatched church as a wealthy and elegant newly-wed wife; had that been the extent of her ambition initially, or was it only the first step along a long and lonely road, the end of which she herself could not foresee?

5

....

Actually it was only the faces around the table that changed over the years, a changing pattern in the candlelight in a house where nothing changed otherwise. Pieter returned and Father passed on, Coenraad left us and Stienie moved in, but the course of our lives remained unchanged and the silence of our communion undisturbed. Our thoughts, our plans, our doubts or anxieties were never declared outright, but slowly and along indirect paths they found their expression.

She was very affectionate – that is to say, she always behaved very affectionately towards us, her fellow-residents and new relatives. She called Mother "Oumatjie", and was inclined to embrace and cuddle her, which Mother endured and in her own way possibly even appreciated. Quite soon Stienie began calling me "Tantetjie", and though she may have meant it kindly, I always found it somehow disparaging and demeaning. She never attempted to embrace or cuddle me, however, and I do not believe she ever felt quite at ease in my company.

When all was said and done, however, Stienie and I managed to live together in harmony. Initially she was still feeling her way, of course, uncertain of my established authority and sensitive to my being so much older, as well as her husband's aunt; she always had her way, but she made her influence felt gradually and revealed her strength carefully, so that there were no outright clashes. But why should the two of us clash? For all those years I had stood in Mother's shadow and obeyed her instructions; why then should it be harder for me to defer to Stienie who would sooner or later be mistress of the house openly and undisputedly anyway? She went ahead carefully and I knew how to yield, and so we managed to live together: the changes she made, no matter how far-reaching, were carried out wordlessly, appearing suddenly as an accomplished fact, and no one could say how they had come about. During those first years of their marriage that Stienie and I lived together here on the farm, I gradually and imperceptibly lost all control over the household and saw how my procedures and methods were done away with and supplanted one after the other. The lines were never drawn, however, and the battle remained covert and secret: quietly, lovingly, affectionately and with utter relentlessness Stienie came to power during the course of those few years and saw the triumph of her own will.

What was concealed under that gentle nature? Occasionally there was a brief episode when the carefully sustained performance seemed to be taking its toll, and she would lose control, so that something of her true feelings showed: for a brief moment a glint of anger or impatience would flare, for a moment the abiding tenderness would be belied by a quick, deprecating movement of head or shoulders, or the voice would take on an unusual sharpness. These were mere moments, as I have said, and they did not occur often during those early years of her marriage, and yet it seemed to me as if that hint of rage and resentment was more honest than the unfailing kindness we were accustomed to.

She bore with me, that is what it boils down to, and why should it still be denied? She bore with my presence in her home because she had no other choice, and when the chance came to get rid of me, she was only too glad to leave me in town alone until she needed me again: let me be honest, for that is how it was. There was never any tenderness or affection for the peculiar spinster aunt she had been saddled with in her marriage. "Oh, Tantetjie has always been shy," I once heard her tell visitors in the voorhuis as I lingered in the kitchen, unwilling to join them; and once, years later, when we were living in the new house, I entered the voorhuis and, invisible behind the net curtain, I heard Stienie, an older and mellower woman by then, remark to her guests on the stoep, "Yes, but you must realise, Tantetjie is strange," with the same deprecating tone that I remembered from years ago. I was standing behind the net curtain in the voorhuis, among the gleaming furniture, and dispassionately and without regret I realised that in all those years I had not even managed to earn her approval. She still merely put up with me in her home and at her table.

To Pieter Stienie showed more or less the same kindness as to the rest of us, for he was family, and she called him "Oom Pieter", but she saw him only at meals or when he accompanied us to town, and so he did not bother her. It took a while before I realised that she always spoke of "Maans's uncle" to others, as if the mention of Maans maintained a certain distance between them; and it took even longer for me to notice that she always avoided addressing Pieter directly or looking him in the eye, no matter how hard she otherwise tried to conceal her distaste. Pieter did not fit into her plans for the future either, though she could not undertake anything against him as long as Mother was still around; later, when Mother and I were living in town, Stienie arranged it so that Pieter no longer joined them for meals, and when I returned to the farm years later, I found that his food was sent to his room outside. He probably preferred it that way himself, yet I never felt that it was right.

At last only old Dulsie remained on whom Stienie as a young housewife could exert her will. By that time the old woman was totally confused and almost blind, but she had raised us and Father before us, and we were used to her, so that she still occupied her place in the corner of the kitchen, her pipe clenched between her teeth, without anyone taking notice of her muttering. However, Stienie maintained that the old woman scared her, and that she was dirty and smelly, and at last she succeeded in having Dulsie moved out to a small room behind the shed where one of the kitchen maids was told to take care of her. I often took her her food myself, though Stienie did not approve, and sat with her in her stuffy, smoky room for a while, but she no longer recognised me and she probably did not even notice when Mother and I moved to town. She died while we were in town, and I do not even know under which of the stone mounds in the graveyard she lies. Did Maans bury her inside or outside the wall, and would he still be able to point out the place today if he were asked?

Thus we lived together on the farm for a few years, Mother and Maans and Stienie and I, but there were many interruptions when Mother and I went to stay in the town house. It could not have been easy for Mother to see Maans, the apple of her eye, so completely under Stienie's thumb, for though he remained loving and considerate towards her, Stienie also invaded that relationship relentlessly, and though Maans still discussed farm matters with Mother as of old, it was Stienie's opinions he expressed, her advice or assurances he listened to, and more and more often Stienie would act as go-between and mediator between Mother and her grandson. Early on everyone naturally expected that there would soon be a baby, and when that did not happen, Mother became impatient and disgruntled, and then it was almost as if she lost interest in Maans and Stienie, just as she had stopped taking an interest in the farm after Father's death, and once again she retired to the town house and consoled herself with the life-style and status she enjoyed there. Two or three years after Maans's marriage – or perhaps it was not even that long, I no longer know – it was more or less wordlessly decided that she would establish herself in town permanently, and equally wordlessly it was presumed that I would accompany her. It is very wise of her, the guests in the voorhuis declared, nodding over their coffee cups; after all, she was no longer young and life here in the new town house would be much more convenient than on the farm, with her daughter to look after her and the church and even a doctor close by. Perhaps; but while they spoke like that, I watched them and noticed how they would pause for a moment and glance at Mother sharply, as if giving her a chance to contradict them and confirm their suspicions about the move. They believed Stienie was behind it, but though they dearly wanted their suspicions confirmed, Mother kept silent. Perhaps the comforts and the church and the doctor did play a role, but in town our lives were not really very different. By the time we moved, Mr Aling had already received his demission, so that for the next five years the congregation was without a minister yet again, and though it was true that there was now a doctor, he never came to our house, not until the end, when Mother was undeniably dying and allowed us to send for him at last.

But whatever the case might have been, Mother decided, and so the two of us moved to town. At first we still went down to the Karoo with Maans and the rest, but in later years Mother did not feel up to it any more and we stayed in the Roggeveld for the winter. Of course Maans and Stienie always came to stay when they were in town, though these visits gradually became less frequent too, for during those years the road down Verlatekloof was constructed and the railway line ran from Worcester to Matjiesfontein in the Karoo, and more and more often we heard that Maans had taken Stienie down to catch the train to Worcester. She visited friends there and shopped, and she always maintained that she had to see the doctor, as if our local doctor could not be trusted. People had a lot to say about this, but it is true that she often complained and, after all, why should she not go to Worcester if it made her happy, for they were still childless and there were no compelling duties to keep her at home. In due course she sent for one of her relatives, a widow, to live with them on the farm, and when she was away old Betta was left in charge and looked after Maans. He came to visit us in town regularly, but we hardly ever saw Stienie except at Nagmaal, and over the years it was almost as if we had become strangers to each other.

For ten years Mother and I lived together in town. Could it possibly have been that long? But it could easily be verified – we came to town in the spring after Mr Aling's departure and Mother died in the same year as Mr Reyneke's wife; the date of her death can be seen on her tombstone. The arrival of visiting ministers and later the regular Nagmaal services when we had our own minister, the post-cart bringing letters once a week and the periodic arrival of itinerant traders and transport-riders, those were the milestones of our existence and weeks and months often passed without any other interlude, so that the weeks and months and finally also the years melted together and, looking back, I can scarcely believe that Mother and I spent ten years together in that big town house.

It was a good time for Mother. The town was not big, but there were distractions we had not known on the farm, with visitors from other villages, people coming in from the farms, and neighbours dropping in. Even during her last years Mother could not have been considered sociable but, unlike before, she now enjoyed it when callers arrived unannounced – for it was always others who came to her, never the other way round. Visiting ministers or other distinguished guests were entertained by us as a matter of course, often spending the night, and she enjoyed the opportunity to impress them with the decanters, the coffee cups and other tokens of our wealth. Moreover, during the years we were without a minister, the elders would often solicit our help with some document that I had to write or read or translate, or a news report that needed interpretation, just as when Father was still alive. They were still a bit resistant and reluctant, for though I was nearly middle-aged, I was still a woman, after all, and they disliked the idea that I knew more and was capable of more than they who were men in important positions. But, as I have said, in the years after Mr Aling's departure, when there was neither minister nor parsonage, our town house filled that gap, and it was at the regular meetings in our voorhuis that church matters were discussed and finally also, I might say, concluded. If I look back over the years with complete honesty, I would not describe Mother as devout or even as a particularly religious person, notwithstanding the claims made in the eulogies after her death, but as Father's widow, as a leading member of the congregation and a strong-minded woman, she exercised an exceptional influence in her own way.

Was that what Mother had finally wanted – the wealth, the status and the power in this restricted environment of town and congregation? I think so. Or perhaps it was not so much the money and the status and the power, as the security these provided, the fact that those people with the wild eyes, the shabby wagon and the scrawny dogs were finally banished to the shadows for good, outside the circle of lamplight where she was entertaining her guests in the voorhuis; perhaps that was the reason for her greater tolerance, the knowledge that the battle had been fought and the desperate effort of all those years was no longer necessary, the last spirits of the past having been exorcised. Only once did she flare up as in the old days, when Mr Van der Merwe came to us as minister, and in his zeal to straighten out the neglected congregation, reopened the question of her seat among the wives of the elders. It was the beginning of a long and bitter battle with wide repercussions that divided the congregation anew, and our home was the scene of much lively debate, and many heated and unruly discussions occurred, for Mr Van der Merwe was quick to make enemies and Mother soon used the conflict to her own advantage. Exactly what was said and done, how they negotiated and planned and schemed, I never knew, for I busied myself in the kitchen or in the garden and took no part in it; but Mother retained her seat in church, and during the short time Mr Van der Merwe served in our congregation he never once set foot in our house, though his wife sometimes called on Mother.

The discord, the angry conferences in the voorhuis and the rows with the church council continued, however, and after four years Mr Van der Merwe received his demission. Mr Reyneke, who succeeded him, was a more cautious and more flexible young man, and he and his wife called on Mother regularly and showed suitable respect for her position, so that she developed a liking for them. Gradually the serious rift in the congregation was mended; but until the very end of her life, when it was no longer possible for her to leave her room or even her bed, Mother retained her honorary seat in church, the black-clad figure increasingly gaunt, but the back as straight as ever. In those years she ordered from Worcester a cape, embroidered with glittering jet, which caused a mild sensation and to which the women of the congregation reacted with spite: such a display of elegance did not suit her, and she was not really comfortable with it herself, but for years she wore that embroidered cape to church every Sunday, glittering among the paler women.

Could it really have been ten years? I looked after the house-keeping and supervised in the house, baked bread and counted the washing when it came back from the fountain at Ouplaas, and tried to protect the paltry flower-beds from frost and drought; I filled the paraffin lamps that were used in the voorhuis and dining-room, and in the evenings drew the curtains against the dark; I followed Mother to church on Sundays and took my seat at the back, close to the door, while she moved among the pews in her glittering jet to claim her honorary seat in front of the pulpit – a good daughter, a model daughter; a blessing in the house. To others it must have seemed a tedious and lonely life, but I never saw it that way myself, for I had learned to distance myself from appearances and to be unaffected by the restrictions of my existence. After church the women addressed me kindly and when I passed them on my way to the store as they stood talking in front of their houses, they graciously tried to include me in their conversations, but I was unfamiliar with most of the matters they were discussing and there were also many things they did their best to withhold from me. Their goodwill was not unlimited, however: sooner or later they lost patience and gave up on their efforts and their verdict was probably the same as Stienie's. Well, you must understand, Tantetjie has always been a little strange; and the bright sunlight falling through the net curtain is diffused, so that the room where I stand alone seems gloomy and mysterious.

I am standing at the window and under my fingers I feel the smooth, straight edge of the splashboard – no, not like that, not that. I am standing at the window . . .What memory comes back so vividly now? It was a different evening; for a moment I feel the window-pane smooth and cool under my fingers before I draw the curtain, and for a moment I linger, because outside in the twilight I see something stirring, a figure at the gate, fumbling for the catch. Must I remember, must I go on to remember what has been forgotten for so long without making the slightest difference? I have been trying to sleep, and because I cannot sleep, my thoughts have been set in motion here where I lie alone, speechless and paralysed in the dark of the sleeping house; I did not want to remember anything, it was never my intention to call up the past and to call up figures in the half-light, to have phantoms step out into the light where their features would be recognisable again. Where does Abraham van Wyk come from now, striding out of the past, out of the dark night to stand at our front door once again, his eyes blinking in the light of the candle I hold in my hand? There was no reason for him to visit us that evening, but neither was there any reason for such a visit to seem strange, for he was an old acquaintance, always somewhere in the background over the years with his bashful smile, his sparse beard and dry cough. His wife had died and there were no children, and now he was suddenly standing at our door without us even being aware that he was in town.

I lit the lamp in the voorhuis, for when we were alone we usually sat by candlelight until we went to bed, and made coffee and took it in, and then I carried on with my chores while Abraham discussed his affairs with Mother. What did I actually know, I who was nearly forty years old? I was never told anything, nothing was ever explained to me and no reasons were ever supplied; I continued with my work without asking questions or expecting explanations and I considered it natural that questions, explanations, feelings remained unspoken, and knowledge was accumulated along other ways, in the form of deductions, suspicions or incidental observations, a few words in the passage, a flash through the chink of a door, a hazy figure in the gloom behind the net curtain. He took his leave of Mother and departed and I accompanied him to the door with a candle; he muttered a few words of farewell and walked to the gate in the dark, and I shut the door behind him.

What did I know after all? Thus I was completely unprepared for the outburst that engulfed me when I returned to Mother in the voorhuis, and it took a while before I understood the gist of those knife-sharp words and realised that her scorn and outrage were directed at Abraham; accustomed as I was to the vehemence of her hostilities and feuds, it took me even longer to realise that this time I was involved too. A loser with a stand barely big enough to keep a handful of sheep alive, a no-hoper who in a million years would not be able to pay off his debts at the store, a weakling who would never even be elected as deacon – Father would have laughed in his face, she declared, trembling with barely contained outrage and fury; Father would have driven him from the house before he had even finished speaking. I listened silently to the biting words without interrupting, for since childhood I had learned to let her attacks of almost demented fury wash over me, and it was only when she began to prepare for evening prayers and bed, still seething with fury and stuttering over the prayer, that I realised, dazed, that it had been for my sake that Abraham had come that evening.

I remember lying awake for a long time that night, quite astonished, trying to take in the events. Father would not have laughed at him, that I knew, nor would he have driven him away: Father's heart had been too kind and loving for that and as far as Abraham was concerned, he may not have been wealthy, but he was a decent and well-respected man who had nothing to be ashamed of. That this unassuming widower wanted to court me, surprised me, but I considered the fact without the rush of panic I had felt when old Tant Mietjie had sent Jasper across the dance floor: instead, the knowledge moved me in a strange way, and I felt a kind of gratitude towards Abraham because he had come that evening, but nothing more. I remember how cold the nights were towards the end of that autumn, and how I lay wide-eyed, watching the bright moonlight move across the floor and listening to the incessant, distant barking and howling of the dogs at the straw huts of the coloured people below the ridge. The offer had been made, I thought, and as far as I was concerned, it had never been withdrawn, so that it would still be possible to take it up; it would still be possible to get up and move soundlessly across the moonlit floor to the window, to swing myself over the window-sill and walk barefoot down the white street to the little church house where he stayed when he was in town, to knock on the shutter until he opened. Would anyone see me; would anyone hear me? Would it matter?

I know I lay like that for a long time, contemplating the possibility, and I realised it was my last chance to flee from this sleeping house; but though I saw that clearly enough, it did not even enter my mind to get up and make my escape along this final route. The possibility existed, but it remained no more than a possibility, something to contemplate and consider without trying to make it real. This was my life, this room where the moon-light moved across the bare floorboards, this large, silent house, and as I lay awake motionlessly, I realised it and accepted it. In some way the choice had been made long ago, without my ever being aware of it, and all I could do was to continue. The next morning I got up, light-headed with sleeplessness, and rekindled the fire and brewed the coffee as usual. My road lay straight ahead of me, not along a side route.

Abraham van Wyk soon married a widow of more or less my own age, and a year later she died during childbirth, both she and the baby. Abraham moved to the Bokkeveld and what became of him then, I never heard. He never came to our house again; I never saw him face to face or spoke to him again after that evening when I accompanied him to the front door with the candle.

Every year on Mother's birthday the town ladies came for coffee and a few of the church councillors came to congratulate her, but she remained so proud and quick-witted and straight-shouldered that it was hardly noticeable that she was growing older. Only sometimes I was startled for a moment as I entered the voorhuis where she was sitting alone, but when she heard me she pulled herself together at once, as if it were only my imagination that had suddenly made her appear fragile and wasted, and naturally I asked no questions. How long did the pain gnaw at her before she finally yielded? I know I sometimes thought I heard her cry out in the night, but when I got up to listen at her door, all was quiet; when I knocked hesitantly, she answered after a while, as if she had been asleep, and then she said it was nothing and told me to go back to bed. It was a long time before she sent for old Tant Gesie who doctored with herbs, and even longer before I was allowed to boil or steep the herbal infusions because she could no longer do it herself. By that time she did not enter the kitchen or eat at the table any more; she mostly sat at the window in the voorhuis, and later she no longer left her bedroom. During all that time of her drawn-out deathbed she never said a word about her illness to me, however, or conceded that she was ill, and never amid the worst pain did she admit that she was suffering, refusing in her wordless pride and stubbornness to yield to the inescapable humiliation and defeat of death.

It seems easy to sum it up in a few words now, those last months or weeks of her life, though while I was a witness to her silent death it seemed an endless drawn-out passing, longer than the ten years that we lived in town together. No relief was possible by this time, though I continued to brew the herbal infusions: sometimes she allowed me to sit with her at night, or at least she did not object, until one night she shrieked with pain, so that I woke up where I had fallen asleep beside the bed, and she told me to fetch Tant Gesie. I still remember how I ran through the dark and knocked on her shutter, and how the bewildered old woman groped for the flint to strike a light, how she gathered her clothes and, panting and groaning, followed me with her medicine chest under her arm, but it was too late, and not even with her herbs and infusions could she provide a semblance of hope any more. It was so late that Mother even allowed the doctor to come, for she knew that he, too, would be unable to do anything, and so she was indifferent to his arrival.

Maans and Stienie came to bid Mother farewell before they went down to the Karoo for the winter. Afterwards Maans sat at the kitchen table, tears pouring down his cheeks, for he had always loved Mother, and Stienie looked away and chattered in a loud voice, impatient to get away and unwilling to show it. They had brought Pieter along, and I still remember how he sat next to Mother's bed, stroking her bony hand slowly, carefully and distractedly, as if it were a strange object he had come upon somewhere in the veld, the feather of a spur-winged goose or the quill of a porcupine, for that seemingly intimate gesture nonetheless held no recognition.

She did not surrender, she did not surrender one step of the way, and to the end she battled with death, but on the inside she was being eroded by the pain, hollowed out like an anthill, and finally she succumbed wordlessly. I sat beside her bed in the motionless chill of the winter night and forced myself to stay awake. Was I expecting anything more, was I still hoping? But there was no word or sign, no gesture of supplication or reconciliation, no sign of love when the last breath in the small, wasted face on the pillow gave out and the end came.

By rights she should have been buried beside Father on the farm, but Maans was still in the Karoo and there was no one to arrange it, and so the funeral took place in town: her grave had to be hewn from the frozen soil with crowbars. There were few people left in town to attend the service and it was a struggle to find enough men to act as bearers. In the bitter eastwind the handful of mourners did not remain at the graveside long, and it was all over very quickly.

The neighbours pitied me for having been left behind so alone: they enveloped me with their sympathy, with small tokens of love, with words of consolation and efforts to help; they offered to sleep in the house at night and invited me to stay with them, they offered to send word to Maans to come and fetch me or to arrange transport so that I could travel to the Karoo. They dearly wanted to do something for me, and I could not tell them there was nothing I desired from them; disconcerted, they looked at me as I stood before them, word-less and tearless, uncomfortable in the presence of their unsolicited sympathy, waiting for them to go and to leave me alone, and at last they withdrew and did not bother me with their offers of help again. The young minister came regularly to support and console me with verses from Scripture and to pray that I might deal with my loss and accept my new solitary state, and I listened to his words of comfort and encouragement and expressed suitable gratitude for his visit. He was doing his duty as well as he could – for he was still young and did not know much about life – but I needed no consolation or encourage-ment, for there had been no bond between Mother and myself other than the one established by years of familiarity and habit, and as far as solitude went, alone in the big house after Mother's funeral that winter I realised with amazement that I was not lonely and that I had never been conscious of loneliness. I could remember a moment of solitude and fear, with the fog billowing in the kloof, there was the long, dark emptiness after Pieter and Sofie had left us and another moment when I had knelt on the muddy banks of a fountain, but that was something else, something more than loneliness and at the same time also something less, and that memory came from long ago and was almost irretrievable in the distant past.

Our village had always been very small – I do not believe there were more than twenty or thirty thatched houses in those years, with their pear trees and vegetable patches lining the two streets that led past the church, and most of these were church houses, occupied only occasionally. A new parsonage had been built, there were a few shops and the little post office, and huddled together to one side at the foot of the ridge were the huts and shelters of the coloured people. Now that most residents in the district had moved away to the Karoo for the winter months, there were fewer visitors than ever: the itinerant traders from the Bokkeveld and the Boland no longer came, the transport-riders rode in from Matjiesfontein less often, and even the arrival of the post-cart was delayed from time to time by heavy snowfalls in Verlatekloof or Komsberg Pass. Few people had stayed behind in the village, and when I had no reason to go to the store, entire days sometimes passed when I spoke to no one except the woman who came to do the housework; when she left in the afternoon, I was alone in the clean, empty, waiting house.

Waiting – yes, I must admit. To the people around me with their fruitless sympathy it seemed as if with Mother's death I had lost my drive and my purpose in life, and in their eyes it was all over: I had been left alone with nothing to look forward to except my own inevitable old age and death; their views did not touch me, however. So much had already changed or been lost over the years, that this was only one more change and loss in the long sequence; I had survived each change and each loss thus far, however, and I knew I would be able to endure this one too, regardless of their expectations.

I remember a heavy snowfall one night during that winter after Mother's death. Snow was not a rarity to us and there was no reason why I should remember that particular fall, except that it was heavier than usual, and I was still unused to my newfound freedom. When I awoke that morning I was instantly aware of my deeper isolation from the silence in which even the scattered sounds of the village were muffled; the cleaning woman did not come and the townspeople remained indoors and made no effort to call; no one thought of coming over to find out how I was doing, and I spent the entire day alone in the house without speaking, or having to speak, to anyone, without duties to take care of or expectations to live up to, the first day of complete freedom I had ever known in my life.

Outside the entire world was white, and the vegetable patch, the narrow flowerbeds and the street in front of the house were covered and obliterated; the snow lay on the stone walls and the roofs, the grey veld on the outskirts was a pristine snowfield and the low ridges to the east were softened by the thick layer of snow on the rocky ledges. The day was grey and colourless, the clouds low over the hills, and the snow had not melted, so that the landscape retained its whiteness all day long. As I moved from room to room inside the house, the empty rooms were lit up by the bright reflection from outside, and when I looked out, the familiar scene of street, houses and church was unrecognisable. I moved through the endless space of the house, from room to room, almost noiselessly as was my custom, not even my dress swishing or a floorboard creaking under my foot, and from window to window I surveyed the new world in which I found myself so unexpectedly. That was all; that was all it was, a heavy snowfall and my isolation in the empty house, for during the night the snow began to melt and when I awoke the next morning I heard it dripping from the thatch in front of my window, and I saw the familiar outlines of road, rock and ridge reappear once more from the melting snow and mud. I treasured the silence of that day, however, and the long silence I had experienced remained a part of me, regardless of the numerous conversations I had again afterwards. What do I mean when I say this now? I do not know, for I did not understand it then and even now I am still unable to explain: that is how it was for me that day and that is what it meant to me. No, I am not trying to justify myself – to whom, and what for? I remember, that is all, and these are the things I remember, alone in the dark at the end of my life, all the small and simple things I cannot explain to anyone, I who do not even remember the birthdates of my brothers and the dates of my parents' deaths. As I lie here in the dark, I remember the empty rooms filled with the bright white glow of reflected light.

During that winter I naturally visited Mother's grave in the grave-yard on the outskirts of town, and I was aware that people were star-ing after me, invisible behind the windows of the houses I passed. In their eyes, to see me walking down the front street to the graveyard in my black dress alone probably made up for my lack of words and tears and other visible signs of grief. Why did I go? Mother was dead and though I did not miss her or grieve for her, it was more than mere duty. I could visit and have coffee with the handful of women in town, I could go to the store on weekdays and to church on Sundays; I could walk down the front street, past the last scattered houses where people were observing me from behind their curtains without showing themselves, and past the last cultivated plots, to the graveyard with its stone mounds and soil and its few chiselled headstones. The grass was dead and white, the veld colourless; the clods of the heaped soil over Mother's grave were frozen solid and when I stooped to touch them, the earth itself was hard as rock. There were no flowers to lay down on the bare earth and no wild flowers could sprout or take root in that frozen earth; there was nothing I wished to say, no feelings I wanted to express or memories I wanted to relive. What was I doing there? I remained at the grave so that I did not have to return home, and with my back to the town I looked in the direction of the road lead-ing through Rooikloof to Verlatekloof and the Karoo, climbing over the rise at Groenfontein to Driefontein and Vloksberg Pass. No roads were visible from where I stood, the cart and wagon tracks among the rocks and shrubs had been half-obliterated by the winter storms, but I knew their course and my eyes traced their lines, through the faded, undulating veld and up the rocky ledges, up to the edge of the escarpment where the sparse snowflakes came whirling upon the wind. After a while I would turn and walk back. On the way back from the graveyard it might have been possible to take a right-hand turn and follow the twin tracks of the cart and wagon wheels through the veld; but I turned left instead and headed back to town.

I might have set my course for some unknown destination like a trekboer family with their wagon and handful of sheep, or a farmhand looking for a new master, his bundle over his shoulder, and if I saw a rider in the distance, I might have crouched among the low renosterbos like a fugitive, until he had passed. Ahead of me I saw the scattered houses of the town waiting for me, the stone walls and the whitewashed walls, the thatched roofs, the bare limbs of the fruit trees and the high white ridge of the church roof. The coloured women gathered harpuisbos in the veld for firewood, the girls tended the goats where they were grazing and in summer they sometimes wandered far, looking for veldkos; there were white women who went to Ouplaas with the washerwomen to do their own laundry there. I could only visit Mother's grave, however, and stand there, looking out over the veld, my back to the distant houses of the town. After a while the young minister came to see me and gently and lovingly and very earnestly pointed out that it is not good to grieve too deeply or to mourn for too long, and that we should not cling to our loved ones or to our memories of them. Even in my loneliness, he said, stuttering slightly, for he was young and still had much to learn, even in my loneliness life still had much to offer and I had a task, no, a duty to fulfil, a solemn duty, here in the congregation where as a member of a respected family I held such an honoured position and was so highly esteemed. Neither would my mother have wished for me to become so absorbed in my loss, he assured me fervently; and after that I did not go to the graveyard so often.

What prevented me from following that white road, those twin tracks among the stones and shrubs, up the slopes to the edge of the mountains and the farm? Mother was no longer there to forbid the journey and no one had remained behind on the farm that winter to whom I would have to explain my sudden arrival; the house was deserted, the kraals and stables empty. I lay awake at night, as happened more and more often during that time, watching the moonlight move across the floorboards and considering the possibilities of my newfound freedom. My shoes stood in front of the bed, my clothes were on the chair where I had folded them on taking them off, my shawl hung over the back of the chair; I only had to get up and reach out my hand, for there was no longer any reason to be quiet, afraid that a creaking floor or a rattling doorknob might betray me. The town slept, its empty windows dark, and the barking of the dogs had died down; where I lingered on the stoep for a moment, the white street before me was as bright as day.

I followed the front street, past the last houses and the stone mounds and the scattered rocks of the graveyard until it stopped pretending to be a street and became a mere road again. Clouds moved past the moon and the pattern of track, shrub and stone flowed together before my eyes, so that I had to wait, light-headed and breathless with excitement. There is no hurry, I told myself, for no one will have noticed my flight, and it will be a long time before they become aware of my absence and begin to search: there is a long road ahead, and there is no sense in breaking into a run yet in my impatience to arrive. When it dawned on me what I was doing, however, I picked up the pace again. The moon had disappeared, its light dimmed, effacing the white track before my eyes, but I did not hesitate, for how could I not know the road home after all those years, and alone and on foot I could travel faster tonight than ever in the past by cart or wagon. Past Groenfontein and up the sloping ridge behind the homestead, suddenly surrounded by whirling snowflakes, icy against my face in the dark. I saw no lights at the farms I passed now and again, their buildings dark and deserted, and nothing was visible save the dark, rolling veld outlined against the murky horizon, nothing could be heard save the beating of my heart and my rasping breath as I hurried along, my shawl wrapped tightly around me against the cold, as I pressed on blindly, my feet finding their own way without waiting for memory to guide them. I stumbled over rocks but soon found my way back to the beaten track; I raced across the miles without wearying, until I could make out the hazy glitter of the dams in the half-light, and the dark buildings of our own farm took shape in the distance amid the surrounding gloom. The doors were closed, the shutters closed, the beams in front of the kraal gates fixed in their slots, but house, stable and kraals lay waiting, and if the doors were locked I could force open the shutters from the outside and hoist myself up over the window-sill into the familiar darkness of the house. I was back. And then?

Then, after that I did not know: perhaps that was why I hesitated and lost my nerve at the last moment, no matter how often I considered the possibilities and rehearsed the details of my flight in my imagination. What explanation would I give when they inevitably found me there, relentlessly demanding reasons and explanations, and what would finally come of my brief escape except that I would be brought back to town, held faster than ever by their watchfulness and concern, guarded with relentless love in a way that would leave me without even the semblance of freedom? That is why I never attempted that long journey. But had I pulled open the creaking shutters to lower myself over the window-sill in the dark, what would I have seen and heard? I turned my face away – it was only later, only now at the end of my life, that I learned to stare wide-eyed into the dark, unafraid of the voices in the silence. It remained a dream; I woke up with the tingling of snowflakes still on my lips and, seated on the edge of the bed, I reached for my clothes beside me to feel whether my shawl and the hem of my dress were still wet, my shoes still muddy from the journey.

When Maans and Stienie returned from the Karoo that year, they came in to town immediately to sympathise and to learn the details of Mother's deathbed. I believe my answers to their questions were vague and confused, for I realised I could no longer remember the details of that distant death, neither did I know how to react to their sympathy. In a sudden upsurge of emotion Stienie advanced on me and I drew back instinctively to avoid her embrace. We rode out to visit the grave and Maans undertook to order a stone from the Boland, and we divided Mother's personal belongings amongst ourselves, though there was not much of value except the gold chain; Maans took her Bible and hymn book, and then Stienie said she would not mind having the chain as a memento of Oumatjie, and declared that she wished for nothing else.

They spent a few days with me in town, and though Stienie chattered and fidgeted nervously and there was a steady stream of visitors to greet and to entertain, the three of us were constantly aware of the question that they were unwilling to ask and I was afraid to hear. Only when they were about to depart, their luggage already loaded on the cart that stood ready at the kitchen door and Stienie's hat already pinned on, only then did she ask innocently and almost in passing if Tantetjie would not be lonely here in town on her own, and quite airily and casually I answered, oh no, not at all, it is so much more convenient to be here in town now that I am growing older, with the minister and the doctor close by and the neighbours always willing to help. At first I did not really know what I was saying, but it was clear as they were bidding me farewell that they were relieved, Maans because he did not have to worry about me, and Stienie because she would not be obliged to take me in. After all, she already had Betta, who was her blood relative and completely dependent on her; why should she have to be stuck with me as well? I stood at the gate, waving goodbye; I watched them ride away, my eyes following the dust from the cart all the way out of town and along the long, straight road that led to the farm. The dark, deserted farm of those winter months belonged to me, I realised, as did the house of my dreams and my unfeasible plans, and I no longer had any interest in the house to which they were returning, the house where Stienie reigned, with Betta carrying out her instructions, and where they would have provided me with a room if I had demanded it of them. It was better to remain here and endure the silent compassion or pity, to attend the prayer meetings and Sunday services alone and, once a week, to gaze out from the graveyard at the edge of town across the grey, rolling veld to where the roads climbed invisibly over the ridges.

The house was filled with a delicate spring light as bright as the reflected glitter of the snow. Sometimes I still found myself waiting or getting ready for something, sometimes I would start up suddenly because I thought someone was calling me, but that did not last long, and I soon became accustomed to my freedom. Sheltered by the garden wall or the stoep, the flowers emerged hesitantly in the cold spring, painstakingly grown, sheltered and kept alive, and in the bare, cultivated gardens of the town the trees, swaying in the eastwind, put forth buds; until October or November every night still held the possibility of frost, every day might bring a sudden whirl of snow across the rocky ridges. Against a stoep pillar of the parsonage the climbing rose Mrs Reyneke planted when she and her husband moved in the year before bloomed, but that same spring she died, and she lay buried in front of the church without ever having seen the first blooms on the young plant, their bright, translucent white petals unfurling in the bleak chill of the Roggeveld spring.

For a while people called on me on their return from the Karoo to convey their sympathy, and each time I heard the sound of horses' hoofs in the street or a vehicle in front of the house, the squeak of the gate or the sound of footsteps across the boards of the stoep, I cringed. Gradually the danger passed, however, and the threat diminished, and it was as if people mercifully forgot about my existence, perhaps because I led such a retired life and took so little part in their activities, a silent spectator on the fringe of their meetings, a timid tantetjie in the background at their social events. Or perhaps they lost patience with my timidity and my silence, and limited themselves to the most basic tokens of politeness and goodwill. Only Maans and Stienie still came in to Nagmaal with Pieter and Betta and spent a few days with me, but it was their house too, though I saw them as intruders each time and their arrival as an invasion. For a few days the house would be filled with the sound of Stienie's high heels on the floorboards and her chattering and her questions, her cross-examination and instructions and rummaging through cupboards – "Why don't you rather do it this way, Tantetjie?" Fortunately Betta kept her company most of the time, for that was her task in life, and after a few days they left again and I saw the cart making its way past the thinly-scattered houses of the town and following the white road back to the farm, and I was delivered once more to my own freedom.

Thus I lived in the town house alone. How did I pass the days? I began to read again, I remember – I never had much time to read before, and Mother was always impatient when she saw me with a book and she would soon find something for me to do. The young minister would sometimes bring me a volume of sermons or a religious pamphlet because he knew Tannie liked such things, and he would smile at my strange pastime, and there were a few other people in town who also had books and who would lend them to me; the magistrate sent over his newspapers once he had finished with them, and when people in the district found out that I read, they sometimes arrived with an old book, or even a case of books they had inherited and had no use for. I read whatever I found, whatever I could, now that Mother was no longer there to complain about duties that were being shirked or candles that burnt down too quickly. "You must take care of your eyes, Tannie, you read far too much," young Mr Reyneke scolded playfully, for he did not set much store by book-learning and his Dutch sermons were full of mistakes.

I wrote. Sometimes someone would still ask me to write a letter, and the writing materials were kept in the drawer of the dining-room table; sometimes I would take them out needlessly, the writing paper and the steel-nibbed pens and the ink, and arrange them on the table, and I would write, not the words someone else was dictating, but my own words that I had to seek and find before writing them down. Miss Le Roux had taught me to write neatly, in even, round letters with fine open loops and regular downstrokes, but when I tried to write for myself, my skilfulness would forsake me completely, and the paper would be rumpled and blotted, like the soiled, wrinkled cloths on which I had learned to embroider as a child. What did I wish to write? I no longer know – not letters, for there was no one who expected a letter from me; I suppose just the things I would have said if there had been someone to talk to, someone willing to listen and to understand, and if my tongue had not been burdened with obstructions. I know that I would sit there for a long time, facing the empty page on the bare tabletop and trying to find words, and when at last I was done, I would fold the paper several times and put it away at the back of a drawer in my wardrobe, behind the stockings and underclothes, where no one would find it. After a while I stopped, however, and one day I took out all those folded notes and burnt them in the kitchen stove without reading them again. It was not that I had lost heart because I found it too hard, only that I felt no further need to do it. And so I lived in town; for a number of years.

Maans had a tombstone erected on Mother's grave, a large white stone from the Cape, conspicuous among all the low, flat headstones and stone mounds, with names and dates and texts from Scripture that the minister had helped him select; I touched it, and it was as cold to my fingers as the frozen clods of the soil that had covered the grave after her funeral.

Maans was doing well, for he was a meticulous, careful and hard-working farmer; moreover, he had inherited well, of course, and rumour had it that Stienie also inherited well when her father died, for she had been an only child. The people in our district loved Maans, solemn and restrained as he was, and they trusted his honesty, just as they had trusted Father all those years; and because he was slow to talk or react and deliberate in his judgement, he never really made any enemies. It went almost without saying that he would be a deacon and later an elder; when our town eventually got its own municipality, he became a town councillor, and when the time came, he was nominated as member of the district council. I do not know whether Maans himself was eager to serve in all these capacities, for he did not really enjoy meetings and conferences and public appearances, but he accepted the elections and nominations and he fulfilled his duties faithfully.

Because of all these commitments Maans and Stienie came to town more often, so that I saw them more regularly. To me it seemed as if Maans never really enjoyed having to drive in to town, dressed up in a stiff collar and tie and a suit or a frock-coat, but Stienie enjoyed it: when she was not in Worcester on some errand, or at the baths in Goudini, she was often in town, and sometimes I wondered if she would not have preferred to live in the town house herself, for I sensed that she was not as happy on the farm as in earlier years. She had dresses made, copied from pictures in the magazines she ordered from Cape Town, and she always wore the most stylish outfits in our little congregation, dresses with bows and frills and tassels and trains, as was fashionable in those days, and small hats with ribbons and flowers, so that everyone looked up on Sundays when she entered and took her place among the wives of the elders. I believe people learned to watch out for her quick eyes and sharp tongue, but because of Maans's position she was a well-respected woman in our community. To look at her, you would not say that she had almost everything a woman could desire, and certainly more than most other women, for Stienie never really seemed happy or content. Could it have been because they had no children? Perhaps, but as far as I know, Stienie had never been particularly fond of children. Could it have been because there was no heir to the farms and the sheep flocks and the family name and status? But how could I understand and explain such mysteries, I who had avoided Jasper Esterhuysen when he was sent across the dance floor by his mother; I who had shut the door behind Abraham van Wyk as he departed and had made no attempt to respond to his offer? I never understood what Stienie's childlessness might have meant to her, neither did I understand the meaning of her eventual pregnancy. These things remained as incomprehensible to me as the other mysterious matters the married women discussed in undertones so that I should not hear, and of what importance were my suspicions and inferences, and who cared about them?

As I have said, old Betta was living on the farm with Maans and Stienie during that time and took care of the household. When they came in to town periodically, they would sometimes bring her along and at other times they would leave her behind, perhaps according to Stienie's moods, but when she did come, she never accompanied them anywhere, and when they went out, they left her with me, where she would crochet and talk about her ailments and grievances, the stout, middle-aged widow with her monotonous, whining voice and the endless stream of complaints and reproofs she poured out without expecting a reply, while her nimble fingers carried on working uninterruptedly and the crochet hook flashed in the light.

Did that liberation, that freedom, that dizzying solitude after Mother's death really last as long as I imagine now? No, it is just my memory playing tricks on me again, my imagination betraying me; it was only a few years, and even then the solitude was constantly interrupted by Maans and Stienie coming to town for Nagmaal or church services or meetings, and by Betta with her flashing crochet hook and her complaints. Only for a few weeks between these interruptions with all the accompanying visitors and noise and upheaval, could I actually enjoy my precious freedom; the visits remained interruptions, and reality was the unhindered weeks in between when I led my own life, alone in the empty house, silently facing the unmarked white page.

That all was not well on the farm, I had realised for some time, no matter how little attention I paid to Betta's tales. Nevertheless, she was a single woman dependent on Stienie, and thus she had no option but to endure and to carry on, and there was no advice I could give her, even if there were any point in getting involved myself. One day I just heard that Maans had brought Betta and her suitcase to town in the cart, and left her with Tant Miemie Olivier, who was somehow related to her; the two of them lived together until they both died, and everyone said, oh, what a shame, poor Betta, it is not right, and shook their heads disapprovingly. In my presence they said nothing, as usual, and Stienie herself maintained an eloquent silence on the subject, while I gave Betta no encouragement to air her grievances when she called on me. "I would rather not say anything," she would remark pointedly, "after all, she is related to you as well", though Stienie was her own flesh and blood. Then she would fall silent resentfully.

It could not have been more than a few months later that Maans came in to town on his own one day, something that did not happen often, and as he sat in the kitchen watching me prepare padkos for his return journey, he asked timidly and in a roundabout way whether I would consider coming to live on the farm with them again. He was so tentative and long-winded that I knew what he wanted to say long before he came out with the request, and I was able to prepare myself while slicing the meat and bread, without having to listen to any more. Why had he been the one sent to ask me then, I wondered, while it must have been Stienie's decision that I should return, and it was clear that he was reluctant to follow her orders? Yes, of course I would come, I assured him when he had finished, and I could see how relieved he was, just like that day when I had told Stienie, no, I do not mind living in town, after she had already decided how it would be. If it had all happened just a few weeks or months earlier, I might still have shied away and tried to find a way out, or I might have tried to delay the matter, but now I simply accepted the new arrangement and prepared to vacate the house, emptying the chest of drawers in my room and packing my things; that must have been when I burned the folded notes in the kitchen stove before allowing the fire to go out. Of course there would have been no point in resisting or delaying the matter, for I was a single woman without any possessions or income, after all, living in Maans and Stienie's house, and just as dependent on their charity as old Betta; but the thought did not even enter my mind. That period of absolute freedom had not lasted long, dispersed over scattered months, weeks and days, and spanning a few years; it was a matter of a single uncertain spring, a single noiseless day when the empty house had been filled with the reflected light of a snowfall; but it had been enough, and I knew it was time to return.

Maans sent Pieter in to town with one of the farm-hands and the cart to fetch me and my possessions, and he slept over in town that evening. It was the first time since his return that I was completely alone with him, and I am at a loss how to describe that evening we spent together, for over the years he had become a stranger to me, so that his presence was as impersonal as that of any unknown visitor that I had to entertain; yet at the same time I knew that this strange, silent man sitting with me in the candle-light was my brother, my very own brother, my beloved brother, and it was because of that distressful knowledge that I was unable to eat that night, and not because I had to take leave of the house where I had lived for so long. He ate his food, head bowed over his plate in the candlelight, and he did not speak except to say yes, please, and no, thank you, in reply to my own words, peacefully retreated into his own distant world, just as we had known him since his return twenty years before, a thin man with grey hair, who handled his knife and cup with stiff, wooden movements and never looked at me. Never again would the two of us be alone together like this, I realised, never again would we be as certain that we would not be disturbed, never would such an opportunity for frankness and openness present itself to me again. I wanted to reach out and touch his hand, I wanted to stretch out and reach for him, I wanted to pave the way for the questions I had kept bottled up for almost a lifetime; but it was impossible for me, still impossible, and I sat across the table from him and did not say a word.

I did not have many things, a few items of clothing, a brush and comb, my Bible and hymn book and a case of books: they were soon packed and loaded. With my hat already pinned on, I walked around the house that morning to make the final arrangements, to draw the curtains and lock the doors of the rooms. Behind the house the cart stood ready, and on a bench by the kitchen door Pieter sat waiting in the morning sunshine, his back against the wall. I went outside, and when I saw him there, I knew this was my last chance, for even if another unexpected opportunity should arise at a later time, it would be too late then, and I would not be able to make use of it any more.

I sat down beside him on the bench and we sat together like that for a while, with the horses snorting and trampling restlessly. It was spring, it was spring again, and Maans and the others had not been back from the Karoo for long; the air was still sharp and cold, but the sunlight was bright and silvery and there were blossoms on the trees. "Pieter," I said at last, softly, so that no one else would hear, even though there was no one near us; "Pieter, what happened to Sofie?"

After his return, Pieter gradually learned to perform certain tasks and to follow simple instructions; he understood that he had to come in to town to fetch me, though someone had been sent along for safety's sake, and that the cart had to be inspanned and the things loaded. As far as we knew, however, he had no idea of the reasons behind the instructions or the connection between the specific actions he performed: how much he remembered, how much he understood, what he thought and felt, if, indeed, any thoughts and feelings were left, remained a mystery to us after all the years, just like Pieter himself, withdrawn from us in his silent world. Perhaps, I sometimes thought, perhaps he knew more than we suspected and he was just unable to express it, like the old people or the bywoners in the district who had never learned to write; or perhaps he had simply reached a point where he felt no further need to speak of what he had experienced and where he understood the meaninglessness of all efforts to communicate. Here, too, as we sat together on the bench at the kitchen door in the spring sunshine his reaction was ambiguous: to me, waiting anxiously and nervously for his answer, it seemed that the name I had mentioned was not unfamiliar to him and that he recognised it, but that the memories it evoked caused him to withdraw into himself, rather than reply to my question. He made no reply, and when at last I turned to look at his face, his expression was gentle and friendly: it was the open, vacant look of a child, waiting for me to give the order to get up and leave. I would get no reply: I would never know.

We got up, we climbed in; there was no reason to delay. We rode away, around the corner, past the church, along the front street, past the last houses and the trees with their sparse, glittering blossoms in the spring sunshine; past the graveyard and out, following the white road through the veld, past Groenfontein and up the rise to Driefontein and Vloksberg Pass at the edge of the world. I was going back.

6

....

That is all, there is nothing more to tell. I want to sleep; I want to rest. Or if that is not possible, not yet, I want to hear the cocks crow in the distance and see the shutters outlined against the first grey light of dawn. No sound reaches me in the dark, however, and the window remains invisible to me. Thus I am still not relieved of the burden to remember, still forced to continue with my long monologue as I lie here waiting to be set free. Why? There is really nothing more to tell.

When it became known in town that I was returning to the farm, the neighbours might have sympathised if I had allowed it. They dearly wanted to gossip about Stienie but, discouraged by my silence, they could finally do no more than shake their heads ruefully and steer the conversation back to poor Betta – what a shame, it is just not right. They were probably expecting the worst where I was concerned too but, as before, I had no trouble with Stienie. She was more difficult now, impatient and irritable and short-tempered, but everything in her house was exactly the way she wanted it and there was never any reason for conflict between the two of us.

During my long absence much had indeed changed, but the house had never been mine, though I had grown up there, and it had been so many years since I last lived there that it had become unfamiliar to me, so that I was surprised anew every time I recognised something from the past. There were glass panes in the windows and a wooden floor had been laid in the voorhuis; there were armchairs and a sofa, and a lamp had been suspended from the ceiling, and large framed photographs of Maans and Stienie, taken in Worcester, hung on the walls. In the kitchen there were more things than we would ever need and, where Mother and I got by with only old Dulsie for all those years, there were now more than enough women to do the housework. My old room was still the same, however, and I unpacked my things there, put my clothes in the drawers, the brush and comb on the chest and the Bible beside the bed, and I knew that this homecoming would be the end of the journey: for a moment I stood in front of the small, old-fashioned window and looked out over the familiar yard and veld, and with undeniable certainty I knew I would die in this room with its dung floor and wooden shutters.

"Tantetjie has not seen the beautiful stone we erected for Oupa, has she?" Stienie remarked at the table. "And Maans had one made for his mother too. We must go and show Tantetjie this afternoon." I had been warned, however, and I followed the footpath alone, past the place where the shed, the outside rooms and the kraal used to be, to the graveyard beyond the ridge where a white marble stone had been erected over Tannie Coba's grave with Sofie's name and date of birth on it and the date of her death that I had entered in the family Bible years ago with Mother standing over me. It was then, as I stood in the graveyard alone, that I realised how completely the farm had passed into Maans and Stienie's hands, and I accepted it: if this was how they wished to give meaning to this nameless grave and this arbitrary date, then this was what it would henceforth signify; only my memory contested this new interpretation, and it was up to me to keep silent and to see that this unsettling knowledge remained unspoken until the final threat disappeared along with me. What had happened was in the past, after all, and how the next generation wished to apply or interpret the relics of the past was their concern: the words, dates and facts they wished to remember were chiselled into the stone, in lead-filled letters, to be read and accepted, or one day to crumble and be lost together with the weathered stone, its last fragments never to be found among the rank bushes and shrubs.

That summer after my return to the farm was the summer of the long and bitter drought, and that also made it easier for me to adjust, for the unaccustomed barrenness rendered the familiar landscape alien to me, as if it were a strange new region that I encountered for the first time. Here along the fertile edge of the escarpment, with our ample fountains and dams, we were more fortunate than the farmers in the drier regions farther into the interior, and Maans still had enough grazing for his own sheep, but by the end of the year farmers from the Riet River district began sending their sheep flocks to us for grazing. By Christmas the veld was as dead as in winter, and we scarcely celebrated New Year, for though it was customary for Maans and Stienie to entertain all the neighbours on a grand scale, no one was in the mood for festivities this summer. Only the people standing on Maans's land with their sheep gathered at the house for a glass of sweet wine; the young people danced a little to the rhythm of a mouth organ and an accordion, and the young men fired their rifles, but it was a joyless occasion and everyone soon departed again. The guests could not have felt very welcome in our home, for no matter how hospitable Maans always was and how willing to help others, Stienie made no effort to disguise her resentment of these uninvited strangers who were abusing her hospitality and destroying our grazing with their flocks, so that they tended to avoid the house. But perhaps I am not being quite fair to Stienie, for it was during this time that she fell pregnant and that might have been why she did not feel like entertaining: the time of the great drought was the time of Stienie's pregnancy.

Nothing was mentioned to me, as usual, and it was taken for granted that I knew, or perhaps they thought I had no business to know. A few months after my arrival, Maans told me rather sheepishly how good it was to have me back, especially with Stienie being the way she was; it was not an easy time, I would surely understand ... He left the sentence unfinished and gave no further explanation, but by then I had noticed that Stienie was less fastidious around the house, that she often complained, that she was wearing light, loose-fitting frocks and was spending more time lying down in her room.

How long had they been married at the time, Stienie and Maans? Fifteen, sixteen years, I would say, and never had there been any mention of a child, so that long before her death Mother had stopped speculating about the possible arrival of a great-grandchild, and even Stienie's relatives had learned not to make any light-hearted allusions any more. Now, however, in these unrelenting months of heat and dust, the veld parched under the empty sky, the bushes shrivelled, the paths trampled to dust and the last fountains drying up, now her body suddenly became heavier and her movements clumsier, her hands and feet swelled with the heat and she lay on the sofa in the voorhuis, fanning herself, or sometimes failed to emerge from her darkened room at all. The child was due to be born only at the end of autumn or the beginning of winter, I gathered, for she said she did not feel up to the trek down to the Karoo in her condition, yet she made no attempt to prepare for the confinement, and at last I began to worry, for I knew enough about birth to realise that there were preparations to be made. There was no sense in discussing it with Maans, for what did men know about these affairs? And Stienie became annoyed and declined to be bothered with such matters. It was strange to see her like that, for I had never known her so listless and indecisive; on the contrary.

It must have been in May that Maans rode over to Komsberg to fetch old Tant Neeltjie Müller, who was the most skilful mid-wife in our parts: it was almost winter, for I recall how long the evenings seemed and how she and I sat in the voorhuis around the fire-pan and how she grumbled because she wanted to join her people in the Karoo, and with a pencil stub she would mark off the days in the back of her Bible. She and I finally made a few pieces of clothing and other items for the baby, but to me she did not seem very interested in this confinement and she took very little notice of Stienie, and when Maans asked how it was going, she just shrugged. He must have paid the old woman well to wait there for weeks on end with winter approaching, and it was probably only for the money that she stayed. At last she persuaded him to pour her a tot of brandy every evening, to which she added a few lumps of sugar, for the gout, she said. She would spoon this mixture from the glass, and soon be regaling us with tales about the difficult confinements and deaths she had witnessed over the years. How clearly I remember those last weeks of Stienie's pregnancy, with the land caught up in a relentless drought, the shrivelled grey land-scape of rock and dust and dry bushes under an empty white sky, the chill of the evenings as we sat waiting in the voorhuis together, the old woman with her cap, her fringed shawl and her little Bible, and the smell of the brandy-and-sugar concoction she was eating with a spoon.

Nothing happened. Motionlessly the land encompassed us, colour-less sky above colourless, dead earth, and motionlessly winter settled around us. Fine snow whirled in the sky for a minute or two, the ice-flakes visible for a moment as they caught the light before vanishing again. Old Tant Neeltjie sat counting the pencil ticks at the back of her Bible, muttering to herself as she counted and checked on her fingers, her feet on Mother's foot-stove that we brought out because she com-plained so bitterly of the cold; with unmistakable resentment she sat muttering to herself, and pushed her glass across the table in Maans's direction so that he could fill it up again.

What exactly happened, I do not know, for I was in the kitchen: it had been a restless night with recurring gusts of wind rattling the doors and shutters. Stienie had not slept well, and Maans had called the old woman to come and take a look at her, which had left her very ill-humoured. The wind was howling mournfully in the chimney and rattling the windows, chasing the dust across the arid veld to swirl in the yard and be blasted against the window-panes; the weather was threatening, yet it did not rain, the veld as desolate as it had appeared for months. It must have been during the tenth month of Stienie's pregnancy that I heard the scream from her bedroom that morning as I was stooping in front of the stove, and we had been waiting for so long that I pushed the kettle over the fire instinctively to boil the water, and turned to fetch the cloths we had prepared. While I was standing there, I heard old Tant Neeltjie's voice in the voorhuis, however, and realised that the two of them were shouting at each other, the old woman from the voorhuis and Stienie from her bed, with Maans trying in vain to restore the peace. There was just enough time to send the servants out of the house so that they would not hear the old woman's language before I went to Stienie, now screaming and sobbing uncontrollably while Tant Neeltjie stood in the voorhuis firing off curses at the door I had closed in her face.

I never found out what had taken place, for Stienie was too upset to speak coherently, and later it was impossible to find out – as a matter of fact, no one ever referred to it again and later it was as if nothing had ever happened – but Tant Neeltjie must have told her that morning that there was no baby, for afterwards the old woman declared that she had stayed there long enough and insisted that Maans take her to town. While he was still hesitating, for a storm appeared to be brewing, she gathered her things – the little Bible, the nightcap and the sewing-case – wrapped in the grain-bag she had arrived with and tied up with string, and sat waiting in the voorhuis, the bundle on her lap, so that there was nothing for it but to have the Cape cart inspanned. I just had time to tell the servants to prepare some padkos, as I had to remain with Stienie: Maans came to say goodbye, but the cart was at the kitchen door and the old woman had already climbed in, thus he had no choice but to leave. I remember how I stooped, the moist cloth in my hands, to steal a glance from under the low eaves, and through the billowing dust and bushes I saw horses and cart struggling against the wind, already almost invisible under the lowering sky; but then I had to attend to Stienie, for during the next few days she demanded all my attention.

I remember the wind that day and the fine dust penetrating between window and casement, and how it became so dark that I had to ask for a tallow candle in the middle of the day, and how cold it was, how icy the water in which I wrung out the cloths to lay on Stienie's brow and to wash her swollen body. I gave her stuipdruppels and made her an infusion of duiwelsdrek to drink, and gradually she calmed down, but I could not leave her alone. Towards the afternoon the wind brought the first raindrops and then the rain came down, obscuring the land from view and breaking the long drought: Maans had probably reached town, but I knew he would not be able to return in that rain; thus I had coals put in the tessie and, wrapped in a blanket and with my feet on the foot-stove, I kept vigil beside the bed. Nothing, I thought to myself; the baby and the pregnancy and the ungainly body, the shortness of breath and the nausea and the fainting spells, the cramps and the swollen feet; exhausted after her ordeal, Stienie slept, her nightgown and her hair clammy with perspiration. It rained all evening and during the night I heard the steady sound of rain when I awoke on the cot at the foot of the bed, alone in the house with the exhausted woman and the maid asleep on the floor in front of the kitchen stove.

The Cape cart did not return before the following afternoon, ploughing its way through the heavy mud churned up by the wheels and the horses' hoofs, and Maans brought the doctor along, his mount tied behind the cart; he, too, would have been paid a lot of money to undertake the long journey to the farm in that weather. He examined Stienie without saying much, and from his silence I gathered there was a lot he was keeping to himself and not telling us. That evening he lay down on the bed in the guest-room, fully clothed and covered by only his coat, and at daybreak the following morning his horse was saddled and he rode back to town through the mud and the brimming streams. He still had not said much, but he left behind powders and drops for her to take.

After this, Maans took Stienie down to the Boland: he waited a few days to arrange matters on the farm and for the road to become passable again, and then they left. The sheep had not yet been sent down to the Karoo and he said he would get a message to Fisantkraal and ask Coenraad to come and help us, but what did Coenraad still care about us? He had probably already left for the Karoo himself but, be that as it may, nobody arrived and at last I arranged the trek myself. Fortunately Maans had dependable workers, something with which Father had never been blessed, and I made them carry out everything in the house and load the wagon, and so we left for the Karoo, Pieter and I and the herdsmen and their families, no longer down the rocky ledges and slopes of Vloksberg Pass, bouncing and jolting from ledge to ledge with the abyss looming below, but by way of the new road down Verlatekloof. The journey was quicker now but it still took a few days, and those few days were once again a time of freedom, with no one to give orders or demand explanations, no one to look and to ask and to wonder, only the silent, indifferent presence of the driver and the herdsmen with their families, and Pieter across from me at the camp fire in the evenings. I had to look after the wagon and the oxen, as Maans usually did, or Father or Coenraad in the old days, I had to make decisions and the farm-hands came to me for instructions, but the burden of responsibility rested lightly on my shoulders, and as our trek with wagon and sheep descended down the narrow kloof, it seemed to me as if our route had been reversed, the direction lost for a moment, as if in reality we were ascending, climbing up the slopes, to the cliffs where the wind swept across the rolling land of the escarpment, to the shadowless white brightness of the light, and I experienced a dizzying freedom as I had that day after Mother's death, alone in our town house. A few days, that is all, that is all it ever was; a week or two at a time is all I was ever granted, but it was enough, and every time the gift of it left me delighted and surprised. We arrived in the Karoo, we settled into the little house Maans had built for them in the meantime as a winter residence, and in due course he returned from Worcester and joined us. He did not say much about Stienie, but she had stayed behind in Worcester where she had relatives and where the doctor knew her; later she went to the baths at Goudini for a while and she also spent some time at the seaside. She was away all winter and only in spring, when we had returned to the Roggeveld and had settled on the farm once again, did Maans fetch her from the Boland.

It was a good time for me, those winter months Maans and I spent together in the Karoo, for he had remained unchanged over the years, a quiet, grateful boy who made no demands, and it was no trouble keeping house for him. Yes, I still say "boy", though he was a man of forty; as we sat together in the evenings in the glow of the candlelight,

I suddenly noticed the first silver in his dark hair, and sometimes when he forgot about my presence and was deep in thought, he suddenly looked tired and defeated, so that my heart ached to see him, for what could I say or do to help? But still, during those few months of Stienie's absence it was as if something of the old closeness between us had been restored and he became to me once more the child that had been given into my care on my return from death's door, the child that I used to carry everywhere on my arm or lead around by the hand, and that I had come to regard as my own.

Of course old Tant Neeltjie spread rumours when she left us and people were curious: what they surmised never came directly to my ears, but I was aware of the barely suppressed eagerness with which they asked after Stienie's health and how long she would be away and where she was visiting, the inquisitive eyes hoping that my expression might give something away that my hollow or evasive words did not give up. I did not know much more than they, however, perhaps even less, given the fact that I did not share in Tant Neeltjie's wisdom. Once or twice towards the end of winter Stienie sent me a note to say that she was well, but more than that she did not disclose and, anyway, Stienie had never been very comfortable with a pen in her hand, so that I was uncertain what to expect when Maans brought her back to us at last after so many months.

It was clear that she had been very ill: Stienie had never actually been slender and over the years she had grown stouter, but now she was very pale and she looked at us sharply, with dark, glittering eyes, in a way unfamiliar to me – "inquiringly" I might call it, but the word is not strong enough, and perhaps "suspiciously"' would be a more accurate description. At first she was very quiet, almost resigned, and asked few questions about the house or the farm and said nothing about what had happened or changed in her absence, almost as if she did not even notice. She was friendly, but preoccupied, uninterested in her surroundings and with an air of detachment towards Maans and me, and yet it was not because she felt listless or weary, on the contrary, for we were constantly aware of a barely concealed energy that might burst out suddenly. It never happened, however, and as we sat down for supper on that first evening together, I realised that there was no need to fear an outburst, for in an unguarded moment I saw her eyes from across the table in the lamplight and, surprised, I realised that she was afraid of me, though it was hard for me to accept it. Over the weeks and months we spent together the knowledge grew in me, however, and I began to understand the reason for her fear: she was afraid of me because I had seen her naked, swollen body, the hair stuck to her brow and the fear and despair in her eyes, she was afraid of the one whose hands she had clung to in desperation and who had covered her mouth with a pillow to smother the sound of her wailing. I had seen and heard too much, I knew too much, and she would never free herself from the shadow of this knowledge or forgive me for the power I had inadvertently achieved over her. I lived in Maans and Stienie's house and depended on their charity, and yet I speak of her now as if she were a naughty child: I must say, though, that after Stienie's return I never had trouble with her again; after her return she knew where she stood with me.

The neighbours naturally devised plans to call on Stienie immediately, though they, too, were uncertain of what to expect. The visits were strained, with much left unspoken; this was true of answers as well as questions, and there was a great deal of feigned affection and goodwill on both sides. No doubt everyone was glad when the visit came to an end, and afterwards people gossiped more than ever, I presume, and made up for their uncertainty with speculation, suspicion and deduction. We went in to town for the next Nagmaal as usual, however, and attended all the services and Stienie received visitors and made calls as usual, though she was quieter than in the old days, with sudden moments of uncertainty and hesitation, and those restless, shining eyes were still noticeable. During the time she spent in Cape Town she had bought clothes on a grand scale and she wore those outfits to church now – well, it might have been what people wore in Cape Town but, as I have said, it was too stylish for our little town and our townspeople, and I always felt slightly self-conscious as I followed her to our pew, even though I might be considered the last person to accuse others of peculiarity. What bothered me, however, was that, unlike in the old days, she did not wear her expensive, elegant clothes because she found them beautiful and wanted to impress people; instead, her choice of clothing had become a kind of challenge, and as I followed her into church and sat beside her in the pew it was evident how nervous she was as she sat up so straight, glancing around with quick, bright eyes without noticing anyone. At New Year we entertained on the farm as usual, and more people arrived than in previous years, probably still out of curiosity, and I recall how Stienie moved among them all evening in her rustling red gown from Cape Town with its frills and lace trimmings, greeting and welcoming her guests tirelessly, and chattering without taking notice of anyone she addressed.

The nervousness remained, the restlessness remained; after her return she no longer seemed to fit into the position she had held among us before, and it was as if she were forever chasing after something new without knowing exactly what she desired. The hunger I had recognised years ago had only been stayed temporarily, and the restless craving of old had been reawakened. I watched and kept silent and waited, and in the new year she began to work blindly and tirelessly at the realisation of her dream: it was during the course of the next year that the new house was built and Maans went to Parliament, and it was during that time that she found Pieter a wife.

Where did it start – with the house? Yes, probably with the house. The homestead on the farm was old, of course, for it was probably nearly a hundred years ago that Oupa had built it, and it was old-fashioned, for in spite of all the alterations it still remained a house of its time with its dung floors in the bedrooms and kitchen, its sturdy walls, small windows and thatched roof, and our town house had always been more to Stienie's liking with its wooden floors and large windows that let in the light. While Mother and I were living in town, Maans had the outbuildings demolished – the shed and kraal and outside rooms, together with the remains of the old homestead that Great-oupa had built – and had them rebuilt farther away from the house, and a room was added for Pieter; but, in spite of Stienie's complaints, he seemed unwilling to go any further. Shortly after my return to the farm, he replaced the roof of our town house with corrugated iron, as people had begun doing, and that strengthened Stienie's resolve to alter the homestead on the farm. The matter dragged on, however, until her illness occurred; but when she returned from the Boland she could not be stopped and Maans was forced to have a completely new house built with wooden floors and match-board ceilings and sash windows and a tin roof, like the new houses she had seen in the Boland. At last Maans gave in, as he usually did sooner or later, and for months the builders were busy on the plain below the old homestead, beside the road and near the dams, while she watched them from the old house, more and more often giving the orders and instructions herself – and why not, for Maans was not really interested, and had other things to do, while Stienie knew exactly what she wanted. It was as if that protracted building process provided Stienie with a new goal in life after her return from the Boland, and equally important to her was the interest it aroused in our district, for as the news spread, people rode over to come and look. For Stienie it was a big thing to walk across with the women, though there was nothing but the extensive foundations to impress them with, and if there were no visitors, she was compelled to ask me to take a walk with her towards evening, and then we always made our way to the building site to see the walls going up. She was oblivious to the fact that I did not share her enthusiasm, nor take any real interest in the building: Stienie never paid much attention to what others thought or felt.

It was during this time, while she was busy with the new house, that Stienie decided Pieter should marry, for it was just then that Andreas Stofberg died. Andreas had always struggled on his farm and the drought had given him a hard knock, so that after his death the farm had to be sold to pay his debts. People expected Stienie to take care of his widow and young daughter, for she was their closest relative, and Maans seemed inclined to help, for he was fond of the little girl, but Stienie showed no particular inclination to take the woman in, not to mention her child. It was too much of an upheaval with the building, she declared, and in the end they went to live in an outside room of the town house, and Maans probably supported them, though Annie earned a little money with her sewing. After a while, before the new house had even been completed, Stienie remarked in passing one day that she wondered if it might not be a good thing for Oom Pieter to get married, and before I could recover from my astonishment, she went on to list all the advantages; she mentioned that he and Annie could live in the old homestead when we moved to the new house. She spoke rapidly without looking at me, but despite her concern about Oom Pieter, I knew that very little of what she was saying was the truth, for she just wanted to acquit herself of her obligation to Annie and get rid of Pieter before the house was completed, so that there would be no danger that they would spoil that new elegance with their presence, or that she might have to take in Annie and her child. Even so, even so, I thought, and did not know whether to laugh or cry; and at last I made no reply to her suggestion, for what would the point have been of voicing reservations? In the circumstances it was probably the best solution for everyone, even if it were conceived mainly to benefit Stienie. Annie was a decent young woman, quiet, neat and diligent, and she would look after him; and Pieter loved children and would accept her little girl in his life: the two of them would never have a true marriage, but he would be cared for, taste some security and warmth and, who knows, perhaps even something like love and happiness here at the end of his life. Thus they were married hastily before the magistrate in town one morning, almost as if it were something to be kept from people, with only Maans and Stienie and me as witnesses; Annie's mourning period had only just passed and she was still wearing her black mourning dress. Pieter was almost sixty by then but during the few years they lived together, I deemed them to be happy, as far as I understood anything about happiness.

I did not know whether to laugh or cry, I have said, and I still do not know today. Actually, as I have said before, I never thought of the silent, good-natured, smiling old man in the outside room on the farm as my brother and, sitting together on the bench at the kitchen door of the town house that morning, I had made a final attempt to reach him and had been forced to turn away in the face of his implacable silence. There was no road leading back to the past, I realised, before me a wall of stones blocked my entry, and behind it in the distance lay the world of my youth, bathed in sunshine, untouchable but at the same time unreachable, with no connection between this smiling, patient old man in his shabby suit of clothes and the laughing youth with the pale naked shoulders on the sheaves, the youth hoisting himself soundlessly over the window-sill in the blinding moonlight. Why should I blame Stienie for pushing him out, as if I had not done it too, as if I had not been just as ready as she to forget about the poor and slightly neglected old man in the outside room?

At the time that Pieter was married, while the new house was nearing completion, Maans became Member of Parliament. Despite being quiet and modest, he had gone ahead in our community, and when they wanted to establish a branch of the Broederbond in our district, they encouraged him to serve on the committee. He baulked then and declared that he was not a man for politics but later, when parliamentary elections were due, they approached him again and he agreed. Why? As he himself had said, he was not interested in politics and he was not an ambitious or assertive man; but no one from our parts had ever been elected to Parliament before, and it was the best Stienie could still strive for, to be a Member of Parliament's wife who goes to Cape Town every year and socialises with all the important people. Thus Maans travelled in the district to talk to the people and solicit votes, and the building was temporarily halted while Stienie accompanied him. "That was the year when Stienie stood for Parliament," Floris van Wyk with his sharp tongue remarked one evening at a New Year's party when he did not know I could overhear, and everyone around him laughed as if they appreciated the joke; nevertheless, Maans was elected, even though Stienie might have done the persuading.

When the building was resumed, Stienie's plans had become more grandiose, and when they returned from their first stay in Cape Town she introduced even more changes, though the house was nearing completion by that time: the wall between the voorhuis and the dining-room had to be knocked down because she wanted to install folding doors, and she had bought a number of things in Cape Town that had been sent along. For a few years it continued like that, and after every trip things had to be fetched at Matjiesfontein, so that our own wagon could not always manage and Maans had to hire the transporters in town with their donkey carts to help. There were chandeliers and floral wallpaper for the living-rooms and coloured tiles for the built-in fireplaces, tasselled curtains with linings and occasional tables and ornaments, a piano for the voorhuis, though Stienie could not play, wardrobes with mirrored doors and brass bedsteads with coir mattresses, a new dinner service, a tea service, brightly-coloured carpets, and who knows what else: every year after their return from Cape Town the men rode over to discuss politics with Maans and their wives came along to inspect the new things Stienie had acquired. Later they laughed behind her back at her pretentiousness and scoffed at her elegance, but all too often it was only because they were envious. "Well, Maans, it cannot be denied, you have built yourself the grandest house in the entire district," Dawid Loubser remarked while they were getting into their cart after their first visit, but Lina and Gertruida pretended not to hear, and to my knowledge no woman in the district ever went as far as good old Dawid in his honest admiration. After a few years Stienie seemed to lose interest, however, or perhaps there was simply nothing more she could still need or want. She stopped buying things for the house, but continued to return from Cape Town with hat-boxes and suitcases full of new clothes.

Yes, no doubt the new house was elegant, at least for our parts, a large stone building overshadowing the old homestead with its thatched roof on the ridge behind it, its tin roof visible from a distance across the veld, gleaming in the light. The old house had been a shelter where we retreated to cook, eat and sleep, a place where children were born and, if you were lucky, where you eventually died in your bed; but the new one, what purpose did it serve, with more and bigger rooms than we could use, more light pouring through its large windows than anyone could need, and all those fireplaces and lamps and brass beds? I wandered about in that big, bright space, jumping at the noise of my soles on the wooden floor and the rumbling of the rain on the tin roof, and sometimes when I ran into Maans in the passage unexpectedly, he, too, seemed strange and ill at ease; but at least Stienie was happy after her own fashion, for the time being, anyhow, or as happy as it was possible for her to be. And, strangely enough, in time I found, after a visit to Annie who now lived in the old homestead with Pieter and the little one, that the old house where I had been born and where I had grown up appeared cold and dark, as if I were getting used to Stienie's new house.

Maans and Stienie went down to Cape Town every year now, where they rented a house, and as Stienie began to feel at home in the city and got to know people there, she began to go out regularly and took part in the social life. Now and then she sent me a note or a report she had cut from the newspaper when Maans had spoken in Parliament, so that I could show it to people, but the reports were few, and later she stopped sending them, for the people in our district tended to make fun of their silent Member of Parliament. On the few occasions when he did speak, however, it was about agricultural matters or farming, and he always voted correctly, and as people are fond of him and have nothing to complain of, he has remained their representative to this day, almost twenty years later, without saying much, without ever creating a stir or drawing attention to himself.

At the beginning Maans sometimes suggested that I should pay them a visit in Cape Town and Stienie always agreed, but too quickly for my liking, and in such a way that it was clear she did not expect us to start making the arrangements immediately. Once he even remarked that it would be good if I could accompany them to manage the housekeeping, for Stienie had many appointments and, moreover, she often felt unwell; he had spoken without thinking and had probably meant it in jest, but Stienie made no reply and he never repeated the invitation. The initial anxiety that they might expect a visit or want my company, gradually disappeared: for Maans as well as Stienie it was more practical that I should stay behind on the farm while they were away, and furthermore I realised that Stienie wanted to get away, not take her life with her to Cape Town as a constant reminder of everything she wished to forget. During this time some of the wealthier people began sending their children to school in the Boland, and there was always someone with a daughter at school or a son at college in Cape Town; but I heard complaints that Stienie did not look out for the children, and people from our parts who went to Cape Town themselves were sometimes rather scathing about the way they had been received by her. As for me, I knew I was safe.

So we continued, with me on my own in the big house for part of the year, and Pieter, Annie and her little girl in the old homestead behind, and in winter we all went down to the Karoo. As a child I had accompanied my parents to Nagmaal at Worcester but that was the farthest I had ever travelled, and for many years now we had had our own church in the Roggeveld, so that journey was no longer necessary. For years my life's journey had been along the same route, between the farm and the town, and in winter down Verlatekloof to the Karoo. I had never been to Matjiesfontein; I had never seen a train or even a railway track. There was nothing I desired.

Pieter had been married to Annie for five or six years, perhaps, when he died, as quietly and inconspicuously as he had lived: Maans and Stienie were in Cape Town when Annie came running over to the house one morning to say that he had died. He had been unwell for a while, and that morning he had been sitting on the bed when he just toppled over against the pillows and was gone. He was not even seventy years old. I helped lay him out, and he was buried on the farm with only the two of us and the closest neighbours at the graveside. Hendrik Esterhuizen led the service: we sent a message to town for a telegram to be sent to Maans, but of course he could not come all the way from Cape Town just for the funeral. An old man who had lived with us on the farm for many years had died, that was all, a familiar dependent, a respected bywoner, and while I was handling the worn-out old body of the stranger, I felt nothing more than a distant, dull ache that I could not really explain.

After Pieter's death Annie and her daughter remained in the old homestead, for she was a reserved woman who bothered no one and it was handy for Stienie to be able to call on her for help when she entertained. She received firewood and meat, and Maans must have given her a small sum of money to survive, for Pieter had had nothing to leave her. Maans was quite fond of the little girl, but Stienie did not approve and the child was never encouraged to come to our house. There was a time that Maans spoke of sending her to school in Cape Town but Stienie objected quite vehemently. She might have been able to teach, or start up a school in town, but Stienie shook her head and pursed her lips as her shiny needle passed through her embroidery, flashing in the lamplight, and so nothing came of the proposal. The girl walked over to Driefontein for a while to attend the farm school there and I helped her a little with reading and writing, but she was not very clever, or perhaps she simply did not try very hard. I knew Maans once suggested that she should get piano lessons from someone in town, seeing that the piano in the voorhuis was never used, but Stienie simply laughed at the idea, and thus nothing came of that either.

After Pieter's death Maans said he would have a stone erected for his uncle, but he had other things on his mind and the years rolled by without anything being done about it. I hardly felt like reminding him, and at last I used my own money and had a stone made by old Oom Appie, chiselled with uneven letters and adorned with floating branches and wreaths: I had only his name and dates engraved on it, and the words Luke 15 verse 32. Maans was in Cape Town when the stone was erected and neither he nor Stienie had any reason to visit the graveyard, so they probably never even knew about it. Thus everyone was dead, Father and Mother, Jakob and Pieter; yes, and I suppose Sofie too – how could Sofie, who was older than I, still be alive and I myself past seventy? Only I have remained, waiting for the dawn, dying in the dark, with somewhere at my feet the regular breathing of the girl in her sound sleep from which nothing can awaken her. Is she still asleep? The silence around me has intensified and I can no longer hear anything, the darkness as heavy as a curtain before my eyes. I have been left behind alone.

Maans always tried to return from Cape Town as soon as possible, for he did not like the city or life there, but Stienie often tried to extend their visit, so that their absence from the farm usually lasted quite long in the end. Furthermore, when they were back on the farm Maans had to travel a great deal to visit the various parts of his constituency and talk to the people, and Stienie almost always accompanied him, her suitcases tied to the back of the cart, for she said she was bored at home. Thus I was left on my own more than ever and often it was I who had to supervise, give the orders or make the decisions. And why not? I had grown up here, after all, and for the greatest part of my life I had watched what the men were doing, Father and my brothers and Maans, and listened to their conversations. For a while Maans tried to work with a foreman, but sooner or later he or his wife would have trouble with Stienie and they would leave, and gradually he realised that we could carry on, as long as I was at home; he appreciated being able to rely on me, I believe, and Stienie once remarked with a certain smugness that it was a good thing they were able to manage without a foreman, though I myself never heard or received a word of appreciation from her.

But wait, that is not the whole truth, for once I did overhear something I suppose could be considered a compliment, even though it had not been meant for my ears. I was coming down the passage behind the maid who was carrying a tray to the voorhuis when I heard Maans remark to the guests in his quiet way: "Tantetjie looks after the farm better than any foreman", and Stienie joined in, "Yes, she is truly a precious old thing." That big new house did have its advantages, for on many occasions I heard or saw something incidentally, on the other side of the door, in the passage, around a corner, or behind the net curtains that veiled the windows. For a moment I remained in the passage instead of entering behind the maid and helping to serve the coffee, as usual. So that was what I was, I thought to myself, a precious old thing; and after almost seventy years an abyss suddenly opened underneath me and I no longer recognised myself where I stood on the opposite bank looking across. I never really had any reason to think highly of myself, but Stienie's unforeseen words – affectionate yet at the same time snide, as was often the case – shook me, and I still recall how I stood there in the passage, teetering over the abyss, watching myself across the distance.

What more is there: as I grew older, more and more freedom came my way, that freedom that I had been anticipating for so long and that I could use so well now. I was often alone on the farm for days or weeks, and there was no one to see or hear, to observe, wonder or disapprove; only the servants in the kitchen, and what did they care about me? Annie led her own quiet life with her daughter and took no notice of me, and the neighbours no longer tried to call when I was alone, for I usually managed to evade them. Gradually during those days and weeks, those months even, I learned how wide the boundaries of my freedom were and how far I could go before encountering any obstacle; I learned that I might come and go as I pleased and wander where I wished, and I rediscovered all the old paths and the favourite haunts of my childhood. That freedom I had once tasted in town, alone in the house filled with the reflected light of the snow, that freedom had always been subject to limitations, and at the graveyard I had to stand and follow with my eyes the route from the outskirts of the town through the greyness of the veld. Now I was free to go where I wished, without even searching for a footpath, and I could stay out all day without anyone wondering where I was.

At first the war did not change our lives on the farm at all – it was something the men discussed where people sat together, and we were unaffected by it until the commandos invaded the Kolonie and the big English camp was pitched at Matjiesfontein. It was during this time that the ramparts and forts were built along the edge of the escarpment and troops guarded the passes leading from the Roggeveld to the Karoo, and on our farm, too, there was an English camp beyond the dams for weeks. Stienie was pleased, for they had considered moving to the town house, but with the protection of the English, at least we were safe, she said. She was especially pleased when a few of the officers came to ask whether they might play the piano, for the piano in the voorhuis was seldom used; and so they came to play, and she served them tea in her best cups and sat talking to them in the voorhuis, for she had learned to speak English in Cape Town. Maans was not very happy about the English on the farm, for although he was a man of peace who tried not to take sides, he knew people in the district did not approve; there was nothing he could do about it, however, and they paid well for the sheep they purchased to slaughter, and for the bread Stienie had the servants bake for them. After a while they departed, however, and we were left to our own devices; the men and the horses and the tents disappeared almost overnight, but the veld beyond the dams remained trampled and overgrazed for a long time to show where their camp had been.

After this there was only a garrison in town and the town itself was barricaded, and commandos came and went on our farm as they pleased. Stienie mentioned again that it might be safer to move to town, but when the town was attacked by the Boers, she decided it would be better to stay with her friends in Cape Town. No one suggested that I should move to the town house, neither did they suggest that I should accompany Stienie for my own safety, and thus Maans and I spent the war alone together on the farm, with Annie and her daughter in the old homestead. There was martial law and the horses were commandeered: we could not ride anywhere, and no one came to visit any more. In the Hantam and the Roggeveld the commandos moved about freely, and from time to time they would suddenly appear in our yard, asking for food or clothing. I do not think Maans was very pleased with these surprise visits, but he could not refuse to give them what they demanded, and many of our sheep were slaughtered for which he never received a penny. One New Year they captured one of Maans's herdsmen and another man at Bastersfontein because they had supposedly spied for the English and, after thrashing them, shot and killed them. Their wives came to Maans to complain and I remember their cries and wails in the yard; I stood at the kitchen door, just behind Maans, and looked out, my eyes blinded by the glint of the sun on the white dust in the yard, but there was nothing I could do for them, and Maans was equally helpless, for it was war and the invaders did as they pleased.

For a long time we could go nowhere and it was safe nowhere, and Maans suggested a bit hesitantly that it might be better if I did not wander about in the veld on my own as was my habit. More than that he did not say; but afterwards I usually went out when he was not at home to worry about me. To me it was different, however, as if the earth and the veld I had known all my life had suddenly changed, as if the familiar places had suddenly become treacherous and the familiar land could no longer be trusted, glistening and dangerous as a yellow cobra slithering away among bushes and rocks. Some of the young men in our district joined the commandos and some of them were shot dead in skirmishes, or sometimes one of them was caught and executed as a rebel, young men I scarcely knew, though their parents or grandparents were of my own generation. In our isolation our only information came from the herdsmen who brought us news of these battles and executions, and the servants knew more about the movements of the commandos and the troops than they ever told us.

Something had changed and when the war was over, life was not the same. Maans returned to Parliament in Cape Town, but he was past fifty and his hair was quite grey: sometimes, when I noticed how old and tired he looked, I was suddenly reminded of the child I had piggy-backed and raised alone, and the schoolboy who had wanted to become a soldier. Did he remember the water glittering in the sunlight among the reeds, I sometimes wondered; was there a vague memory from his childhood of tears pouring down my cheeks as I knelt in the veld, and did he ever wonder uneasily where this obscure image came from or what it meant? Or had even that been forgotten?

What would have happened if Father had allowed him to leave? Would he have been happier now, or unhappier? Who can tell? Stienie spent even less time at home during these years, for she often complained of her health and said she had to stay in Cape Town to be close to the doctors who could treat her, or else she would be some-where at the seaside, or at the baths at Goudini or the sanatorium at Caledon. When she was at home, she was restless and unhappy, and the only time she seemed content for a while was when visitors came over or she could find a reason to entertain. Her eyes remained rest-less and searching and her voice took on a sharp and whining tone. As she grew older, she gained weight and she dressed more and more outrageously in clothes she brought with her from Cape Town: she had always been a little grand for us but dare I say she now became flamboyant, with her gussets and frills and trains, the hats with their flowers and ribbons and veils and large hat pins and the ostrich feathers – Stienie had always loved ostrich feathers. Where people used to smile good-naturedly about her dress style before, their remarks were less charitable now, and especially the women were quite vicious at times. Oh, it was mostly the younger people who did not know her well who were less than kind in their opinions and quicker to appoint blame and pass judgement, and they sometimes made her seem more ludicrous than she really was.

Maans continued to be as well-respected as always, but yet there was a new sharp edge to people's feelings towards him that had not been evident before, for the war had brought discord to our district, and certain people felt he had collaborated too well with the govern-ment, while others thought he had been too friendly with the com-mandos on the farm. Where people had teased him for years about having so little to say in Parliament, he was now blamed by some for not contributing enough, and by others for what he said when he did speak. I heard him being disparaged, in the kitchen I overheard the words, in the passage where the door stood ajar, at the fringe of the company, behind the backs of those who had forgotten about me, as usual, and with increasing certainty I knew that he could no longer count on the same affection and trust as earlier. What had happened? I did not know myself, for it was something from outside, that bright serpentine path of gold, flashing in the sun, making its way across the faded landscape.

In the end Maans himself became aware of these feelings. He might never have become involved with politics had it not been for Stienie, and had it not been for her, he would probably also have retired a long time ago, for the duties and responsibilities and the long absences from the farm had become an increasingly heavy burden for him, and it became clearer from one year to the next how reluctantly he shouldered it. However, each time he mentioned retiring, Stienie interrupted with that quick motion of her head and shoulders, and laughingly made some deprecating remark to show he did not really mean what he was saying; but at last, when there was talk about a Union, he said he would stay on only until the new Parliament had been elected, and this time Stienie did not interrupt, but listened to his words in silence, staring at her rings as if she had no interest in his decision. He had grown old, this child I had raised, and there was more silver than black in his hair; when I looked up at his words and saw him like that in the lamplight, I was suddenly afraid, as if I had just been reminded how quickly the years had passed. And if Father had allowed him to become a soldier when it had been his one desire, would it really have made a difference?

I could look across the table in the lamplight and see; I could stand in the dim light of the passage or in the voorhuis behind the lined curtain, and hear – that was all. There was nothing I could do to prevent anything, or to change the course of events, and over the years I had withdrawn so far from these affairs that no sense of involvement remained. I still went in to town for Nagmaal and attended church services with Maans and Stienie but afterwards, when the house was filled with visitors, I began taking the liberty of withdrawing from the company, and if people initially noticed my absence, they soon became used to it. On the farm I gave orders in the kitchen when guests arrived and saw that coffee was served in the voorhuis, but I never joined the company any more, and though at first Stienie had frowned at my lack of manners with that impatient little shrug of her round shoulders, she did not say anything, and in all honesty there was no one among the visitors who requested my company or who missed me.

Once I attended a wedding with Maans and Stienie unwillingly, the silent and disregarded guest at the fringe of the merriment, and I heard the women clustered together in the light of the chandelier discussing Stienie over their glasses of sweet wine. "Yes," one of them remarked disapprovingly, "Maans is seldom at home these days. His mad old aunt looks after the farm for him." I no longer remember who spoke those words, I do not even recall whose wedding it was or where it took place; I just remember being seated in the shadowy corner and hearing that observation that no one contradicted, and then the sudden silence that fell when they realised I had been sitting there all the time and had overheard their conversation. For a moment the yawning abyss returned and I found myself on the opposite side once again, almost indistinguishable in the distance; but then they quickly changed the subject, and where I sat, excluded from their circle, I was overwhelmed by the realisation of my own freedom. After this I deemed it unnecessary to attend any more weddings or funerals in the district. I still went in to Nagmaal with Maans and Stienie and attended church with them, but my last discernible connection with the people around us had been severed.

When I was a child, we had no mirror in the house and thus I never had the chance to see my own face. In these years I learned to live without mirrors again, as I had no further need of them, for I knew very well what I looked like: a dishevelled old woman, no longer capable of sensible conversation or any form of intercourse with her neighbours, unsociable and slow of speech, with a peculiar scar across her forehead, scorched by the sun, tousled by the wind, half-wild as a result of her strange and isolated existence. That was all; and this is all that has finally remained: an old woman alone in a bed in a dark room, voiceless and paralysed, so far retreated into herself that no return to life is possible any more. All.

What does it matter? Let the girl sleep on the cot at the foot of the bed: she is young and her life lies ahead of her. Why should she wake and get up? There is nothing more she can do for me.

What did I expect when I kept listening for the cock's crow, peering through the dark to try and make out the first grey light of dawn; what could the morning bring that the night had not already given me? I have remembered what I had forgotten, I have articulated what I did not want to know, and my mission has been accomplished; I am tired now, and I want to rest, undisturbed by anyone, or by the day with its bustle and noise. The pattern has been laid down and the slivers and fragments joined together, my task fulfilled, and it is not for me to judge whether it has been done well or poorly. Only one more thing, seeing that I have gone so far and said so much; only one more thing, even though I do not understand why, and then it will be enough.

During these last years after the war, when I had detached myself from all the affairs of the district, people began to look me up in my isolation on the farm, just as they had done in the old days when there had been few educated people in our parts and they had come to ask me to read or write their letters. Again it was the simple people who came to me, poor people and bywoners, and when I was not at home when they arrived, they simply sat in their carts in the shade of the wall, waiting for me to return; sometimes there were coloured people in a cart drawn by mules who had come a long way from the Riet River district or the Nuweveld because they seemed to have heard of me. Timidly these visitors described their ailments to me, and I discovered that they credited me with a special knowledge of plants and herbs, for this was how people in the district explained my solitariness and my long rambles in the veld, and in their simplicity they interpreted my loneliness and isolation as signs of wisdom and power: humbly they revealed their sores, their ulcers, their swellings to me, and then looked at me expectantly, confident that I could cure them. There was nothing I could do for them, however, for, faced by their suffering, I was as helpless as they and I felt ashamed by the trust they put in me so undeservedly: I could only mutter an apology, suggest a few remedies that I happened to know of and give them some balm or solution from the medicine chest, and shamefacedly watch the rickety cart struggle down the road again, its passengers returning home with their pain and their sorrow. Perhaps there was no one else to listen or help and they appreciated my care and attention, but over the years they kept coming, for they truly believed I knew how to alleviate their pain; and how annoyed Stienie was when these ramshackle vehicles came struggling across the yard when she was at home, and how scathingly she denounced these visitors, though never in my presence. What could I do, however, caught between her disapproval and their groundless faith and only too painfully aware of my own inadequacy? These sufferers were the only people who still needed me, no matter how unfounded their faith in my abilities, and their infrequent visits the only connection that still tied me to the world.

One day while Maans and Stienie were away in Cape Town, a rickety old wagon came to a halt some distance from the house. I was sitting at the dining-room window, for I had been feeling tired all day, so I did not go out to see what they wanted, though I heard a man speak to the servants at the kitchen door. They have come for advice, as always, I thought, but actually it was not the case, and the maid came to tell me that there was a white man asking whether he might stand on our ground for a while and let his sheep graze. I sat with him in the kitchen while he drank the coffee he had been served, for lately Stienie did not want these people in her voorhuis any more, and even in the kitchen they were not really welcome. He was a youngish man, though he looked old and tired in his dusty clothes and worn shoes, and while we were sitting there, he spoke politely yet indifferently of the long road he had travelled, from beyond Sak River and Riet River and down through the Nuweveld. I showed him where he might stand, and as he was taking his leave on the threshhold of the kitchen, he remarked almost in passing that his wife lay ill in the wagon, not as if he wanted or expected any help from me, but as if merely recounting another of the many woes of his itinerant existence that he had been listing for me while drinking his coffee.

It was not often that a white man trekked around to find pasture for his sheep any more, dependent on the hospitality and the mercy of others, neither were these ramshackle old wagons as common as during my childhood. As I sat at the window, I could not help thinking of the past and of many long-forgotten memories, Oom Ruben with his barefoot children and Jan Baster's meagre trek on its way to Groot River. I wanted to lie down and rest for a while, but after the arrival of the stranger I was uneasy, and the old memories stirred up so many feelings inside me that I could not find any rest. At last I took the medicine chest and went across to the wagon.

The man was alone except for his herdsman, and there was no one to help. His wagon was old and rickety, the canvas worn and torn, and it shook unsteadily when I climbed in; the woman lay on a bed of skin-blankets that had been made for her on the cot, and was not even aware of my arrival. I searched among the remedies I knew, but she took no notice of me; the man thanked me almost submissively for my help, as if he had not been expecting it and was unused to such solicitude, but he seemed to know that no medicine would be of any help. There was nothing more for me to do, so I left them alone. I sent them a little food from the house; but later that evening I took the lantern and walked across again.

The herdsman had already fallen asleep at the remains of his fire, and inside the wagon the man sat at his wife's bedside by the light of a candle-stub that had been fixed on a chest. He sat motionless, his shoulders sagging, and he did not look up at my arrival or move aside as I bent over her. I looked at her in the uncertain light and knew there was nothing more I could do for her, and so I sat down on the camp-stool at the foot of the cot to keep vigil with the stranger. Why did I do it? I might just as well have gone back home, for he had as little need of my presence as his wife. In the flickering light of the tallow candle I surveyed the scant belongings in the wagon – the chipped basin, the cracked cup, the knife – and this tired, defeated man and the dying woman in the bed. How old could she have been? It was impossible to say, for years of poverty and suffering on the road had left deep lines on her face, but her hair was still dark where it fell across her damp forehead and it was even possible to believe she had once been pretty – who could know? I got up and bent to wipe the sweat from her brow, for the man made no move and did not attempt to do any-thing; when she moved her hand feverishly and uncertainly over the blanket, the fingers searching, he did not even notice, and it was I who leaned forward to grasp it, and that was how she died, with her hand in mine.

We sat like that for a while, without moving, until the flickering candle threatened to go out, for I did not want to disturb this rare moment of insight with any ill-timed word or movement. Sofie had died like this, I knew as I sat with the dead woman's hand in mine, or in a similar way, somewhere in a wagon or a tent, in a shelter or an outside room, in the desolation of the Great Karoo, Bushmanland or Namaqualand or in the region across the Groot River, in similar isolation, in similar poverty, in similar despair, and it was from a wordless deathbed like this one that Pieter had at last been brought back to us. For fifty or sixty years I had wondered and had carried my uncertainty and unasked questions around inside me, and now the questions had been answered and the circle completed: in a final gesture of tenderness and reconciliation I could reach out across all the years and touch her brow, could reach out and hold her hand while she was dying, and bid her farewell. Now the inscription in the family Bible could at last be made and the date chiselled in the stone.

The next day the man and his helper dug a grave in the graveyard in a place that I allotted them, next to where Jakob lay buried; only the two of them were present and Annie and her daughter and I. After they had filled in the grave, they heaped stones on it, with upright stones at the head and foot, and the man thanked me with a few gruff words before moving on to the next stand with his rickety wagon and mules and his handful of sheep tended by the herdsman. His wife remained behind in our graveyard: on one side of Jakob's grave was Sofie's headstone with the date taken from the family Bible, and on the other side was her grave. After the man had left, Annie suddenly remembered that no one had asked the woman's name; but who would ever erect a stone for her, and, in truth, who could believe an epitaph, even if it were chiselled in stone?

The next day I walked out to Bastersfontein, the first time since that day when Maans had been a little boy and I had taken him there. It had been a long way for a girl with a small child, but it was an even longer way for an old woman who was returning reluctantly and hesitantly to the place she had avoided for so long: I was almost afraid to see it again, but there was no reason for my fear, for nothing had remained, only the low line of the rocky ridge and the grey shrubs against the faded blue sky. The last remains of the dilapidated huts I had once still found there had vanished, and among the harpuisbos and on the rocky ledges I searched in vain for the place where they had once stood; neither could I find any trace of the fountain among the rock layers, no sign of muddy soil or moisture, of bulrushes or reeds, or of softer earth that might have retained a footprint. I found only the heaped stones of two graves, almost invisible among the greyish shrubs: they belong to the herdsmen who used to live here and who buried their people here, I thought, but then I saw bunches of wild flowers, not quite wilted, that had been placed among the stones, and I realised that this was the place where the two men thought to be spies had been shot by the Boers during the war, and I remembered again the women at the kitchen door, wailing, and how Maans and I had been unable to do anything to help them. Now the war had been over for a long time and no one spoke of it any more or remembered what had become of the men's families; yet, years later there were still people who remembered, nameless people who came here through the veld to place the wild flowers they had gathered among the rocks on the two graves.

I sat there for a long time, for I was tired, and I listened to the wind growing stronger. "The sorrow and the pain," I remembered from long ago, "O the sorrow and the pain", but I was unable to recall where I had first heard the song or who had sung it, for the voice of the singer had been forgotten, as insubstantial as the wind. There is no plant in the world that can offer a cure, I realised, no shrub that can guarantee oblivion. We are doomed to remember and to bear our burden, right up to the end.

After a while I realised I had to get up and go back, no matter how impossibly distant the house might seem, for the clouds had been gathering over the escarpment, and so I began to walk, shuffling and stumbling over roots, stones and gullies. The daylight grew dim in the wind; sunshine and shadows moved across the veld, and the landscape rippled before my feet; under the deep blue of the darkening sky and the threatening storm, in the shrouded light of the sun, the grey renosterbos glittered with a silvery gleam, radiant before my eyes, and I stood there blinded, so that the day surged over me and the earth was washed from under my feet. I stumbled over a root or a rock, my foot sank into a porcupine-burrow, and I fell.

When I was a child, they noticed my absence and searched for me and a herdsman found me in the veld and carried me home, reclaimed from death's door; slowly and painfully, unaware of my surroundings, I had wrested myself from the dark depths and risen, back to the light, but that was a long time ago, and there was no reason why I should still desire to live. I would rather lie where I had fallen, close my eyes and listen to the rustling of the wind through the renosterbos, until the radiant landscape was cloaked in darkness and I could descend into the depths, noiselessly and without resistance, carried by the weight of my body. I was getting too old for these solitary journeys, I realised drowsily, and this would have to be the last one.

After a long time I got up painfully, my body stiff with weariness and bruised by the fall, and slowly I walked back through the rolling and surging light and shadows, the silver glow of the late afternoon and the threat of the approaching storm, amid a splendour I had not witnessed for many years, until I saw in the distance ahead the dams glittering in the sun, and I knew I was home. There was no one to witness my shambling return, my clothes dusty and torn, my hands and face bruised. In my room I made an attempt to brush off my dress, I put up my hair and poured some water to wash, but then my hands fell away from me, and I toppled backward into the darkness I had craved for so long, that merciful dark in which I could go to sleep right there on the floor of my room. But not yet: the maid discovered me and called Annie, and the women carried me over to Annie's house, to the old house, to the house where I was born and the room where I had slept as a child. I was aware of their frightened voices, I saw their anxious movements in the candlelight, but I no longer heard their words. Cloistered with my thoughts and memories, I was waiting for the words to end and the candle to be snuffed out, waiting for the nightlight beside my bed to burn out, for even the regular breathing of the sleeping girl on the cot to quiet down. For a moment I was afraid of the darkness and the silence that was vaster than anything I had ever expected, for a moment I was afraid of what I had to remember, but now the anxiety has been conquered, the knowledge attained and the wisdom acquired, and with eyes wide open I behold the dark.

There is no daybreak any more, only the dark; first darkness, then sleep. The dark has obliterated the moonlight, the dark has snuffed out the candle-flame; Pieter falls wordlessly from the window-sill, back into the darkness whence he had come, and only Sofie's black dress still glistens for a moment as she dances alone to the rhythm of the soundless music until she too disappears, a shadow in the shadows. They have found peace, and now this life can end too, the report delivered, the account given and the balance determined. The water has dried up and the soil did not retain the footprint. The darkness obscures it all.

I wished to get up and move through the sleeping house, I wished to go out in search of something, but that desire has also passed, as did the anxiety and the memories, and everything has been engulfed by the vast darkness, and surrendered. What could I still search for now? Let others come, other people one day long after us. Amongst the burgeoning undergrowth where the porcupines have dug their burrows they may find stones for which there is no apparent explanation and the weathered remains of inscriptions that can no longer be deciphered or understood: they may make out a single name or year, but who could determine its authenticity or say what it had once meant? Where the stacked stones of an old wall have fallen apart, among shrubs and stones and grass, no one will ever search for the remains of wood or metal that was once hidden there, and even if splinters or fragments should be found, who would still recognise them for what they had once been, a cross or a ring? The stones once stacked there, have broken up and fallen apart, and there is no sign of them among the rocky ledges, outcrops and ridges in the flat, faded landscape of stone.

GLOSSARY

....

BASTER: person of mixed race; half-breed (sometimes derogatory)

BASTERSFONTEIN: a place name, fountain where the Basters live

"BLINK JAKOB": Shiny (Sleek) Jakob

BOERS: inhabitants of the Transvaal and the Free State in the time of the Anglo-Boer War

BOTTERBLOM: African daisy, *Gazania krebsiana*

BRANDSOLDER: fireproof loft

BROEDERBOND: fraternal society for Afrikaner men

BOEGOE: buchu, *Agathosma* species

BYWONER: share-cropper, person with no land of his own, farming on the land of others

DASSIE: rock-rabbit, Cape hyrax

DOMINEE: reverend, clergyman, also used as title

DUIWELSDREK: asafetida, a resinous plant gum with an ammoniac smell used for medicinal purposes

GEELBOS: yellow bush (lit.); *Leucadendron salignum*

GOUSBLOM: marigold; Namaqualand daisy; *Arctotis* species

HARPUISBOS: resin bush, *Euryops* species

HARTBEESHUISIE: mud-and-daub house, also known as wattle-and-daub hut

KAREE: Karoo tree, or bastard willow; *Rhus lancea*

KAROSS: blanket or mantle made of skins with the hair left on

KATSTERT: cat's tail, *Bulbinella* species

KIST: box, chest

KLIPSPRINGERTJIE: small antelope, African chamois

KNEG (pl. KNEGTE): farm labourer with slightly higher status; overseer, foreman

KOLONIE: the Cape Colony

KRAAITULP: *Homeria* species

MEESTER: Master (title given to schoolmaster)

NAGMAAL: Holy Communion

PADKOS: provisions for a journey

PERDEUINTJIE: *Babiana curviscapa*

PLAKKIE: *Cotyledon orbiculata*

REEBOK: a small South African antelope with sharp horns

RENOSTERBOS: rhinoceros-bush, *Elytropappus rhinocerotis*

RIEMPIE: leather thong (used for making riempie-seat chairs)

SETIES: dance, also known as schottische, or Scottish polka

SJAMBOK: short, heavy whip, originally of rhinoceros-hide

SLAMAAIERMEID: Malay woman (derogatory)

SPEKBOS: shrub of the genus *Zygophyllum*

STUIPDRUPPELS: anticonvulsive drops

TESSIE: container with handles for hot colas, placed inside a foot-stove

TREK: long, arduous journey, especially on foot; can also refer to travelling by ox-wagon

TREKBOER, TREKKER: migrant farmer

VELDKOS: veld foods, edible wild plants and fruit

VOORHUIS: front room, living-room, parlour

WILDE ANYS: wild aniseed, *Pharnaceum lanatum*